Osgood Riddance

The Spectral Inspector Book II

COOPER S. BECKETT

HORROR &
CARNAGE
PRESS

Cover Illustration by Anthony Diecidue

Book Design by Cooper S. Beckett

1 2 3 4 5 6 7 8 9 10

Published Internationally by Horror & Carnage Press

ISBN: 978-1-946876-21-8

BISAC: Fiction / Horror

Horror & Carnage Press - Chicago, Illinois

CooperSBeckett.com

"**O**sgood?"

The voice stabbing through the darkness awakened her pain, which emerged from behind her left eye and sashayed back to her ear. The voice repeated her name.

She debated whether to open her eyes, but it seemed like it'd be so much work.

"I don't even know what to say," he told her, expelling a sigh. His voice she knew: friendly, warm, shaky with age. He sighed again his papery fingers found her wrist; puffing out a breath as he ran his index finger over the jagged T-scar from years ago...how many years had it been now? He paused at the small semicolon tattoo on her wrist. "She has a pulse," he said. "For now."

Osgood frowned. Of course she had a pulse. Of course she was alive. She intended to tell him that. She frowned and squeezed her eyelids together. She couldn't let too much light in at once or it just might kill her. Nevertheless, the migraine surged, and her left ear began to ring, drowning out the old man, her old friend, Albrecht. She kept her eyes shut and instead told him what she'd planned to demonstrate. "She is, in fact, alive."

"Wonderful," he said, relief in his voice. "I'd begun to doubt if you'd ever come to see me again."

She frowned and turned her head toward him in the dark, feeling the surface below scrape against her. Hard, rough, cold. Stone? Slate, perhaps? She felt it against her back, too. "I just saw you last week," she told him, irritation in her voice.

He laughed, a wispy and ancient sound. Tired. "Dear Prudence." He elongated the U lyrically in his quiet voice.

"Don't call me that," she told him, loathing both the name and the idea he might be getting ready to sing to her.

"I'll call you what I like when I find you perhaps dead—"

"I'm not dead." After several deep breaths, she took another run at opening her eyes. *This'll hurt.* She managed to open the right just a bit, though she felt the crusts of sleep tugging at her lashes. His visage hovered before her; a blurry thumbprint that seemed ungodly bright. She closed her eye again, satisfied that her conversational companion was indeed Albrecht. Judging from the haziness past her head and the solid foundation, she surmised she was lying on the floor.

"I said *perhaps* dead," Albrecht reminded. "On my foyer floor." The sound of his footsteps drew further away.

She turned her head to follow him in her internal darkness. She knew the geography enough to know that he'd moved to the fireplace in his living room. She took a breath and gave the left eye a go, feeling the tug and rip as her eyelashes held to one another. "So bright, so goddamned bright." She closed it again and returned to the comfort of darkness.

"The blessing and curse of picture windows," Albrecht said, then abruptly changed his tone. "Do me a favor and wiggle the fingers on your left hand."

"What?"

"Indulge me."

Osgood, confused, did so. "And here's my right. Are we concerned I had a stroke?"

"No."

"Alcohol poisoning?"

Albrecht sighed again. "We're going to try to sit up, now."

"Oh," Osgood sighed at him. "Must we?"

"Unless you want me to call 911."

911? thought Osgood, the emergency number sending a chill through her. "Are we..." she began, then stopped, realizing what she really wanted to ask. "Am I alright?"

"That's what I am trying to assess, Prudence."

"You only call me Prudence when you're mad at me," she told him.

"I am not mad at you," he said, attempting to sound reassuring but instead hitting desperate, the tone you use when assuring someone that yes, they may have cancer, but they're going to be okay. Of course.

"What's happening?" she asked him.

"I have similar questions for you, my dear."

"I'm afraid I won't have any good answers." She pressed her palms onto the slate tiles of the floor in the foyer of Dr. Donald Albrecht's house in the woods and sat up. *What're you doing here, Pru?* she asked herself. She realized, faintly amused, that Audrey's voice had usurped her mother's as her inner critic.

"We can cross that bridge when we come to it," said Albrecht. She felt him take both of her hands and pull.

She had a vision of the old man crashing down atop her and pulled away her hands. "Please," she said, her calmness beginning to waver. "Let me do it."

He snorted a miffed sound and declared, "I am going to

3

prepare tea." She heard him shuffle away, grumbling as he went.

Okay, thought Osgood, *step one: open my eyes.* She took a breath and braced for the impact of the migraine. Slowly she opened both eyes a crack, and blurry light blasted her visual cortex. As she opened them further, the world began to come into focus and she saw that she, indeed, sat on the floor in Albrecht's foyer. She looked into the living room, two steps down from the foyer, where light poured in through picture windows that sprawled up the walls and across a good four feet of angled ceiling. The fireplace, surrounded by large chunks of stone and a massive reclaimed wood mantle, smoldered. Above the mantle hung a painting that hadn't been there before. Had he changed it so recently? The art assaulted her eyes: a purple seated figure, screaming

(when the screaming thing rises in the east)

behind velvet ropes. "Francis Bacon's screaming pope," she said to herself and felt a shudder course through her body. "Odd painting for over one's fireplace," she called in the direction of the kitchen.

Albrecht didn't respond, though he seemed to be having a conversation with someone else in there. She was pretty sure he didn't have a girlfriend. Who would he be talking to? She had no idea of the time, but it felt early. She patted her pockets for her phone, coming up empty. She stopped patting for the phone when she felt skin.

Osgood surveyed her clothing. She was wearing her gray sweats, though God only knew how they had remained on her body. They were ripped to shreds, torn and tattered, exposing thigh and leg and even a sprig of wild bush. Huge smudges of dirty black crossed the sweatpants in several places. She touched a spot of black and felt it come off on her fingertips like soot. What the hell had she done?

"I'm going to go to the bathroom," she called. Again, no

response, though Albrecht's conversation in the other room grew in intensity.

She pulled herself to a wobbly standing position, gritting her teeth through the dull throb of her legs waking up, as though they'd been asleep throughout the night. She wondered how long she'd been on the floor. A stab of pain on the back of her head from the tiles caused her to explore with her fingers. They came away with flakes of dried, dull crimson.

"Shit." Osgood found her way to the bathroom. A hazy blue light lit the room softly, and she laughed when she saw the blue canary nightlight. "Maybe it'll watch over me, too." She flipped the switch. In the harsh white light from above she saw a monster in the mirror. But no, she realized, no monster, just Prudence Osgood. What had become of her? Her hair had lost its color, now a dull brown streaked with the grays of age. It stuck out around her head, tangled and knotted. She brought her hand up to the right side and felt a surprising amount of hair between her fingers, where just a week ago she'd taken clippers with a number three guard. Her brown eyes seemed lighter, the rims of her irises faded like her grandmother's had at the end, and the circles of flesh beneath them were dark purple and sunken. She looked thinner than she'd seen herself in maybe years. Not only were her sweats shredded, but her shirt, an old favorite, Cthulhu for president, was torn across her chest, exposing her left tit and a bloom of purple and black bruise over her sternum.

"That's where the Lord of the Hinterlands slammed his hand into my chest." She'd said it, yes, and knew she was saying it, but still took it as new information. "What the fuck happened to me?"

She turned on the sink and let the water run from cold to tepid, then splashed some onto her face and into her hair, pulling it back across her head, wrestling it into something that no longer resembled a fright wig. As she did, she squinted. Hadn't her hair been purple just yesterday?

As she re-emerged from the bathroom, she noticed a Northern Illinois University sweatshirt and a pair of navy sweatpants on a hanger on the door across the hall. She smiled at them and felt grateful that, whatever was happening, she was here with Albrecht. He'd always understood her. Well, if not understood, then accepted. Beginning with her brief stint in college as his student in literature and writing courses and through the years that had rolled by since, Donald Albrecht had been a constant. A surly counterpoint to her own misanthropy.

She dropped her blackened sweats and socks, briefly wondering where her shoes had gone to, then pulled the remnants of shirt over her head and threw it atop the rest. When she was clad in the softness of a fully operational sweatshirt and pants, she returned to the living room.

Now able to see without squinting, she walked to the picture windows to view the forestry surrounding Albrecht's driveway in St. Charles, Illinois. Immediately, the reason for the overwhelming brightness struck her. The ground, the trees, everywhere was covered in a deep blanket of blinding white snow.

"Your tea," said Albrecht, stepping up next to her. He handed her a tan mug, still steaming, with a tea bag in it.

"Caffeinated?"

"Oh yes."

The man beside her looked ancient, his wispy curly blond hair was almost entirely white. Had it been blond when they first met? It hadn't been quite so thin, then, when she was his student. Wouldn't she *always* be his student, though?

"Thank you." She took the mug, but didn't drink, didn't take her eyes away off his face.

Albrecht ignored her gaze save for some quick sidelong

glances. The corners of his mouth turned down within his snowy beard, dragging lines through his craggy skin that seemed to start at his eyes. How could he have aged so much since she'd last seen him? It had only been a few—

But she wasn't quite sure about that, was she?

"So…" she said, making sure to drag the O out as long as she could.

"Yes," he said. "Quite."

"Who were you talking to in the kitchen?"

He didn't say. He sipped his tea and stared out the window down his driveway.

"Okay." Osgood could feel the stress in her chest spilling out into her voice, first a low rumble, then rising. "I don't know what I'm doing here. I don't know what happened to my clothes or, or my hair. And you're acting like we didn't just see each other…" she hesitated. "A week ago?"

He took another sip and looked down into his mug.

Osgood laughed. "I came to your office, remember?" She turned away from the snowy outdoors, the sunlit forest feeling oddly oppressive now. "I put my feet on your desk, and you drank Scotch by the fire." Her eye caught the Bacon painting and her stomach dropped like she'd just reached the end of the climb on a roller coaster. The pope's mouth was a right horrorshow. Her mind flashed to the broken mouth and eyes of the Lord of the Hinterlands, like holes in a cracked egg, set in smoke.

Albrecht sighed. "We didn't see each other last week."

"The week before, maybe," suggested Osgood. She stomped away from him and threw herself into his easy chair. He didn't turn, so she stared at his back. He wore an Oxford shirt and brown cords. "You're dressed for work."

"Yes."

"What," she began, but immediately felt silly. These were the things people asked you when you were hit on the head.

Do you know what day it is? Do you know who the president is? While she was quite certain about the latter and didn't want to talk about that poor excuse for a man, she realized she had no idea about the former. "What day is it?"

"Thursday." Albrecht's voice was tight and clipped, his terseness clearly withholding something.

"What aren't you telling me?" she asked him.

"What aren't *you* telling *me*?" he asked her. He finally turned from the window.

"Who were you talking to in the kitchen?" she asked, more firmly this time.

"The college. Told them I wouldn't be in today."

"Are you sick?" she asked.

"Am I—? No."

"Then why?"

"Because of you," he said.

Osgood felt the pressure in her chest and head rising, and her eyes began to sting. She knew tears were coming; tears of confusion, tears of creeping panic. But fuck that. She had no intention of crying here, no intention of showing such weakness. "Because of me," she repeated quietly instead.

Facing her, he was nothing more than a silhouette backlit by the brilliance of a morning that was most definitely not September.

"What, um," she choked on the question. "What month is it?"

"December," he said. All his usual florid stylistic quirks had vanished. He gave away nothing.

"December," she repeated and looked down at her tea. She noticed her black ring was gone from her finger, without even the hint of the pale band that usually replaced it when she took it off. "Okay," she said and drew a very long breath. "It's December. The last memory I have is of early September. My hair is different. My clothes are wrecked." She ran through possible scenarios: abduction, falling and hitting her head. Nothing seemed to fit. "Two months," she said instead. "Two months that I can't remember."

Albrecht's stoic face, the one that accompanied his flat voice, fell. "Osgood, darling girl—"

"Don't—" she began but stopped herself. This time, instead of her usual snarky reaction to the infantilization and dysphoria, she took comfort from his words. "What?"

"You've been gone for nearly fifteen months."

Osgood laughed. When she heard it, raspy and choked, echo back down from the cathedral ceiling, it turned into a gasp. She dropped her mug. It banged into her kneecap on the way down, sending a jolt of pain both up and down her leg, and spilled its contents across the taupe carpet, flicking the tea bag against the wall. She saw the pained expression on his face and fear in his eyes. He sipped his coffee once again and turned his head back to the window as a black Jeep rolled up.

"Good," said Albrecht. "Your friends are here."

2

"Hi," said Osgood, wondering if she should add anything, but uncertain she had anything more.

Audrey and Zack stood just beyond the threshold of Albrecht's front door. The frigid winter air poured in over them. They didn't respond to Osgood's greeting, just stared. Audrey had tears in her eyes. Zack seemed utterly perplexed and focused, as though trying to force this all to make some rational sense.

"I'm going to start the water for more tea," said Albrecht. "This one already spilled hers."

A *pfft!* from Osgood.

Albrecht nodded at her, then addressed her friends. "Please take care to not let out all of my heat."

"Right," said Zack. His voice shook.

Osgood took a step back and to the side to let them into the foyer. The triangle remained the same, with her at its apex. Twice Audrey opened her mouth but said nothing. Finally, Osgood waved. "Hey, hi."

"Hey," whispered Audrey, and the tears fell from her eyes.

Osgood felt the impact and pressure as Zack tackled her

in an embrace. He squeezed her until she could barely breathe. She was about to thank him and shove him off when she realized how much he must need this. Never an affectionate friend or partner, this was...different. She could smell the familiar scents on him. She didn't know if it was his deodorant or aftershave or something else altogether, but it was a smell that had no name she was aware of beyond *Zack*.

"We missed you," came Zack's whisper, muffled by his head buried in the fabric of Osgood's sweatshirt.

"I... Well, I'd say I missed you, but..." began Osgood.

Zack stepped back and he and Audrey resumed staring. The look on Zack's forlorn face made Osgood rethink her sentence. Audrey's few tears had dried on her cheeks and a layer of skepticism had fallen over her. Osgood felt herself being studied.

"I missed you," Osgood assured them. She waited. Waited. Nothing but wide-eyed wonder. "Guys," said Osgood.

"I'm not a guy," said Audrey, without passion or inflection.

"Fair enough," said Osgood with a laugh, which turned to a cough that brought pain. She pressed her hand to her chest.

"On the podcast you complained about pain," said Audrey, her voice still flat.

Osgood had no recollection of that. "Well, it hurts like a motherfucker right here." She tapped her chest lightly with her index finger.

"Where your bruise was," said Zack.

"Still is, actually," said Osgood. She grabbed at the stretchy neck of the sweatshirt she'd been given and pulled it down enough to expose her sternum. Both started at what they saw, and Zack averted his eyes.

"Judging from your reactions, it's worse than you thought it'd be. And Zack is still a prude afraid of seeing my nipples."

"I'm—"

"Osgood," said Audrey firmly. She held out her hand, palm

down. Not the type of gesture you make when re-encountering an old friend after a long time. The kind of gesture you make when you're trying to convince everybody in the motherfucking room to be cool and put down their motherfucking weapons.

"Yeah," said Osgood. "Yeah, I'd love it if someone took charge here."

Zack opened then closed his mouth. He turned to Audrey.

"Let's sit down," said Audrey.

Osgood followed her into Albrecht's living room.

Zack hesitated. "I'm going to...grab some gear."

Osgood looked up at him and was about to reply when Audrey did it for her, "Perfect, Zack."

Uninterested in staring into Bacon's twisted mind now, Osgood sat in the love seat facing the windows, leaving The Screaming Pope painting to face Albrecht's empty oversized couch. Audrey sat in a recliner all the way across the seating expanse. She let her fingers drift over Albrecht's pipe on the table next to her. She pursed her lips.

"Okay," said Osgood, dialing up the edge in her voice. "I can't tell if you're pissed at me for some reason, or scared, or—"

"I'm on hyper alert," said Audrey without a waver in her inflection.

"Alright," said Osgood.

"Did Albrecht tell you *when* it is?"

"December," said Osgood. "Gone for a year."

"468 days, actually," said Audrey, betraying some deep emotion in her voice.

Osgood exhaled sharply. She laughed a nervous laugh. "Whatcha been up to?"

"Did you run?" asked Audrey, clenching her jaw.

"Did I what?"

COOPER S. BECKETT

"Did you run away?" Audrey's face reddened with a combination of anger and sadness.

Osgood couldn't figure out the question, even as it seemed straight forward. "Run away? No. What?" After a moment she added. "Wherehow?" without a break between the words.

"I'm afraid she doesn't seem to be very aware of the duration of time." Albrecht emerged from the hallway with a tray containing multiple mugs, an assortment of tea bags, and a teal ceramic teapot. He set the tray down on his coffee table and glanced between the two of them. His eyes narrowed at... what? Their distance? The tension? Finally, he poured them each tea. He set a mug down in front of Osgood. "Do keep a hold on it."

Osgood gulped at the tea, even as she felt the mild scald. She paused, looking back at the four eyes staring at her from Albrecht and Audrey. "I'm exhausted. And I spilled the last one. Made Albrecht very grumpy, it seems," she told them and then resumed drinking her tea. When it was gone, she set the mug back on the coffee table. Albrecht reached down, lifted her mug, and slid a coaster under it. He took his seat on the end of the couch closest to Osgood. She felt a twinge of gratitude that he'd sat near her, that he showed genuine affection for her. Despite... Well, despite who knows what?

"Alright," said Osgood. "Since you seem rather angry and I have limited answers, I'll just—"

A pounding on the front door.

"Did you lock it when you left?" bellowed Albrecht toward the hall.

A pause, then quietly, "No," from Zack.

"Then it stands to reason that it might remain unlocked."

Another pause, then a click and the door swung open. The icy wind whistled through and sent rivulets of cold bouncing into the room. Zack, replete with two large black bags, closed the door and kicked off his shoes, one flopping off the welcome mat and over the side of the step down into the living room. Albrecht looked over his shoulder, following the shoe all the way to his carpeted floor.

"Sorry," said Zack.

Albrecht shook his head and turned back to Osgood. "You were saying?"

"Yes." Osgood nodded. She *was* saying, but what? She scrambled to grasp at the thoughts floating through her mind like fliers caught in an updraft. She caught one. "The last thing I remember was being wheeled into an ambulance. The EMT was pretty, but I played it cool."

"You wondered out loud about the Florence Nightingale effect," said Audrey, and the barest inklings of a smile poked at her cheeks.

"To her?"

"Yes. And I didn't have the heart to tell you that the Florence Nightingale effect is when the nurse falls in love with the patient, not vice versa."

"Ah." Osgood had no memory of this. "But I probably wanted her to fall in love with me." She heard an odd crackling to her right, not by the fire but behind, over her shoulder. She flinched at a dingy brown disc on the end of a metal wand being run over her shoulder and down her arm. The other end of the wand led to a box in Zack's hand. She stared at his face, but his eyes didn't leave the box. "Zack."

"Yep," he said without looking at her. He brought the pancake probe back up and ran it across her chest.

"We're using a Geiger counter on me?" asked Osgood.

"Well," he threw his eyes first to Audrey, then to Albrecht, then back to meet hers. "Yes. Thought it was the most—"

"Are my tits radioactive?"

Now he looked up at her. "We can't be too careful," he

said. "Audrey had symptoms of radiation sickness for three months after we—"

"You what?" asked Osgood.

"I'm okay," said Audrey. "Though my doctors have all conspired to frequent cancer scavenger hunts. The Geiger counter is now part of our stock kit."

"And you splurged for the oldest one you could find?" Osgood asked Zack.

"I—" he began.

"We didn't give enough thought to gear before we went in search of the Hinterlands," said Audrey.

"The rest stop area has been cordoned off by the government," said Zack. "They found elevated radiation levels there. Our evacuation was the excuse they used to wall it off." He waved the paddle over Osgood's face.

"The point is," said Audrey, "something happened to you, and we have no idea what that something is. But the thing that happened to the three of us, Zack to the least extent—"

"I *did* get shot," he reminded them.

"Right!" said Osgood, mouth dropping open.

"You forgot?" The hurt spread from Zack's eyes to his mouth.

"No!" Osgood exclaimed. But she had, hadn't she? She had vague ideas about what had transpired in realm of the Lord of the Hinterlands, but she'd forgotten so much.

He set down the Geiger counter near the hearth and moved to the couch, taking the seat nearest Audrey. He turned to her. "Nothing concerning."

"Good," said Audrey. "Do you want to set up the big camera or—"

"For this, let's go with phone and tripod."

Osgood watched the back and forth between them, waiting for either of them to acknowledge her again as something more than just their subject. She turned to Albrecht and gave him an aggressive shrug. With his hand on his cheek, elbow resting on the couch's arm-lean, his return shrug was far more mellow. She looked back. Zack had set up a tiny plastic tripod on the table and was wedging his phone into it. Audrey had a notepad in her lap and flipped to a blank page.

"I guess Zack's essential to *you*, now," said Osgood. She knew as she said it that this was nothing but petulance, but after the morning she'd had, she'd go ahead and feel whatever the fuck she wanted.

"Prudence," said Albrecht, reaching out to put his hand on hers.

Startled by the touch, she yanked hers away. "No, I'm starting to feel—"

"Okay," said Zack.

"Okay?" asked Audrey back.

"Recording."

"Recording?" asked Osgood.

"Recording," confirmed Audrey, now hitting Osgood with her steel blue eyes.

All at once Osgood felt she was seeing Audrey for the first time. Her friend's hair had regained its natural curl and taken on a richer tone. Her face had filled back out so that her cheekbones no longer looked sharp. She had color in her cheeks. Color she hadn't had last time Osgood had seen her. Color that Osgood didn't have now, she realized, looking at her own hands. "You've gone from someone who looked like she had cancer to—"

"Thanks, Os," said Audrey.

"And now I'm the mystery," said Osgood as she ran her right hand over her left. She could see the vague blues and reds of veins and arteries in the back of her hand. She looked up again at the small rectangle with the dual lens circles at the top. The mystery. The subject. Being watched by three friends and a little camera.

"At this moment," confirmed Audrey as she took a deep breath. "You are the mystery."

Hearing it repeated knocked Osgood's wind out. She looked inward for a moment, but only a moment. "Well then, what's the score here? What's next?"

"Let's start again with the last thing you remember," suggested Audrey. "We'll go from there..."

"Okay," said Osgood, closing her eyes. "Let's do it."

3

"We were in the Hinterlands. Audrey, you stabbed the Lord in the face." Osgood opened one eye and cocked her head. "It was a bitchin' move, by the way."

"Thank you," said Audrey allowing a slight smile.

"Then..." Osgood closed her eyes and tried to get back, but the imagery had grown fuzzy. She remembered a burst. The thankful final death of the horrible red star above her. Then... "The Hinterlands crumbled, and we wound up outside the rest stop, where Zack was okay..."

"Transport between worlds cauterized my wound!" exclaimed Zack.

"That is quite impressive, dear boy," said Albrecht.

"And we were loaded into an ambulance?" Osgood made it a question instead of a statement. The memories were fuzzy here, but she did remember one thing, vividly. "I told you I love you."

"You did," said Audrey, and her voice caught.

Osgood resisted opening her eyes again. The longer she stayed in the dark, the likelier something would rise to meet her. And she wouldn't have to see them looking at her like a puzzle to be solved. She pressed her thumbs into her eye sockets, something she'd done ever since she was little. Her ocular nerves would fire vague colors and motion across her visual cortex. Sometimes it led somewhere. Other times, like now, it just hurt. It also reminded her of something else. "Um, hey." She opened her eyes after all, and the light flooded back in, sending a stabbing pain through her head. "No one bothered to bring my glasses, did they? These lenses have been in my eyes for over a year; it's no wonder they hurt."

"I did," said Audrey. She reached into the pocket of her hoodie and pulled out Osgood's crimson-framed specs. She half stood and reached across the expanse of the coffee table.

Osgood met her halfway and took the glasses. She reached up to her left eye. "Albrecht, do you have a tissue, or..."

He extended his hand out to her, beneath her face. She felt a tremendous amount of love for him at that moment. They might barb and banter, but his arrival in her life had corresponded very closely to her mother and father's exit. He'd taken up the vacancy with aplomb. She popped her lenses into his hand and saw him blurrily stand and leave the room. The world came back into focus when she slid on her glasses.

She held her eyes closed for a while, feeling the relief of moisture saturating her eyeballs. She refrained from pressing her thumbs into them again. Flashes came to her, things she remembered. The looming presence of the Lord of the Hinterlands, his undulating fabric extensions, herself but not herself unzipping her mouth to reveal... Something wouldn't come to her. The truth of the Lord's form, the reality of it.

"Os?"

She nodded at Zack's gentle prod and zipped forward to the blank space on her tape, between being loaded into an ambulance by the faceless but cute EMT and waking up here on the floor. The reel missing from the film in her mind. "I remember a voice. A woman's voice. She told me it would be okay." She could hear the voice as she said it. It echoed through her mind, full of kindness instead of animus. For a moment she thought she could see a face there in the darkness, way in the back. But the figure stayed hidden, reminding her, *It shall be okay.* "She said shall. Not will." Her hand drifted lazily to her chest. "And I think she grabbed me and pulled."

Osgood could hear the tone in Audrey's voice change as her friend switched tactics. "Do you remember overnight in the hospital?"

"No."

"Your parents came to see you."

She scrunched her face and opened one eye. "What did the Osgoods think?"

"They were concerned. I didn't tell them much, but did tell them that our friend got shot. Zack was still under observation at that point."

"My father didn't make the drive," he said.

"Wait, were we still in—"

"Northwestern Minnesota, yeah," said Zack.

"The ambulances didn't take us back to Chicago!" said Audrey with a laugh.

Now Osgood opened both eyes. "So, you're telling me that Cynthia and Basil drove all the way to Minnesota to see me?"

"They did," said Audrey with a nod. "You should call and tell them you've—"

"Jesus," said Osgood. Her parents driving six hours to see her was the kind of thing she'd have thought impossible. "They won't even drive the hour to see me in the city."

"They might today," said Zack.

"Why, what's today?" asked Osgood, before the absurdity

of her question struck her. Her observers opened their mouths to respond. "Never mind. But the hospital. Because of..."

"Your nasty bruise," said Audrey, pointing toward her chest.

Osgood yanked forward the neck of the sweatshirt and looked down at herself again. The purple and black bruise between her breasts looked even more black than she'd expected. Small lines radiated out from it, the kind of tracks that in movies usually meant blood poisoning. "We should probably stop at an urgent care. Before you take me..." She trailed off, realizing. "Do I even have a home anymore? I haven't paid rent in...fifteen months?"

"You do," said Audrey. "Well, *we* do." She gestured between herself and Zack, then Osgood. "I took care of your rent for a few months until I couldn't— Until my divorce was final, and we had to sell the house. Then I moved into the spare room. Zack moved in later."

Osgood blinked. "Into my room?"

"No," said Audrey. She looked at Zack. "Look, Os, there's plenty of time to catch you up. But I think it's more important to record any lingering thoughts. You went to—"

"The space between," Osgood whispered, more to herself than to them or the camera, but she considered the phrase as she said it. Where it had come from.

Zack gave her a mirthless laugh, the kind supposed to suggest that everything is a-okay. "Love that song."

"The woman said that, too," said Osgood, hearing it in the same voice from beyond. Kind and gentle. Calm. "I call it the margins," she added.

"You?" asked Audrey. "Or the woman?"

"Me," said Osgood. "Like we talk—*talked* about on the podcast: the margins between worlds, between life and after-life. The margins are..." She nodded. "The space between."

"More tea? Anyone?" asked Albrecht.

"Have any Scotch?"

"Look who you're asking," he said, again disappearing down the hall.

Audrey leaned forward. "It's a little early—"

"I'm a little paranormal jet-lagged," Osgood snapped back.

Her friend leaned back in her chair and put a hand to her face, looking at Zack, who silently met her gaze.

Again, Osgood felt that ping of jealousy, almost resentment, that the world had apparently gone on without her. How dare it?

"Okay, so you can't remember anything, so—"

"I remembered 'the space between,'" said Osgood.

"You remember very little," said Audrey, correcting herself. "I want to try something." She flipped through her notepad a few pages, then held it out to Zack.

"You sure?"

Audrey nodded.

"Want to let me in on it?" asked Osgood.

"Do you remember a diner?" asked Audrey.

Osgood snort-laughed. "A diner?"

"A planetarium?"

"What are we doing?" asked Osgood.

"I was going to save this list for confirmation," said Audrey.

"Was going to?"

"Since you remember—"

"Very little," interjected Osgood.

"Yes. We're going to have to change tactics. So please, just yes or no. A subway or L platform?"

Osgood frowned and looked between them. She felt their eyes. They saw her...but not really her at all, was it? They saw something that looked like her, acted like her and— "You don't believe I'm me."

Both seemed startled by that.

"That's it, isn't it?"

"No," said Audrey, slowly.

"Yeah, you think something *else* came back, and I'm still—"

"Osgood," said Zack.

"—floating around somewhere. Or maybe dead!"

"Pru," said Audrey, calm, compassionate, her face softening.

Osgood pursed her lips at the name. The name her mother had always used for her. The name she'd once loved being called. The name she'd left behind when she— "Put away childish things," she said to herself.

"Hmm?"

A slow, dramatic, and entirely-for-their-benefit sigh came from deep within Osgood. "Continue with your list."

"Do you remember a library."

"No."

"A theater."

"No," said Osgood, but for a moment, she could see curtains. "Wait."

"You remember a theater?" asked Audrey, a twinkle of hope in her eyes.

"I—" Osgood could see nothing more in her mind than red curtains, and they looked like curtains around the screen at the Catlow Theater, one of the old movie palaces that had showed cheap movies in her childhood. "Might not be from... Come back to that one?"

Audrey made a check on her pad.

Osgood felt glass against her fingertips and looked down to see Albrecht handing her a finger of Scotch.

"Lagavulin," he said.

"Really?" she asked.

"Worth celebrating a friend's return," he said. "Even a drop of spring water."

Osgood smiled at him and raised the glass. Looking down at the surface she could see the water interacting with the liquor, spreading, spiraling outward. As she moved the glass, it changed and spread in other directions. Every movement caused a cascading fractal of changes in the dissemination of the water into the Scotch. She lost herself within it, seeing the growing spiral at the center, a jetty, a vortex, a hole. A hole in her. "Shit," she said.

"What is it?" asked Albrecht.

She looked up at him, and saw his face was filled with concern. "Oh, the Scotch is fine, but I don't think I'll have it after all."

"Alright," he said, taking the glass from her and knocking it back.

"Damn, Albrecht."

"What is it, Os?" asked Audrey.

"I remember a hole," she replied, no difficulty in saying the words, but trouble keeping them in an order that made any sense.

"At the rest stop?" asked Audrey.

"When the music played," said Zack, "a hole appeared in the wall."

"No, not that—"

"The one in the Lord of the Hinterl—"

"Stoppit!" shouted Osgood, louder than she expected. She leaped to her feet, instantly regretting the move as it caused terrible pain in her thighs and legs. *So much for the idea that the Hinterlands cured your chronic pain, Pru.* Her inner voice, still Audrey and not her mother, was right. She had briefly considered that possibility, but not seriously.

"Os," said Zack.

Albrecht was at her side immediately, one hand gripping hers and one on her left elbow. She looked at him, about to assure him she could handle this herself, when her legs fell out from under her. He kept her from cracking her head open on the coffee table, lowering her slowly to the ground. The sudden loss of bodily control had come from an image, one she didn't understand. A motion that didn't make sense.

A spiral, a hole, a—

"There was a hole in me." She pointed at her chest, noticing that Zack and Audrey had come to her side. "And—" The image kept replaying and replaying but still didn't make any sense to her. She couldn't see it for what it was, because it...wasn't. She knew one thing, though—what the image represented, what it meant. "I fell inside me."

With a snap, she felt the reality, the gravity of the image, even if it still didn't make sense to her. She had been sitting at her microphone in her office, talking to the Specterinos. She had felt pain in her chest, pain where the Lord of the Hinterlands had slammed his

(tendril? tentacle?)

arm. She'd said it, on the air. 'Cuz that's the kind of podcasting hack she was, right? Just say what's happening. The way newscasters used to say, *Tommy has just come into the studio and handed me*— "No!" she said aloud, slamming her hand on the coffee table hard enough to knock over the camera. Zack quickly righted it.

She knew she needed to stop letting herself run away, she almost had it. "I was sitting at my desk, and my chest hurt, and—" Osgood's throat closed as it made sense. Now she knew it. "He punched a hole in me. And I went through it." She looked at the three of them, all looking back at her with the same expression. "Literally!" she said. "And I'm not saying literally meaning 'figuratively,' I'm saying literally that I looked down at my chest and suddenly my face pressed in between my tits and through my skin, and I could hear scraping as I moved through my ribcage. Scraping in my *brain!* I saw my heart, and then—"

Suddenly it all felt so real, so vivid. She saw herself and the incident. She saw it happen in horrible detail. "I turned inside out," she told them. "And I fell into the margins."

4

Osgood ignored the first knock, only stared at the door from her vantage point on the floor of Albrecht's first-floor bathroom, holding her hand to her head, fingers gripping a mass of messy curls. She could see them in front of her eyes, the silver bits glistening, nearly opalescent. The knock came again. "I'm almost done, for fuck's sake!"

"It's Audrey."

"Well, Audrey," said Osgood, "I'm almost done, for fuck's sake." For good measure she reached out and flushed the toilet next to her.

"I don't believe you're using the bathroom."

"It's a powder room," said Osgood.

"I think you're hiding."

"Oh, really?" snapped Osgood. Hiding? *Of course,* she was hiding. Hiding from the year and change she'd been absent from the world. Hiding from the newly recovered memory of being pulled through her own body, sliding through to be reborn in the darkness, shooting out into the margins, sticky with some cosmic afterbirth. How much of that last part happened had and how much was her mind filling in the blanks that came after her ribs cracking open to accept herself? She could still hear the scraping, against the bone. That had been... *Real?* she asked herself. There's no way she could consider that memory "real" without dramatically changing what the word "real" meant. It had happened, for sure, that part anyway, but it wasn't even in the same fucking ballpark as real.

"I'd like to talk," said Audrey.

"To interview me more? Your newfound mystery?"

"No." Audrey sounded closer, maybe leaning her head on the door.

"Must suck to have resolved one missing person and then gotten a new one just a few days later." Osgood regretted the words as soon as they left her mouth, but her scrunched lips wouldn't allow for an apology.

"Osgood."

Just that. Just her name. Osgood looked at the door, at the faux golden doorknob, at the wood grain tracing lines up and down which mirrored and repeated on the other half. And here she sat opposite. Osgood. Just that. Just her. "You can come in," she allowed.

Audrey opened the door.

"No camera?" asked Osgood.

She shook her head. "No."

"Just you?"

"Just me."

"Well!" said Osgood, hitting a jovial tone so hard Audrey flinched. "The rug there has memory foam in it." She pointed at the turquoise rug in front of the sink.

"Should I sit?" asked Audrey.

"Jesus."

"What?" Audrey looked at her with wide eyes, a frown on

her face not of anger but of confusion, exhaustion. "What do you want from me?"

"I—" Osgood stopped; she wasn't certain. "Not this. You didn't trust it was me."

"Trust, but verify," said Audrey quickly. She sat across from Osgood, crossing her legs beneath her.

Osgood remembered when she could do that, when the pain hadn't been unbearable. She looked at Audrey, noticing for the first time that her friend wore a pair of tortoiseshell framed glasses. "Those new?" asked Osgood, reaching out and tapping the frames.

Audrey jerked her head back.

"See."

"What?" Audrey scowled. "You tapped my glasses. Most people would jerk away from that. Yes, they're new."

"Not 'cuz you're fucking scared of me?"

"Os, honey," said Audrey. She put her hand on Osgood's shin.

The contact through the bulky sweats felt...well, she wasn't even sure.

"I'm not afraid of *you*!"

"Then what?"

"Okay," said Audrey, folding her hands and leaning forward from her sitting position. "We need to be really honest with each other here."

"I've *been* honest with you this whole time."

"Not about that."

"What then?"

Audrey stared into her eyes, the intensity of the blue almost overpowering, and Osgood willed herself not to look away. "Hey, Os, a woman reappeared after fifteen months with no rhyme or reason."

Osgood sighed. "I see what you're—"

"Her clothes were tattered, and judging by her pre-disappearance wounds and hair length, she doesn't appear to have been gone for that long, either."

"Gee, is she also surly?"

"Always," said Audrey, allowing a smirk. "But I want to know what you think, 'cuz we're rather stumped."

Osgood leaned toward Audrey as much as the pain would allow, to the point where she could nearly hug her knees. She wanted to tell Audrey how silly this was. She had no idea where she'd been, really. The margins were a great abstract suggestion, sure, but in practice what the fuck did that mean? But she knew deep down that Audrey was just trying to make sense of something paranormal. Because what had happened to her was pretty para-fucking-normal. "Okay."

Audrey's smirk turned into a genuine smile, and she waited.

Osgood leaned back to the wall and looked at the upper corner of the bathroom, where a tiny spider had made a tiny home. She knew Albrecht would never evict it, so long as it didn't move down to the waterfront property next to the sink. "Okay," she said again, to buy herself a little time. *Pretend you're not part of this.* She wanted to tell her inner Audrey that she knew that's what she was supposed to do, but she realized the voice now wasn't Audrey or her mother. This voice was familiar, like something heard in a dream, something other, something outside. "I would look at the circumstances leading up to the disappearance."

"Chest pain from a wound inflicted by an interdimensional being while in his interdimensional world."

"There's some inference there. The chest pain could be incidental."

"Alright," said Audrey.

"I could have been having a heart attack! Addict and all," said Osgood. Her snark was short-lived, and she looked away as her face grew hot and her nose stuffy. Here came tears, again. Tears for— "I missed you so much." The words surprised even her as they tumbled out.

Audrey looked surprised. "Really? I mean, I missed the hell out of you, but you don't really even remember being gone more than—"

"No," said Osgood, shaking her head and covering her face. "Before." She yanked on the roll of toilet paper, but it didn't tear, just came spiraling off the roll toward her. She wiped her nose, folded twice, then wiped her eyes. "I missed you before."

"Oh," said Audrey.

Osgood hoped for more, but none came. "Remember, in my timeline, it's been only a week since you re-entered my life."

"That's—" began Audrey before looking down at her hands in her lap and considering that. "That's true, and worthy of extra consideration.

"I hate that I can't remember."

"I know."

"No," said Osgood. "It's more than that. Memory is all... I watched both of my grandparents on my father's side go through dementia and Alzheimer's. I've seen traces of it in my mother. And that was so long ago, who knows where she's at with it now. My father probably doesn't get to dodge that bullet, either, despite seeming strong as hell last we spoke. With two parents having it—"

"Bad odds," said Audrey.

"Bad odds," repeated Osgood. "When Grandma Osgood got bad, she basically reset every day. She could remember us mostly, but every morning it was like yesterday, last week, last month, all of it hadn't happened. She was trapped in the hell of waiting for my grandfather to come home. Waiting without being able to comprehend or make peace with the fact that he was in her 'heaven,' waiting for her to come home."

Audrey nodded but didn't respond.

What was there to say, anyway? *I'm sorry?* Osgood had lost her paternal grandparents decades ago, it would be silly to expect condolences now.

"I asked my father on our drive home once, if you can't remember something does it really matter. He had tears in his eyes, and that was a big deal because it was one of only maybe two times I saw it, before— Well, before the 'we don't agree with your lifestyle, blah-blah-homophobiblah.' He told me that things matter, whether we remember them or not, because they happened. We should never let go of the things that happen to us.

"'What if we're forced to,' I asked. Forced to, like Grandma with Alzheimer's. Forced to let things vanish from our minds, like illness can do, like apparently getting spear-fished by a cosmic deity can do."

Audrey laughed but turned it into a cough in a dramatic about-face.

"He didn't want to talk about it, and he made that clear. But I couldn't stop thinking about it. I asked Mr. Budzich, my science teacher, the same thing. He said he wanted more information, the 'why's' of my question, before he could weigh in. Rather than tell him about the Alzheimer's, because I wasn't in the mood for pity-face at the moment, I suggested a scenario where I was going to be the first woman on Mars."

"Impressive," said Audrey. "Very you."

"He thought so, too," said Osgood with a small smile. "We'd been talking about Mars that week and how it's something like 150 or 175 days to get there. I asked if we could be given a pill at the beginning and at the end of the trip that would guarantee we'd forget about what would likely be a very long and dull and probably tense trip, forget like when you fall asleep on a car ride and suddenly you're home. Would we just sorta 'wake up' on the other side? Does lack of memory make the time lost irrelevant, if not actually gone?"

Audrey considered it. "I guess I'd side with the idea that you'd still experienced all of it, whether you forgot or not, it would still have happened..." She trailed off, becoming very focused on her thumbnail.

"But that's it, isn't it? If you experience it or if you don't, neither matters, because in the end it's gone."

Now, Audrey gave her a slow nod. "I guess."

"Well, I've just arrived at Mars this morning, Aud. I got the pill that guaranteed I wouldn't remember. I don't know where I was, what I did, what I saw or felt, or even *who* I was in the margins. As far as my memory goes, someone took some scissors to the film and then spliced it back together from last September to now." Osgood ran her fingers through her hair, three times coming upon knots of curls she needed two hands to untangle. "I *know* I'm a mystery right now. And you're right, if I were getting this story from someone else, I'd be all over investigating immediately." She reached out and took Audrey's hand. "But right now, at this moment, I just want to go home. I want to get a fucking burger at Mary's. I want to pretend that everything's normal, for just a little while."

"But it's—"

"Not," agreed Osgood. "Most surely, most definitely, most unbelievably *not* normal. But could that something for Future Osgood to deal with?"

Audrey nodded and stood, moving out of the cross-legged sit admirably. She reached down and offered her hands to Osgood, who rose with creaks and aches.

"I'm fucking old," said Osgood.

"Yeah," said Audrey. "Turned 40 outside the world."

"Does that mean it doesn't count?"

"If you want to be 39, Os, you can be 39." Audrey wrapped her arms around Osgood, holding her tight. Osgood sank into the hug and didn't want to leave. "You probably should call your parents."

Osgood leaned back; her brow furrowed. "Could that be something *Future* Future Osgood does?"

"That's not my call," said Audrey. She let go the embrace and took Osgood's hand, then turned back to face her. The blue of her eyes pierced Osgood's. Audrey was waiting. For what?

"Permission," said Osgood.

"Permission?" asked Audrey.

"Yeah, you were waiting for mine, to leave this safe space."

"Albrecht's?"

"The bathroom," said Osgood.

"It's a powder room," said Audrey.

"Bitch," said Osgood.

"I think I'm going to text your mother to meet us at—"

"Don't you fucking dare," said Osgood.

They left the safe space of the powder room. Osgood stopped and turned back to flip the light switch off. The blue glow of the canary in the outlet gave her comfort. The things that moved in the darkness did not.

5

The apartment was still home, but only barely. Looking around it gave Osgood the impression that an attempt at continuity had been maintained for a while, but likely had fallen away as the months trucked on. Zack had clearly gotten ahold of her office. Her grandfather's desk had been moved to a place of reverence by the windows, and an IKEA monstrosity filled the vacant corner space. Multiple microphones on goosenecks, with big pop filters and vibration reducers, hung around the table. A mixing board and computer sat off to the side.

"Looks like The Spectral Inspector has moved up in the world," she said to herself. She wondered if she'd ever be interested in podcasting again. She certainly wasn't just now. *We must not make life decisions from the middle of confusion.* Osgood frowned, wondering still to whom that voice belonged.

She felt another wave of sadness. The ache, the yearning for a past she didn't have. She'd felt it the entire drive home. As they'd come down Clark Street nearing her apartment, the pangs had begun. She'd seen the barbershop with the rainbow flag in the window, where she'd gotten the first haircut that made her feel like herself. Her true self. She'd seen the Philadelphia Church, with its garish marquee declaring that *Jesus Saves!* She'd wondered what would happen if she walked in there and dropped some knowledge about the things that existed between worlds. That their lord wasn't the only lord. If he even *was*. These were her landmarks, places she'd passed every time she walked to the grocery store, or on dates with people she occasionally liked. The Andersonville neighborhood. Where they'd eat on patios in the summer, surrounded by others like them. Interesting folk. On the side of a brick building were large painted letters. *Anything is possible,* it had proclaimed, just some motivational phrase the way *You are beautiful* had been before she'd...gone. But this one felt pointed. Like a spectral spear to the chest. She'd sighed at the loss. A year had been stolen from her. It wouldn't be coming back. And the only thing she felt was regret for lost time.

"Anything is possible," said Osgood in the office that had once been hers and was now apparently "theirs." She sat behind her desk and turned in her chair to look out the windows at the street below. Flurries drifted, adding to the gray slushy messes on either side of Clark. People bustled up and down the street. Hearty Chicagoans. Foolish Chicagoans.

This reprieve, her privacy, wouldn't last long, she knew. Their dinner at Mary's Diner and Bar below would be tension-filled, with the unspoken elephant not just in the room but seated in the fourth seat at their table. As much as Osgood craved normalcy and routine, she had a feeling that she wouldn't be finding it for quite some time.

"Unless I figure it out," she told the street below, her breath fogging the window. She lifted her finger to the window and made two downward swipes and a dramatic frown.

Despite Audrey filling her in on the time after their jaunt

to the Hinterlands, despite knowing everything leading up to her final podcast, it didn't feel real. It felt like it happened to someone else. Someone who looked a lot like her, and sounded a lot—

"Huh," said Osgood, interrupting her own thought. She woke her computer up and pulled up the file browser. The icon next to it was for her web browser. She could open it and see what'd happened, what'd gone on in…the interim. But she resisted that urge and instead clicked through scattered and progressively less helpful folder names until she found *Podcast New New 0000 (copy)*. She double-clicked and scrolled to the bottom, finding a file named with a date just after their investigation had begun. Below that was a file labeled *temp (autosave)*. She double-clicked, and, after a moment, her own voice began to play. The voice was exhausted but exhilarated and spoke of confirmation of the afterlife, the margins, the place beyond and between. Her exhaustion and enthusiasm were broken only by mentions of pain in her chest.

"*What I can tell you,*" she'd said to her audience, "*beyond the rest of this scattered micro-cast, is that my team survived. We all came back. Each of us a bit worse for wear, sure, but Zack's recovering and should be going home tomorrow…*" She looked up at the recording setup across the room with guilt in her chest.

Zack deserved the space he wanted. "He took a bullet for us."

"*And me,*" the version of herself that she couldn't remember continued. "*Well, I'm still me, still Osgood, your— Jesus that stings. Still your Spectral Inspector. Looking forward to what the future— Fucking hell!*"

Then came silence.

Osgood frowned. There had been— What? Something in there was tugging at her gray matter. But what. She clicked the back button and listened again, feeling the same curious tug, still not hearing anything obvious, anything that stood out. But she felt a growing discontent, a growing concern. What was that?

"Still your Spectral Inspector."

Osgood slapped the space bar. "There," she said aloud. She zoomed in on the track so she could slide back and played it again.

"Still your Spectral Inspector."

"Zack!" she called through the closed door. When she got no response, she nearly screamed it.

Audrey opened the door. "Jesus, Os, what's up?"

"I need Zack," said Osgood.

"Send him a ping," said Audrey, pointing over her shoulder. "He's all the way in the back."

"The back?" asked Osgood. "The kitchen?"

"There's..." Audrey trailed off and then frowned. "There's more to this whole... Let's deal with that in a bit." She took her phone out of her pocket and thumbed a message. After a moment, she nodded. "He's coming."

"What's in the back, Audrey?"

"We rented the warehouse space next to Mary's. It's where Zack does...Zack things."

"Aha," said Osgood, feeling the missing-out-sads swimming back. She shook her head. "Fine. Listen."

"Still your Spectral Inspector."

"I thought you didn't want to deal with—"

"What do you hear?" asked Osgood, impatiently.

"I hear you, from that last broadcast."

"And?"

"And nothing. I think you said that right before you started complaining about pain."

"Listen again," said Osgood. She reached forward and turned her computer speakers all the way up, then turned them both to point away from her at the desk, toward Audrey in the doorway.

"Still your Spectral Inspector."

"Yes," said Audrey.

"You don't hear it?" asked Osgood.

"Maybe I would, if you told me what I was listening—"

"What's up?" asked Zack, appearing in the doorway next to Audrey.

"Nice setup." Osgood pointed at the podcasting studio.

"Oh." Zack gave her a phony chuckle and looked down at his feet. "Thank you."

"Now listen to this."

"Still your Spectral Inspector."

"That's you," said Zack.

"From her last broadcast," said Audrey.

Osgood looked at them and repeated, "Last broadcast." The words held such finality.

"The last one... So far!" said Zack, holding out his hands in a reassurance pose.

"But what do you *hear*, Zack?"

"Still your Spectral Inspector."

Zack opened his mouth slightly but said nothing.

"She won't tell me what we're listening for," said Audrey.

"Because I want to make sure you don't fake hear it when I tell you."

"I," began Zack, then fell silent. He shook his head. "I'm sorry, Os, I don't hear—"

Osgood scowled. She zoomed even further in on the waveform and selected a single word. Then she clicked the infinite repeat option, and the word "*spectral*" began to play over and over.

"Does it have to be this loud?" asked Audrey.

"Wait." Zack held up a finger.

"That's not me," said Osgood. She clarified. "The rest is, but that word is not my voice."

"What is—"

"Wait!" Zack insisted this time.

Audrey fell silent and leaned against the wall next to the door. Osgood looked at Zack's face. She could see the deep concentration, his eyes darting back and forth as the word *"spectral"* echoed over and over through the room.

"We didn't do deep analysis on the audio," he said.

"No," said Audrey. "We didn't think—"

"There's something there," he said. "It is your voice, but there's sorta..." He moved to Osgood's desk and shooed her out of the chair with his hands. "Let me drive."

"With pleasure," said Osgood. She turned to Audrey. "I'm *not* crazy."

"I never said you were."

Zack opened two other programs and copied and pasted the audio clip. Then he zoomed out. "She's right," he said.

Audrey walked around to look at the monitor.

"Her voice has a consistent form." He pointed to the waveform for the sentences before, and the peaks were all very similar. "I bet if I pulled another episode, it would look the same. It's almost like a fingerprint. Not 100% identifiable, of course, but it's certainly enough to—" He looked at the two of them and must have seen the impatience on Osgood's face because he zoomed back. "This is the word 'Spectral.'"

He hit the space bar, and *"spectral"* played again.

"Notice how different the wave looks." He brought it up and then opened a new window below it. He played through the beginning of another broadcast until he found Osgood introducing herself as, "The Spectral Inspector."

"Okay," he said. "So, these two, while they won't ever be *the same*, should be reasonably close. The whole phrase matches here at the beginning. But in this one, 'Spectral' stands out."

"Yes," said Osgood. "Your color, as always, appreciated. Now, *why* does it stand out?"

"Well, I think it *is* your voice," he said. He pointed to peaks on her last broadcast and then on the one below. "But it's not *only* your voice."

"Can you isolate the part that isn't?"

"I don't know," said Zack. He zoomed deeper and deeper until the form on the screen resembled curved waves, no peaks, no deep valleys, just a smooth, relaxed curve. He slid through that wave. Out of nowhere was an interruption, a jagged peak in the middle of the calm. "That's odd."

"Why?" asked Osgood.

"At this zoom level, it should all be smooth. These are microseconds. Less even."

"So that is..."

"Well," he said. "It looks like a full word or phrase, crammed into a tiny bit of time."

"Faster than people can talk," said Audrey.

"Faster than people can think!" said Zack. "Like gunshot fast. Faster."

"What is it?" Osgood asked.

"Working on it," said Zack. He'd copied and pasted it to a new window and was applying filters and slowing it down. He hit the space bar, and what came out sounded like a voice but was choppy and distorted. "Still sounds like you."

"Oh," laughed Osgood mirthlessly. "Didn't I tell you I developed *uber*-fast-talking abilities in the Hinterlands."

Zack looked at her, perplexed.

"I didn't really... C'mon Zack."

"Well, I don't know!" exclaimed Zack. "Gonna try a different program." He again copied and pasted the waveform into a new window and opened a filter menu. He clicked one after another. "Okay, this should give us something remotely understandable." He hit enter, and status bars next to each step started sliding across the screen. He turned back to Osgood. "It *is* possible that this is just a file glitch from the saving, that it had some data it didn't know what to do with and—"

"Yeah," said Osgood, pointing at a new pop-up reading **Complete** on the screen.

Zack selected the finished track and hit play.

While Osgood had been sure that the word "*Spectral*" hadn't been in her voice, this one was, making her wonder about the first again. It was still broken, distorted, and garbled, but she heard herself. "I don't know Latin," she told them.

They looked at her in confusion as the phrase repeated and repeated. "*Aperiam in porta.*" Over and over and over.

"I don't know Latin," Osgood insisted again.

Audrey opened an app on her phone and held it toward the speaker. Then she leaned forward and hit the space bar herself, stopping the repeated phrase. She pressed a button on her phone.

A friendly computerized female voice said, "'*Aperiam in porta*,' Latin. Translated to English: 'Open the gate.'"

6

Osgood traced lines with her index finger in spilled
sugar on the Formica tabletop as Zack and Audrey
tried to fill her in on details from her gap, the hole
in her world. She didn't lift her eyes from the table as they
spoke, and after a while, their voices grew muffled, seeming
so much further away. She should feel safe and comfortable
here at Mary's Diner and Bar. Over the years she'd lived above
it, Mary's had been her sanctuary, her church, her pickup
locale, her security blanket. This space had always been one
of few in the world where she could be herself. A bar with a
theater space that routinely ran drag burlesque versions of
cult 90s TV shows surely was a place where Prudence Osgood
could be all she could be.

Today, though, as Zack and Audrey droned on with something about a podcast, *her* podcast, she found the once warm
and inviting purples to be cold, as though some great cosmic
being had adjusted the color temperature of her life.

Winter brings cold, a voice assured her. The voice. The calm
female in her mind. Not Audrey. Not her mother, Cynthia
Osgood. Someone else. Someone she didn't know. A voice

without judgment or malice or cynicism. After all, malice and cynicism were her job.

So does vanishing from the world for fifteen months, she assured the voice, her spectral friend.

Quite true, came the reply.

Osgood frowned. Her voices didn't generally converse with her.

"Harper Collins wants the book to encompass the podcast content, as well as dig deeper into the history surrounding Rhapsody in the Shallows, and the mythological history of 'deals with the devil,'" said Audrey, plastering a needy smile on her lips. Needy because it seemed desperate. She seemed desperate. Desperate to have Osgood mirror one back? Desperate to have Osgood agree to whatever was happening? Desperate, regardless.

"Podcast content," repeated Osgood. She knew they'd spoken about it but couldn't recall what had been said.

"Our podcast..." said Audrey, slowly.

"*Your* podcast," said Osgood. She looked into Audrey's eyes and got a flinch in return.

"No, Os," said Zack, "*our* podcast. *The Spectral Inspectors.*"

"I seem to recall only one *Spectral Inspector.*"

The two of them made brief eye contact, the kind that asked, *Well what the fuck are we supposed to say to that?* Osgood couldn't help but see the hurt on Zack's face. After all, he may not have been *the* Spectral Inspector of note, but he was certainly a major part of the show, of the investigations, of—

"I'm sorry," she said, quiet, low. "You were— *Are* essential, Zack." And Audrey? Well, Audrey would've certainly been a Spectral Inspector, had their relationship not blown up years ago. Decade and change. So why was she this way? *Why so furious?* Osgood asked herself in the voice of Heath Ledger.

Zack mumbled, "Thank you." The entire table fell silent.

Osgood knew that she needed to salvage this, to somehow

claw her way above the hurt feelings that were in no way her friends' faults. "When you leave..." She found the words as she said them and knocked more sugar to the table on which her fingers could focus. "Like when you go on vacation, or sabbatical, or overseas, you expect the world to go on without you." She looked between her two companions. Zack's eyes were still downcast, but Audrey's held hers steadily. "On the other hand, you don't expect the world, your friends, your podcast," she laughed without humor, "to have moved on for over a year when the last memories you have of it all were from two days ago."

"I know, Os," said Audrey, in a reassuring voice.

"I'm not angry that the two of you continued the podcast without me."

"It's about—" began Zack.

"I'm not angry that you moved into my apartment," continued Osgood.

"To help hold—" started Audrey.

"You both keep defending things I'm telling you I'm not angry about." Osgood stopped and stared. They both looked back, assaying patience. Waiting. "I don't belong in this time-line. Not yet." Osgood finished what she'd thought was a figure eight in sugar on the table, but realized, with its elongated shape, she'd managed an infinity symbol. "I need to catch up. And that's not going to happen immediately after emerging from wherever at Albrecht's place this morning."

The two of them nodded and returned their eyes to the tabletop. It seemed fortuitous timing, as a couple appeared in the doorway of Mary's that shocked Osgood to her very core. The woman's blonde hair came to a point below her chin, almost an arrow toward the pearls around her neck. Her tight lips had a slash of crimson across them and age lines radiating from the corners. She looked shocked. By what, Osgood didn't know, but the look on her face wasn't new; it filled the same creases that it always had. The man's eyes were sad, his hair grayed on the sides and receding on top, the out-of-place traditional mustache below his nose still the vivid brown his hair had once been.

Osgood scowled and put both her palms on the table, leaning forward toward Audrey and Zack. "I'm going to ask this calmly, but you should know that I am anything but calm as I do so. Who the *fuck* invited my parents to our dinner?"

Her friends seemed to mirror each other as they put their arms on their chair backs and turned to look over their shoulders at the pair moving toward them.

Osgood pursed her lips and began to count to ten. She closed her eyes, hoping beyond hope that they were a figment of her damaged imagination and that when she opened them again, Cynthia and Basil Osgood, in the flesh, at Mary's, would be gone. She reached ten and re-opened her eyes. Far from gone, her parents stood above her. Both wore inscrutable expressions that seemed to vacillate from anger to concern to relief. She took a deep breath. "Cynthia, Basil."

"How about Mother and Father," offered Cynthia in a clipped voice.

It'd been so long since Osgood had heard that voice for real. She couldn't remember the last time they'd spoken. Years, certainly. Long before her rumspringa from reality. That voice, though, had lived within her mind, judged every thought, every action. "How about give me space?" Osgood snapped back.

"Pru," said her father.

"Os," said Osgood.

"Prudence!" asserted her mother.

"Well," said Osgood, "I'm so glad that you both came to remind me that you still don't have any concern for what *I* want."

Her father crouched next to her. His classic scent wafted

off him, the kind that came in a bottle with a ship on the label. That scent brought back childhood, better times. The two of them barbecuing on the Adler Planetarium peninsula before a Saturday afternoon sky show. Going to see the snakes at the Lincoln Park Zoo. Before times. Way before. Before high school. Before she'd begun to be herself. Before she'd even known who that was.

"If you want to be called Os," Basil said, "I'll call you Os." His accent, still resoundingly Northern UK, had faded in the last years, now a mutt combination of the intercontinental generic-ness of the American accent. He looked up at Cynthia. "*We*," he emphasized. "We will call you Os."

"Why didn't you call?" asked Osgood, closing her eyes to blink back the tears.

"Why didn't *you*?" asked Cynthia.

Enough.

Osgood leaped to her feet. "When?" she yelled at her mother. "Before I..." what? "I called enough," she told the woman with the clenched fists. "I told you what I was doing. I told you about the ghost hunting. About the podcasting. And you told me that I continued to be a disappointment and a blotch on the Osgood family name, and hasn't it already had enough—"

"Honey." Basil put his hand on her shoulder.

"Embarrassment!" She shook away from him. "Didn't want yet another fraud Osgood in the family. Didn't want *this* Osgood." She pointed to her chest.

"Such histrionics," said Cynthia.

Osgood laughed. "Histrionics? *Histrionics*, Mother?" She gave the title Cynthia had asked for such venom. "Is there anything I've ever done that you've been happy ab—" She shook her head. "You know what? Fuck that. I'll save you from asking the question: Where have I been? I have no fucking idea. I'm disoriented. I'm confused. I'm afraid. I'm barely processing it with my *friends* here. People who like me. People who understand me. Just barely handling things. And to have you—"

"Oh, Prudence," snapped back Cynthia, an oddly blasé tone in her voice. "I assumed you were on a drunken bender. Maybe dead in an alley in some—"

Osgood slapped the woman. Hard. Hard enough that Cynthia reeled backward and grabbed for a chair at a nearby table. Osgood couldn't hold back her tears any longer, and they began to stream down her face. Tears at the confrontation with her mother. Tears for the lost time with her father. Lost time when she *had been* in the world. Tears for her confusion around what had happened to her. Around what Zack and Audrey had been doing. But she wasn't about to let Cynthia Osgood have those tears. "Stay away from me, Cynthia."

"Pru— Os," said her father, grabbing at her upper arm. "Please give us a—"

"What, Dad?" Osgood swung around on her father, his mouth open, his eyes wide. "A chance? The benefit of the doubt? I heard you came to the hospital to see me last year. And here you are, now that I'm back. You know, I was here for years. Right up there!" She pointed at the pressed tin ceiling of Mary's that was only a foot or so below her apartment. "Here and alive and... And *me*. All you had to do was make the drive."

"You know that—"

"No, Dad." She clenched her fists and shook her head. She looked over her shoulder at her mother, holding a pale hand to her cheek. Osgood looked to her friends at the table, to the staff of Mary's. All seemed to be wondering if something should be done and, if so, what that something might be. "You don't get to walk back in now. When I needed you—" She grinned to bring her tone back down. Don't let them get her goat completely. "'We know you're gay, but do you have to be *so* gay?'" She stared at her father, watching him remember the words. "You didn't say it, she did."

"Don't call your mother 'she,'" he said, quietly.

"That's what you're taking away from this?" asked Osgood. She shook her head at him and yanked her arm away. She grabbed her coat. The maroon leather felt like a shield as she threw it around her. She walked away from the table, stopping immediately next to her mother. She leaned in so her lips were no more than an inch from Cynthia's ear. "Yes, Cynthia, I do have to be so fucking *queer*. And you'd have understood, if you'd ever listened. If you'd ever asked. I *also* must be this fucking difficult. This fucking standoffish. All the things you wondered in that fucking tone if I must be. The answer is yes!" She shoved past her mother and turned back to the group. Audrey and Zack sat at the table, looking shell-shocked. She wondered which of them had called. With her father standing next to the table and her mother leaning on the chair of a neighboring table, the cold purples of Mary's had never felt less inviting.

"Do me a favor, all of you. Fuck right the fuck off for a bit," said Osgood, before walking out to Clark Street, where snow had again begun to fall.

What now? she asked herself. But she honestly had no idea.

🐀 7 🐀

With the privacy curtains closed and the knowledge that no one had lived there for quite some time, the tomblike atmosphere of Osgood's bedroom was exactly what she needed. She wasn't sure how much time had passed since she'd left Mary's, and she wondered if her friends had remained with her parents. "Friends," she muttered. If they were all there, they were talking about her, and if they were doing that, she intended to give them a piece of her mind. A huge fucking piece. With her door and curtains closed, the only light came from a dim bulb in a lamp on her bedside table. Osgood put her head on her pillow and stared at the ceiling where the ceiling fan lazily spun, sloughing off dust bunnies as it went. "Fifteen months' worth," said Osgood.

A jolt of pain hit her sternum. She pressed her fingers against it, trying to offset the internal pain with external. A momentary thought of razor blades in her medicine cabinet stopped her cold. The pain grew more profound, as though burrowing from the crimson, black, and purple Rorschach blot on her chest through to her spine. She squinted at the ache and sat up, feeling her head swimming with a migraine in response. She grabbed the lower hem of her t-shirt and pulled it over her head.

The bruise, the mark, the blot, had grown darker, with a new center line as black as pitch. She gingerly dabbed at it with a finger and flinched with each touch. The burrowing sensation continued.

She reached to the bedside table and grabbed the phone Zack had hastily spun up for her before they went to

(ambush)

dinner. She swiped to the camera and brought it behind her. The flash fired off, and she looked at the capture. Out of focus, sure, but flesh tone. Her back, just that. Overexposed. With a...

"Huh," said Osgood. She reached around to her back and felt similarly tender areas, none approaching the sharp and focused pain of the bruise on her chest, but still there.

She left her bedroom without putting on her shirt. *It's still my fucking place,* thought Osgood. She closed the bathroom door behind her and stood opposite the medicine cabinet's mirrored door. The bruise on her sternum looked horrifying. If she didn't know that she'd somehow been living with this for fifteen months, and before that had been cleared as uninjured, she might rightly panic at the sight.

But that line in the center does *look darker now.*

She turned around and looked over her shoulder. Under the harsh lights of the bathroom, the short side of her hair sparkled with her grays. She thought about dying all of it, long and short, or maybe taking the clippers and just cutting it all the way off.

Along her spine was another line of pitch black surrounded by bruise, this one smaller, but just as angry. Had that been there? Had it been there *then*, and they just didn't notice? Had no one seen? Was that even possible? "No," she insisted, "that's not fucking possible."

As though proclaiming its own reality, the bruise on her spine radiated pain both upward and below, reminding her legs, her hips, her neck, her entire body of the decades of chronic pain she'd treated with a bootleg oxycodone tincture. She had no more of that here, of course. She'd sucked down the last just before her jaunt to the Hinterlands. "My kingdom for some fucking pain relief." She'd had pot, at least before she...went. Probably still in the tea tin in—

As I built my kingdom, so have you built yours.

Osgood froze. She knew that the voice had been within her own head, but it seemed to echo off the bathroom tiles. Where had she heard that? Who had said it? "Prudence," she told herself. Yes. The false Prudence from her time outside the world. The false Prudence that the Lord of the Hinterlands had used as a mask.

"My kingdom," Osgood repeated. Her kingdom had been a terror, hadn't it? A punishment trap for her alone, taking that horrible intersection near DeKalb, the one with the blinking amber beacon, as its model. Why her subconscious had chosen that place, the site of her eight minutes of death, the site where a semi-truck had flattened her Buick Skylark, she had no idea. Guilt? Desperation? Fear? She hadn't the faintest idea what the Lord had meant anyway.

The knock was light, just two raps. It betrayed hesitance.

Ignoring the deference, Osgood yanked the door open, startling Zack twice, first with the force of the door swinging open and then with her exposed and blackened chest. He looked away, saying only, "Oh," once and then again.

"Are they here?"

"No," said Zack.

"Did you invite them?"

"No," repeated Zack. He tilted his head. "Well..."

"Well." Osgood repeated. She grabbed his chin and turned his face back to her. His eyes darted between hers and her chest. Ages ago, she might've thought he was checking out her tits. Today, though, she knew that Zack couldn't help but look at that black area in the center. Skin shouldn't be black. Black skin meant—

He gasped a breath before explaining. "The listeners are just so invested."

"The listeners?" questioned Osgood.

"*The Spectral Inspector* listeners."

"Ahh, my—"

"Our," asserted Zack.

"—podcast listeners."

"Yes," he said. "Since you've been gone, they've been doing all they can to help with the search. We thought we had you a few times. One man still insists you're in Dubai."

Osgood frowned. She felt her anger ebbing.

"Once we knew we had you," said Zack. "Like for real, not a maybe, I posted on social media. That's where your parents must've gotten—"

"My parents don't use social media," scoffed Osgood.

"Your father is a patron of the show."

She didn't know what to say to that. It felt so out of character that her father, prim and proper and very British Basil Osgood, supported the supernatural musings of a show dedicated to finding his queerdo daughter. "I..." she began but stopped.

"We're on your side," said Zack. "Everyone is—"

"Cynthia isn't."

"Okay," conceded Zack. "Everybody else." His voice wavered. "*I* am."

Osgood looked at her feet.

"Could you please put your shirt back on?" Zack asked, voice cracking like a teenager. "Your boobs are—"

"Distracting?" Osgood couldn't help but snicker.

"Yes," he said.

Osgood nodded and went to her room. She opened her drawer where the jumble of t-shirts looked exactly as she'd left it. This whole place was a time capsule from the last time she'd been in here, wasn't it? She pulled a black shirt out, slashed red text gave hail to the Crimson King, his eye sigil within it. "Very me," she said to herself, and then she returned to the hall.

She moved slowly, hearing Zack and Audrey conversing in the living room. She stopped midway, her attention grabbed. On the wall between the bathroom and guest room was a photo she hadn't seen in decades. Tall and gawky young Prudence, maybe eighth grade, still in braces, stood flanked by two nearly identical girls, prettier than her, more mature in appearance too, if one took the tightness of their shirts into account. Audrey and her sister Caroline. The sister that had vanished. The sister that had led them all to—

"I put that up," said Audrey from the end of the hallway. Behind her was the light from the living room.

Osgood looked from her friend's face to that in the photo. She could see vectors that led from one to another, but time had changed so much, hadn't it? *Thankfully, in my case,* she thought.

"What did your parents say?" asked Osgood. "I assume you told them..." Told them what? That their daughter had been kidnapped by a cosmic entity because of the music she listened to. Told them that Caroline was really for real dead, and Audrey had helped set her free into the afterlife.

"I told them what they needed to know." Audrey sighed. "That they'd been correct that she was dead. I wrote them a letter with the rest and told them that they didn't need to know what was in it, but it would be there should they choose."

"Hey, that's how I came out!" laughed Osgood mirthlessly.

"I remember."

"We're not your enemies, Os," said Audrey.

"I didn't say you were."

"Not in so many words. And you have every right to be out of sorts, to rail, to fight. But maybe you could do it *to* us instead of *at* us. Because there's still a lot—"

"I think whatever this is..." Osgood pressed her finger to her chest above the crimson eye, "has moved to my back as well."

"It's getting bigger?" asked Audrey, alarm in her eyes.

"I don't know. I never saw it on my back. But, of course, I don't remember much beyond having it in the first place, and—"

"We can go to the doctor tomorrow."

"I don't have a current primary care—"

"I'm sure we can figure that out," said Audrey. "Come into the living room?"

"For an intervention?" asked Osgood.

"Is there something in need of intervention?"

Osgood considered that. "I've actually been sober for the longest span of my adult life. Doesn't really matter if I don't remember it, does it?"

"Come into the living room, please," Audrey requested again.

Osgood nodded and followed.

8

"Sit?" Audrey gestured to the couch. Osgood took the seat silently.

Zack sat to her left in an armchair, remote in his hand. The TV in front of the couch, much larger than the one she'd owned, showed a logo proclaiming The Spectral Inspectors with a cartoon ghost on it. Osgood thought it looked entirely too similar to the *Ghostbusters* logo for her taste. Audrey took a seat in the La-Z-Boy recliner to her right.

There the three sat in silence, Audrey and Zack exchanging meaningful looks, their eyebrows sloping outward, eyes slightly widened. They gestured with their heads. Then each lifted a finger slightly to point at the other.

Osgood realized something surprising, as their eyes kept darting to her. "You're afraid of me."

This stopped the pantomime. Audrey stared blank-faced at her for a moment, seeming to call up the appropriate emotion when she suddenly smiled and ejected air in a *pssht!* sound. She shook her head.

Osgood turned to Zack, who tried to mimic Audrey's casual yet transparent denial. She narrowed her eyes at him, and he looked at his lap, then back up. "A little."

"Zack!" exclaimed Audrey.

"Thank you for being honest with me," said Osgood. "Refreshing," she directed pointedly at Audrey.

"I am not afraid of *you*," insisted Audrey, driving home the point with a gesture toward Osgood.

"But you are—"

Zack jumped in. "Maybe we should tell you about some of the things that—"

"Yes," said Audrey. "There are some things that you need to—"

"Get on with it, you two. It's been a bizarre..." Osgood glanced at her temporary phone on the coffee table, seeing from the clock that it was just after eight. *Jesus,* she thought. "Only thirteen hours?" She leaned back into the couch and looked at the ceiling. Her voice dropped to a whisper. "It feels like so much longer. Days."

"Zack?" asked Audrey, though it sounded more like a direction than a question.

Zack pointed his remote at the TV. A hastily shot video appeared, a vertical image with two large black bars filling the rest of the screen. A crowd. Sunbeams kept flashing over the image as the person filming moved through the crowd. The videographer seemed to have a singular purpose as they moved. The sounds of wind rushing over the phone's microphone occasionally obscured the chatter of the crowd.

Osgood turned to Audrey, who seemed engrossed in the video footage. "Should I be looking—"

"Wait." Audrey held up a finger. She looked at Osgood and then insistently pointed at the TV.

Osgood looked back. The crowd seemed to be made up of mostly teenagers and adults. In the background, she glimpsed an unfamiliar skyline. "I really wish you'd tell me what I'm supposed—"

"Upper. Left."

Zack's terse delivery gave her pause. Out of her peripheral vision, she saw that his eyes hadn't left the screen. Osgood squinted. At the upper left of the image was a fountain. A figure stood before it, back to the camera. She felt a tingle in her chest, the warmth of embarrassment, that feeling of getting caught being bad, but she had no idea where it was coming from. "Okay, uh..." began Osgood. She frowned, noticing, "Wait." The figure began to resolve as the camera got closer. What had been silhouetted and dark now became maroon leather. An ill-defined head began to show shape, but more importantly, color. Purple. Purple curls. With a shorn side opposite. "What the fuck?"

"Osgood!" came a voice from very near the video's microphone. "Prudence Osgood! The Spectral Inspector, right?"

The video stopped moving forward, framing

(me)

the woman fully in the vertical image. The woman didn't turn around.

"Okay," said Osgood. "That's not me."

"We don't think so either," said Zack.

"But—"

"Wait," said Audrey.

The video moved slowly closer and closer. Again, the videographer, a male voice now sounding more nervous, asked, "Prudence Osgood?" The question seemed to hang in the air, not only on the video, but in the living room on Clark Street. Finally, a hand reached out to tap the shoulder of the woman that Osgood was now less confident wasn't her. The tap lingered and the woman did nothing. Another tap, the name asked again. Still nothing.

Then the figure turned a full 180. The camera shook as

though the questioner had flinched, then refocused on the figure.

"That's not me," said Osgood, in a whisper this time. She was both incredibly sure and not at all that the person on screen wasn't her, despite the identical features, identical freckles, identical lines around her eyes, identical hair, identical teeth. "That's not me," she said again.

Now not-Osgood began to speak, quickly, only her mouth moving.

"Can you turn it up?" Osgood asked.

"We've tried," said Zack. "We've filtered, we've done everything we could to the audio, there's nothing. She's not speaking."

"Out loud," said Audrey.

Osgood watched the lips of her doppelgänger move, trying to make out what she was saying. Usually, she could read lips reasonably well, but here she came up blank.

Abruptly, not-Osgood stopped. In a single motion, she turned back around completely and stood, statue-like. The camera work turned shaky again, struggling to keep its view on the woman.

"Aah! Stop!" exclaimed the man filming. The image tumbled, people then sky. An Indian man in his twenties covered his ears with his hands and squeezed his eyes shut. "Stop!" he screamed.

"What's happening?" asked Osgood.

"Well, we know what he said happened," said Zack.

"What did—"

The Indian man opened his eyes again and uncovered his ears. The tension on his face had been replaced with fear. He grabbed for the phone and turned it back to the fountain, showing that the woman by the fountain, not-Osgood, was gone. The phone shook, and the view jumped. Now his face filled the frame. "She's gone," he said. "I don't know what *tem*

—" He gulped a stuttery breath. *"Tempus, tempus descensus,* means.*"*

"He could hear her," said Audrey.

"Her screams. Fuck," said the man, with tears in his eyes. "How could she scream so loud?" He pressed his hand to his forehead and breathed, looking down as he did so. Then he looked back into the camera. "I don't think that was really her."

Then the video stopped.

The three of them sat in silence. Osgood looked between Zack and Audrey. "So," she began. "What the fuck?"

"We don't know," said Zack.

"What does *tempus descensus* mean?" asked Osgood.

"Time to descend," said Audrey.

"There's a fake me speaking Latin out there, and you didn't think it worth mentioning when we found Latin in my last podcast?" Osgood scowled at them.

"There's more," said Audrey. "And we wanted to ease you in."

"*Ease me*—" Osgood stopped herself, feeling the needle in the red. Deep breaths. The concern on Zack and Audrey's faces was quite genuine, she was sure. She needed to center for a moment. To recognize. Deep breaths. "Okay," she said after a while. "I'm putting on my Spectral Inspector cap—"

"Oh," said Zack, perking up, "Do you like them?"

"What?" asked Osgood.

"The—" Zack stopped himself. "You weren't talking about a literal cap."

"No, I was talking— There's a literal cap?"

Zack nodded and walked to a box by the window, from which he pulled out a black baseball cap with the same cartoon ghost logo on it. "I made them." He extended it to Osgood.

Osgood looked at it, smiling. "You have merch."

"Need to pay the bills," said Audrey.

"Make that paper," said Zack with a grin, then regretted his slang. "Sorry."

Taking the hat, Osgood felt her sadness grow, her regret. "You have merch, and I missed it."

Audrey moved from the La-Z-Boy to sit on the couch next to her. "You were always there. It was always about you."

"Every episode we counted the days since we last saw you," said Zack.

"And updated with every possible sighting and every tip."

"And that's where..." Osgood pointed at the TV.

"One of fourteen videos," said Audrey.

"All by that fountain?"

"All over the world. That one was Budapest, by the way. The cameraman was in the country for school."

"Most of the others are from far away. Each is pretty much the same. The videographer notices, well, someone who looks like you. Wearing your coat, which really tipped us off, because it has stayed right there since you—" Zack pointed to the hook holding Osgood's maroon trench coat. "Only one other gets close enough for you, um, it, to talk. Can't hear it then, either. In that one, the battery dies almost immediately after it, she, starts talking."

Investigate, Os, it's what you're good at. Osgood nodded, looking down at the hat in her hands. She nodded again and put the cap on her head. She looked up at them. "Fourteen videos," she said. "Is it one other me? Evil Pru? Or are there fourteen of them?"

"Well, they're projections," said Zack, before qualifying it with a less confident, "We think."

Audrey nodded. "No one has reported any interaction at all, beyond the looking and talking without making a sound."

"Projections," repeated Osgood. On the TV, the video had

looped back around, and the projection, the mimic, the not-Osgood was moving her lips again. *"Tempus descensus,"* real Osgood whispered, then shivered when her vocalization perfectly matched the lips of her doppelgänger. "That phrase is familiar."

"Do you know from where?" asked Audrey.

"I don't," said Osgood. She looked at them. "Do we have to have a globetrotting adventure and track down all these doppelgängers? Cram all the clowns back in the car?"

"Projections," corrected Zack.

"Whatever."

"Well," began Zack.

"Actually?" asked Osgood, pointedly fixing him with a look that caused him to shrink in his seat.

"I just mean..." He sighed and looked to Audrey for help; she looked back at him across the coffee table with her head cocked. Osgood thought she saw a bit of, *Go ahead, dig yourself out*, on her face. "Doppelgängers are traditionally bad luck omens, seen by the, um, original."

"Me."

"Yes."

"And since they're just out and about in the world?" Osgood looked at herself on the screen. The hair, the coat, the eyes. Everything matched. "The shirt," she said, pointing. "That's the shirt I wore to the rest stop. To the Hinterlands."

"The one that came back shredded," said Audrey.

"I'll take your word for it," said Osgood.

"The EMTs cut it off. The one you liked, in fact. You asked her, 'Like what you see?'"

"Did she?" asked Osgood.

Audrey guffawed in a way that seemed to surprise her.

"The doppelgängers," said Zack.

"Projections," corrected Osgood.

"Doubles," said Zack in a huff.

"They were never seen in the same location," said Audrey. "Do you have the map, Zack?"

"Yeah," he said and set to clicking on his laptop. "They don't interact, they can't be heard, they're like…"

Osgood frowned. "Residuals."

A map of the world appeared on the screen. She saw a handful of red dots across Europe and Asia, but most were collected in North America.

"Have you ever been to any of these places?" asked Zack.

"You can wipe everything outside North America off the 'places I've been' list." Osgood frowned. "For them to be residuals…"

"You'd have to be dead?" asked Zack. "We did worry about that, once people started—"

"Actually, no," said Osgood. "*Usually* residual hauntings are from people who died. But the living, when there's enough…" She moved her hands and looked at the ceiling. Why couldn't she find the right word?

"Intensity? Catharsis?" offered Audrey.

Osgood snapped her fingers and nodded. "Intensity in an action. With enough, the living can leave an imprint that lingers after they've left. But that's not what this is," she said. "I was gone. I was outside of—"

Tempus descensus.

She stopped. And repeated it in a whisper. "*Tempus descensus.*"

Zack and Audrey looked at her with matched expressions of uncertainty.

"Right," said Audrey. "Does that mean more to you than it did?"

"I—" Os shook her head. What could she tell them? *I hear voices in my head? In fact, sometimes it was you, Audrey; usually, it was Cynthia, but now it's this... Jesus, Os.* She had to tell them something. They had to know. They had to— "I remember a woman's voice," she said, finally. "A voice in the darkness."

"While you were—"

"Gone," confirmed Osgood. "She was kind and calm. Her voice...Has stuck with me."

The look on Zack's face held mixed embarrassment and fear.

"See!" shouted Osgood, pointing at him. "That's why I didn't tell you!"

"What?" exclaimed Zack.

"You think I'm crazy?"

Zack made a sour face. "You really shouldn't use the word crazy any—"

"Os!" exclaimed Audrey. "We visited an alternate plane of existence because of voices we heard in records. A voice in your head isn't *that* difficult to go along with."

Osgood jumped up. "She said that!"

"What?"

"Tempus descensus! She told me that just before..." Osgood squeezed her eyes shut. When she opened them again, she knew. "Just before I woke up on Albrecht's floor."

"Time to descend," said Audrey.

Osgood nodded, remembering hearing it in the darkness, hearing the words with echo and weight, and then feeling a pull. "She pulled me back to the real world." She stood on shaky legs.

"Are you alright?" asked Audrey.

"I need," began Osgood. What did she need? She wasn't sure. This was a lot, and she needed... "Rest, maybe."

"Alright."

Zack nodded. "We can get back to this tomorrow."

"That might be..." She felt her head swim. "Yeah. Rest."

She closed the bedroom door behind her, not wanting anyone to follow her in and put her to bed like an infant. In the darkness of her bedroom, she heard the voice again, *Tempus descensus*, and felt the pull in her chest.

She took a deep breath and was asleep before she let it out.

9

Bits of gravel dug into Osgood's knees and her left palm. In her right hand, she held a piece of chalk ground down to a nub. She looked at her fingers holding it and saw angry red scrapes on the tips. She closed her eyes. "No. No fucking way." In the darkness behind her eyelids, she reluctantly took in the world. She felt the asphalt under her. A frigid breeze blew over her. Semis barreled down a highway in the distance. But she couldn't be here. Not now, not again. She'd spent so much time, so unbelievably much time, here. She turned her face up, holding her eyes closed for a moment longer. She heard her breaths, steady. *Open your eyes when you're ready.* Would she ever be? No, decided Osgood, she would never fucking be ready to be here again. Opening her eyes confirmed what she'd already known but didn't want to. Above her, on cables reaching in four directions, was the yellow metal housing of a four-way amber beacon. It flashed north-south, and with a *ca-chick*, it switched to east-west.

She felt betrayed, by what, she didn't know. Maybe her body. Definitely her mind. She couldn't remember much of anything after the Hinterlands, of course, but she'd had a sense that her horrid recurring dreams involving trucks and cars meeting at high speeds, and the rending and churning of metal and flesh, had ceased. She'd thought they might no longer haunt her.

Yet, here knelt Prudence Osgood in the middle of the crossroads.

She pushed herself back and landed on her ass, thankful for the cushion of Albrecht's sweatpants.

"Wait." She said it, then did it. She wasn't sure if she was telling herself or asking. Something felt off, different. She pushed herself to a shaky standing position, feeling the screaming aches of her body, which seemed magnified. Perhaps drawing power from this place, from their origin.

She looked to her left and saw the yellow dashed line of the street, dimmer the further it got from the flashing amber light above her. Beyond it, she saw skeletal branches in the dim waning crescent moon's light. Even further, a work light hung on the outside door of a barn. She narrowed her eyes and looked to her right. Well past the circle of amber light, she saw an evergreen with a few rounds of upsettingly bright blue-white LED lights. Maybe thirty feet beyond, a pole jutted out of a snowbank, sending white rope lights up to a cross, similarly lit. She looked forward and could see the pinkish-orange glow of fluorescent lighting at a factory bouncing off the low gray clouds of a winter's night. Only behind her was dark, well beyond the circle.

"I've never been here in winter," she said and heard her voice echo then be drowned out by the whistle of wind across the fields. She shivered and looked down her body, finding that she seemed somewhat reasonably dressed. Her leather trench coat was warm-ish, and a rainbow-striped scarf hung down both her chest and her back. She looked at her fingers and saw how pink they were, beyond the scrapes from the—

Wait.

She looked at the chalk in her fingers, worn almost all the way down. Then she looked past the chalk and couldn't quite comprehend what she saw. The entire intersection, perhaps ninety feet square, was covered with intricate chalk-work. Circles intersecting with others, spirals ebbing and flowing, squares, leaves, curly garlands on corners. The sharp points of stars.

Osgood let her mouth gape as she stepped out of the intersection, realizing faintly that this spot, this grassy edge which tonight was covered in snow, was where she'd died on a hospital gurney two decades before. She *had* died,

(*They merely cannot comprehend what you are.*)

hadn't she? Here at the crossroads. She'd died for eight minutes and sixteen seconds. Some kind of—

"No," said Osgood. She dropped the chalk nub and saw it bounce, break, and scatter into the darkness. She felt an urgent need to bolt, to run away, but she couldn't just leave... this, could she?

With shaking hands, she reached into her coat pocket and felt palpable relief as her fingers closed around the cell phone. It rejected her fingerprint once, then again, before finally accepting the impression. She held the phone up and snapped a photo of the intersection from her corner, then made her way to each of the others.

"Be objective," she told herself, cramming her flight reflex way down deep as she took dozens of images. "This is chalk. It'll be gone at the first bunch of cars driving over it." She nodded, could see the intricate design already striped here and there with tire tread. She moved to the center, carefully stepping over lines as she went. She swiped and switched the phone to video mode, then began a spiral, working her way further and further out from the center. Zack could assemble something from that, right? He was magic or something. Before tapping the red button and ending it again, she took stock. "It's December—" Her voice gave out as the vastness of her missing time struck her. She took a few deep breaths and continued. "December 10. 3:07 in the morning. I assume the photos will be location tagged." After a moment, she realized. "Timestamped, too, I guess."

She flipped the camera to the front to show her face, alternately lit by the dim fingernail moon and the amber beacon. "I am Prudence Osgood. I don't know how I arrived here. I appear to have drawn all the shapes you see in the pictures. This is the intersection where I died." She looked back up at the beacon and watched it flip back and forth. "And I'm here for real, this time."

Osgood pressed the red stop button on the screen and looked around, entirely unsure what to do next.

⚡ 1 0 ⚡

"Twice in 24 hours." Albrecht squinted at her from the threshold to his home. His voice betrayed exhaustion but, somehow, not annoyance. The porch light glared in both of their eyes. He shivered as a cold breeze passed directly through his light linen pajamas.

Osgood nodded. "Yes, sorry, I—"

"No need for apologies ever, my dear," he said. He stepped back from the doorway and gestured her in. "Explanations, on the other hand, would be most appreciated."

"I don't have any," said Osgood.

"Pity," said Albrecht.

"Did I wake you?"

"At 4:30?" he asked her.

"Right."

He closed the door behind her and flipped the switch in the foyer, bathing both of them in bright light. "Shall I call the school? Tell them I won't be in today, either?"

"What day is it?"

Albrecht let out a sigh. "Today is Thursday, my dear."

"No, I won't be here..." Osgood looked around. Why had

she come? Proximity, yes. Albrecht's house was between the crossroads and her apartment in the city. But she knew the real reason. "I don't know if I can take that look from my friends again."

"Which look would that be?" he asked. He flipped another switch, and the sunken living room exploded with light. He stepped down the stairs.

"The one they gave me this morning," she said, not moving out of the foyer, not removing her coat. "That combination of pity, skepticism, and fear."

"I see." Under the living room's lights, Albrecht's snowy hair and beard glistened a brilliant white that almost seemed to pulse.

She felt the throbbing begin and put her hand to her head. Not an ocular migraine, not now. Not so far from any sort of medication or treatment. Albrecht was an old hippie, but she didn't think he was a pothead.

"Apologies," he said. He moved to the row of switches and dimmed all the lights in the room by half. "Are you going to join me or remain in my foyer?"

Osgood nodded, then removed her coat, kicked off her dirty Chucks, and joined him in the living room. She sat opposite him, where earlier...yesterday, now, Zack and Audrey had sat.

"I guess I don't look at you that way?"

"You look at me the way you always have," said Osgood.

This got a chuckle from Albrecht, who covered his mouth with his hand until he could return to stoicism. "And what way is that?"

"Like a curiosity."

The chuckle came again, and he didn't try to hide it this time.

Osgood nodded and smiled as well. "From the moment we met, you knew I was different; strange and unusual."

"This is true."

"And you've always approached me as someone from whom you're uncertain what to expect."

"Also true."

"Zack and Audrey... They look at me like someone who lost... I dunno." Osgood laughed and felt a drop on her cheek. She dabbed at it, wondering where the leak was that had dropped it onto her. Surely, she wasn't crying. "Lost my mind."

"I don't believe they think that," said Albrecht. His tone had dropped, and she knew he'd noticed the tear.

"What if I have?"

"Have what?"

"Lost my mind," said Osgood. She felt her cadence rising and speeding up. The bruise on her chest pulsed with her heartbeat. "Like my little walkabout from reality there in the Hinterlands." She stopped and looked at him. "Which I realize you probably don't know a lot about."

"I've seen the videos, I subscribe to the podcast," he said. "I am, my dear, a Specterino." He said the word with relish.

Osgood sat in silence. She didn't even know there were videos. From the Hinterlands? She wanted to see them, to see if her vague memories were accurate, to see— She stopped her mind from running down the track and refocused. "I drove to an intersection tonight. *The* intersection. The one where I—"

"Your accident."

"Yes. And I have no recollection of doing so."

"You've experienced significant trauma to your psyche, Prudence," said Albrecht. He leaned forward and folded his hands on his knee. "It's not unreasonable to ask for more than 24 hours to sort your mind out."

She found it unreasonable. Untenable as well. She needed

to get her shit together. Figure out what had happened to her. What *was* happening.

"That intersection was a monumental spot in your formative life," said Albrecht. "To say nothing of your night terrors. It's unsurprising that you would return there..." He twirled a hand in the air as he looked for the right words. "On autopilot?"

"I also did this on autopilot," said Osgood. She opened her phone's gallery and handed it to him. "Is that unsurprising?"

Albrecht reached into his robe pocket and pulled out a pair of black-rimmed reading glasses. Even wearing them, he extended his arm out as far as he could as he swiped through the photos. She tried to read his expression and couldn't discern anything in it. "You did this..."

"Tonight," she said.

"It must've taken you hours." His voice held a note of awe. "It's something like 20 degrees out. Maybe five with the windchill."

"Yeah. And I wasn't wearing gloves," she said, holding up her hand with its scraped fingers. "Yet my fingers haven't turned black and fallen off."

He stopped swiping, and she heard wind rushing past the phone's microphone, then her voice. "*December 10. 3:07 in the morning.*" He watched the video, tilting his head this way and that, then the phone. In his expression was puzzlement but also fascination. A long way from pity and fear. When the sounds of the wind stopped, he handed back the phone. He leaned back in his chair and rubbed his hand over his mouth and down his beard, tugging at the longer hairs on his chin.

She waited, knowing that if she was to get anything at all from Albrecht, and she'd be the first to admit she hadn't the faintest idea what that might be, she'd have to let him process and arrive at it in his own time.

"I need not remind you that my training is in folklore, not parapsychology."

"You need not," agreed Osgood.

"Much of this looks like abstract art," he told her. "Loops, shapes. Intersections. Some pieces look runic. Some appear..." He trailed off and looked at the ceiling for a moment. "Some would not be out of place in a book of Germanic or other European occultism. How much of that have you studied?"

Osgood opened her mouth and then closed it again. Studied? None. "I look things up as I need them," she admitted. "Or have Zack do it."

"Then you also don't know Latin."

"Only what I learned today. *Tempus descensus* and..." she couldn't remember the other one. "Something that means 'open the gate.'"

"Time descent?" asked Albrecht, furrowing his bushy brow.

"Something my doppelgängers were saying." She saw his eyebrows register this statement. "Right! Apparently I've been showing up around the world and saying that. Then screaming."

He lifted her phone to look again. "Locked," he told her and held it out to her.

"Irritating," said Osgood. "Zack is *really* into security." She thumbed her print in again and handed it back.

He took it back, offering nothing. She watched as he swiped through pictures. Again, again, again. Then he stopped and stared for a while, then zoomed in with his fingers. He turned the phone first to the left, then right, then upside down.

"Why did you ask if I speak Latin?"

"*Antecursor*," he said without looking up. "It's..." He shook his head, distracted as he manipulated the image on the screen with his fingers. "You wrote it on the street. Means before. Precursor. It's also English but very rarely used."

"Precursor. Before." Osgood frowned at him.

He stopped and looked at her. His eyes had gone nearly wild with curiosity. "More than before. *Ante* is before. *Cursor* is...runner?" He shook his head, dismissing the idea and seemingly the conversation to return to the phone. "Forerunner, scout, vanguard." He waved his hand through the air again. "Harbinger."

An eye opened in the corner of the room. But was it in the corner? It was enormous. She could nearly see nothing beyond its horrible orange iris. "Harbinger," it hissed at her. Osgood screamed.

Albrecht leaped to his feet. "What is it?" He scrambled to grab at the phone but lost purchase and dropped it to the floor. He followed her eyes to the corner, which was just a corner again. Nothing there. Nothing that could speak. Just a shadow cast by the drapes around the picture windows.

"I—" she said, cutting herself off with a gasp of breath that brought daggers of pain. Her chest ached, her back as well, at that line on her spine that had also turned black. "I saw...something. An eye. And it said 'harbinger.'"

"I said harbinger." Albrecht sat beside her.

"I know," she said in a tone that implied rolling her eyes so strongly she didn't even have to do so. "It said it, too." She pressed her fists into her eyes, cutting off the light, feeling the steady headache growing across her entire head. For a moment in the dark she still saw the eye, but it faded like ripples in a pond, and she found she couldn't remember much of anything about it. An eye. Harbinger. She could tell him, but then he might drift toward that thought as well. That she'd lost her mind.

"Never mind. What was so interesting on..." She pointed at her phone on the floor.

"Oh dear." Albrecht lifted the phone. "I'm very sorry."

She saw that the screen had shattered into an elaborate spiderweb of cracks. Behind it, though, remained her photos of the chalk drawings. "It's," she began and then shook her head. "What is that?" She pointed at the screen. On it was a symbol that looked like a T with an arm and a curly S on top. Unlike most of the things she'd seen

(drawn)

tonight, this one looked very specific.

"You said people saw doppelgängers of you," said Albrecht.

"Yes."

"And I assume, by doppelgängers, you mean—"

She rolled her eyes. "I know that doppelgängers are something different. I don't have *all* the good words."

"This," said Albrecht tapping the screen and re-centering the symbol, "is the symbol for Tulpa."

"Tulpa," repeated Osgood. "What is that?"

"It's a Buddhist concept," said Albrecht. "A sort of...

emanation? Sometimes they're called thought-forms. It is thought that someone who has achieved an overtly contemplative life can...create an external—"

"Projection," said Osgood.

"Yes," he said. "The concept has been theorized as the basis for particularly vivid imaginary friends, omens, astral projection. Many things. But if I were reading folklore about someone who was seen while in an otherworldly space, and who drew this symbol, then I'd say that while you were...outside?"

Osgood nodded. "That feels like a good way to put it."

"I would imagine you may have created Tulpas of yourself. Perhaps to communicate with the world. Perhaps to help return you to it."

"How would I know?" she asked. The idea of random doppelgängers appearing around the world was odd enough, but the idea that she'd somehow created them from Buddhist mysticism. "I don't believe I've achieved an overtly contemplative life, either."

"You don't remember your missing time, Prudence," said Albrecht. "Who knows what you achieved?"

She opened her mouth to push back, but he was right. She nodded instead. "I should go."

"You are always welcome here," said Albrecht.

"I know," she said. "Maybe that's why I chose here to come back to in the first place."

"I hope that reason was my hospitality," said Albrecht with a smile.

Osgood stood. "Do you think I could just create these things? The Tulpas?"

"I don't know," he said. "I've not known anyone who has."

"And if I can't," she walked up the steps out of the sunken living room and sat down to put on her shoes. "Does that mean that some...thing else did it?"

"I don't know that, either." Albrecht followed her to the door. He lifted her coat off the coat tree and held it out for her.

In her regular life, Osgood often found such attempts at chivalry annoying, but this felt warm.

"If I were you, my dear Prudence," he said at the door. "I would monitor myself more intensively. Cameras. Tracking."

She nodded, irritated at the very idea. "Because I'm the harbinger?"

"Let's hope not."

11

She knocked again, still pulling her knuckles each time. Then once more.

Audrey opened her bedroom door, squinting at the dim light in the hallway. "What's going— Why are you dressed at—" She threw a look over her shoulder. "Six?"

"Something's happened," said Osgood. "We need to talk."

"Now?" asked Audrey.

"Yeah." *Because if I wait, I won't tell you at all,* thought Osgood. *If I wait, we can just pretend my jaunt out to the really-for-real crossroads wasn't a big deal at all.* But it was, wasn't it? Big fucking deal. "I'm going to go wake Zack."

Audrey opened her eyes fully and blinked into the hallway at Osgood. For a moment, Osgood thought she was going to change her mind, say, "Fuck this," and go back to bed. "I'll make coffee," she said instead.

The relief that washed over Osgood frightened her. So relieved that her friends would be able to put a harder watch on her. Monitor. Make sure she's not

(*antecursor*)

a threat. That's what was concerning her, wasn't it? That she might be dangerous.

She walked to the kitchen and out the back door of her apartment. Once, this had led to a structurally unsound set of back stairs down to the alley. Shit, last time she'd been out here, she'd smoked a joint and ate out Carla. Once that whole deal went south, she really hadn't enjoyed the balcony. Now, though, it was a hall to a staircase.

"Very industrial," she said and heard her voice echo across the narrow stairwell. At the bottom, to the right, was an imposing steel door she assumed lead outside. To the right, a nondescript red door. She knocked lightly, drawing a deep breath. *Don't mean to impose*, she thought wildly and laughed to herself in dismay.

"You'll have to go in."

Osgood looked back up the stairs and saw Audrey leaning against the wall.

"He sleeps like the dead."

"He won't get pissed?" asked Osgood.

"I didn't say that." Audrey vanished back into the kitchen.

Sleeps like the dead. Zack. In her apartment. Well, below and to the side. Osgood shook her head and opened the door. The space felt cavernous, a converted warehouse or storage area. It was dark, nearly black, save flickering LEDs everywhere. Racks of equipment lit up across the board in reds and greens. A command center with a multi-monitor display bounced a screen saver clock from monitor to monitor, from corner to corner. Before the monitors was a keyboard with backlit keys and a mouse that wouldn't have been out of place in *Tron*. She realized that she'd never seen Zack able to fully spread his wings.

5:58, read Osgood off the clock. She looked to the left and to the right, both directions revealing more flickering lights.

"Zack?" she called, and that call echoed back from the ceiling and off the racks.

"Os?" asked an exhausted voice.

"Yeah," she said.

"What's going on? What time is—"

"It's six," Osgood told him in the darkness. "I stole your jeep."

"You what?"

"I filled it up when I brought it back. I used a gas card I found in the glove compartment. I will repay the gas once I get re..." Osgood considered what she even meant by this before finishing, "established." She didn't know.

"Is everything alright?" he asked.

You could lie, suggested a voice in her mind. *You don't have to tell them anything.*

"No," she said, after a long contemplative pause. "No, it's not."

"Jarvis. Lights thirty percent."

"Yes, sir," said a mechanical voice with a British accent.

The room brightened and Osgood saw Zack staggering toward her in plaid boxers and a t-shirt featuring a cartoon character she recognized vaguely but not enough to name. He rubbed at his eyes.

"Jarvis? Really?" asked Osgood.

"Custom name patch for the automation."

"I would think you'd be concerned about privacy."

"I built it. It's not hard to hack down Google or Amazon stuff and pull their spyware out."

"I'll take your word for it," said Osgood. "I need to talk to you two upstairs in...10 minutes?"

"Sure," yawned Zack.

She turned to leave.

"Os," said Zack.

"Yeah?"

"I shouldn't have posted that you came back. I should've let you do it. It was a dick move."

Osgood nodded without turning back to Zack.

"I was just excited," he said. "Couldn't believe we were so lucky to have you back. And there's a whole world of Specterinos out there who are just as thrilled as we are."

"I..." She looked at her red Chucks. She ran the heel of her left over the toe of her right, leaving a dirty streak. She wondered how much dirt she'd left in the apartment. "When I...left, we had about 70 reliable Specterinos."

"Yeah."

"I'm not sure I know how to be available to the apparent throngs we have now."

"I'm sorry."

"We have bigger concerns," she said. "Audrey's making coffee." Without looking back, Osgood walked to the door. She lingered just a moment to call over her shoulder, "I'm not angry with you," and then climbed the stairs.

Back upstairs, Osgood stood in the bathroom, looking at herself in the mirror. Her left eye had a pool of red along the edge of the iris. "That's not fucking good," she said then splashed cold water on her face. Would have to be dealt with, wouldn't it? Would have to be examined. The bruise too, no? She lifted her shirt and noted that the black tendrils had spread further. "One thing at a time," she told the person in the mirror who looked only vaguely like Prudence Osgood. "One fucking thing at a time."

She found them on the couch, both still in pajamas. Both held mugs of coffee branded with the Specterinos logo; both wore the same concern and expectation on their faces.

"Black," said Audrey. "Like a moonless night and such. Isn't that how you used to order?"

Osgood smiled that Audrey had remembered it. "Yes, it is. But I will decline, as I have enough adrenaline coursing through me." She remained standing before them and stared at the ceiling for what felt like a solid minute before figuring out where to start. "I took three melatonin pills to sleep last night."

"So you wouldn't dream?" asked Zack.

"No," said Osgood. "I was unusually unconcerned about dreaming, and, as far as I know, I didn't dream. The dosage was just about keeping my mind from cycling all night."

"That's reasonable," said Audrey.

"I know," snapped Osgood. She closed her eyes and shook her head. Without re-opening them, she took a breath. "I need you *not* to coddle me. Not to pity me. Not to worry. Because what I'm going to say will need investigation. And I should not do this myself." She opened her eyes again and looked at them.

"We're here, Os," said Audrey. "We're with you."

"Yeah," said Zack. "Absolutely. Always."

"Next," continued Osgood. "Until we know what's happening, or until we absolutely *need* their help, the Specterinos don't need to know anything."

They agreed.

"And last." She took a long breath. "If my parents call or come here. I'm not fucking here. Ever. Period. 'Osgood is permanently out.' Got it?"

They agreed on that point as well.

"Okay." Osgood ran her hands over her face. How to talk about this without sounding—

"You can tell us anything," said Zack.

Osgood looked at him. His face seemed devoid of the pity-fear that had irked her. "Can I?" she asked. Was she asking for confirmation of truth or permission? Osgood didn't know, but she spilled. The stolen Jeep, the crossroads, the missing time, the shapes on the pavement. Then onto Albrecht and the Tulpa.

"You drew a Tulpa symbol?" asked Zack. Osgood couldn't tell if his tone was excitement or confusion.

"What is a Tulpa?" asked Audrey.

"Something I'm disappointed I didn't consider," said Zack. He shook his head. Osgood gestured toward him to cede the floor.

"While my father didn't buy into the practices, especially after my mother died, I grew up in Buddhism. And some of my older cousins were very interested in the...superpowers aspects of the religion."

"Buddhism has superpowers." Audrey's tone indicated a statement but begged the question.

"Well, Tulpas are about being able to conjure a friend. My cousin Dinh bragged about his fuckbuddy Tulpa." He looked up at Osgood. "I don't believe he actually managed to create one, to be clear. But the idea was always that you could create an entity with your mind. Once you did so, though, things got a little vague."

"So, Osgood's projections..." began Audrey.

"Could very well have been Tulpas." He looked from Audrey back to Osgood. "I mean since you don't remember what you did in... out of..."

"Yes," said Osgood.

"Then the idea of you creating projections, perhaps to notify us you needed help, or to herald your return. Or—"

"Or to herald something else?" Osgood frowned. "I also saw something. Or somethings. Twice now. At Albrecht's yesterday, when you picked me up, I saw movement in the darkness in his bathroom. And then...well, at Albrecht's again..." She shuddered at the thought, unable to pin it down in her memory. Something in the room with them. Something that saw her. Something that seemed to grow vaguer every time she considered it. "Something proclaimed 'harbinger.'"

"Did Albrecht see—"

Osgood cut Zack off by shaking her head vehemently. "There's every chance these things are in my mind, and that greatly concerns me. Because it supports the crazy—"

"Really need to not use that word—"

Osgood gave Zack a rapid sniff. "Supports my instability. And if I'm unstable, I can't help." She sat in the La-Z-Boy and leaned toward them. "Something is wrong, but I don't know what it is. I need you to analyze the stuff I drew in the intersection." She reached into her pocket and retrieved her phone for Zack.

"You broke it *already?*"

Osgood held up her hands. "Actually, that was Albrecht."

"Alright," he said, staring at the shattered screen with a forlorn expression. "I'll replace the screen."

"Then put a tracker on it. And maybe don't keep your keys anywhere near the front door, so I can't steal your vehicle."

"Os," said Audrey, a calm tone, her hand out. "You don't want us to be your keepers."

"No, I don't." Osgood shook her head. "Look, don't tell me what to do, where to go, where not to go. But if I'm sleepwalking to your Jeep in the middle of the night, it might be valuable to wake me up, or stop me, or fucking follow me."

They both nodded.

"Also, you don't need to steal my Jeep," said Zack.

"Fine, Zack, borrow it."

"No," he said. "What I mean is that your car is in the back."

She cocked her head as she looked at him, feeling the warmth on her cheeks and in her throat. "You got it...for me?" Osgood hadn't herself been certain where her little green car had gotten to, but she'd had some suspicions. "From impound?"

Zack nodded.

"I thought you needed to be on the registration to pick up—"

He stopped her. "You have a lot of friends, Os."

Osgood expelled a literal, "Hah!"

"No, really," said Audrey. "I don't think you understand. Most people didn't really believe the whole 'musicians sold their soul to a demon who then kidnapped your kids' angle."

"When you put it that way, it's rather—"

"But," interrupted Zack, "those who did were grateful for closure."

"As I was," said Audrey.

"Well," said Osgood as the warmth crawled higher on her face.

"A lot of people were happy to do anything they could to see you returned, and to see that your return would be as comfortable as possible."

"When you say a lot..." Osgood said.

"Ten to twenty thousand."

Osgood took a long deep breath. "All the more reason why I ought not to go around scribbling occult nonsense on intersections."

🜨 12 🜨

Osgood tried unsuccessfully to nap, but even in the darkness of her room with the blackout curtains drawn, she found her thoughts drifting and head pounding. She had never wanted the sweet haze of oxy and liquor more.

You were on a supernatural detox, she reminded herself. Maybe not time to go chasing that rabbit again.

She focused on her ceiling fan, visible in a slim shaft of light poking over the top of the blackout curtains. It turned so lazily that it couldn't possibly be circulating air. This speed felt good, though; she could watch a spot of dark dust on one of the blades circle again and again without dizzying herself. She closed her eyes again, but in the darkness, she saw herself, her duplicate, in front of a fountain.

Tempus descensus.

"Shit," she said.

Osgood sat up and slowly moved her legs to the side of the bed. Her chronic pain seemed to have lessened a bit, but this move was always the worst. Today, the pain in her calves and thighs and knees was hot but manageable. Her lower back felt on fire, but that was nothing new. She rolled her head around on her neck, surprised at the flexibility it had found somewhere in the darkness, in the margins. She took a deep breath and held it before letting it out. She saw her small chest of drawers in the corner, that special chest. Special for what it contained, her collection of dildos and vibrators. She could masturbate. That might help clear her mind. Rejecting the idea out of hand, she stood and went to find clothes, but all those in her drawers smelled musty, old.

You haven't washed them in over a year, Pru, she reminded herself.

She dug in another drawer where the scent wasn't quite so noticeable, found a shirt and a hoodie that were far less difficult to be around than the rest, and threw them on with jeans. When she left her room, she stood at the threshold for a moment, listening both forward and back, toward the kitchen and living room, for voices. If she heard them, she'd bet they'd be talking about her. What to do. How to track her. What's to become of Prudence Osgood, pariah?

She heard nothing, though, and walked toward the living room. The transition from the darkness of her bedroom to the windowless hall to her front living room, which was lit brightly from bay windows overlooking Clark Street, was rough, and she shielded her eyes.

Audrey sat in the bay window, scrolling lazily on her tablet.

Osgood tilted her head and watched this beautiful woman in repose. She wished she could preserve time, or at least this simple visual. How long would it be until the two of them could again share space in the simplest of fashions? It'd be hard now. *Now that you're the mystery, Pru.*

The sigh had apparently been loud enough to rouse Audrey's attention. "Hey," she said.

"Hey," said Osgood.

"Couldn't sleep?"

"Couldn't sleep." Osgood nodded when Audrey held her gaze, waiting for more. After nothing came, Audrey returned to her tablet.

Osgood realized that, despite her instinct to protest, this was the simple interaction she craved. How much more could there be? If Audrey were to get up and come to her, offer to lie with her, spoon with her, help her drift off, well, that would be extraordinary circumstances, wouldn't it? And wouldn't Osgood doubt the overture? *Of course, I would,* she thought. Because Audrey knew that she didn't cuddle when she slept. That would be a show of over-concern, over-control. Of getting what she wanted, not what Osgood did.

But right now, it *was* what Osgood wanted. Just to be comforted. Held. Told that things were all right, that she wasn't broken, at least no more than usual. She opened her mouth but closed it again. The room looked nearly the same as it had before she'd gone, something that surprised Osgood. Audrey had very different decorative tastes than Osgood, whose style ran to, "What color were the walls when I moved in? Let's leave them that way," and just looking for places to stick odds and ends. The twin bookshelves that flanked what once was a fireplace and now was a painted brick alcove were overstuffed with books in various positions and conditions, some turned in, some out, some hardcover, some soft.

A large blue...something...caught her eye. As she moved toward it, she saw that it was a record album, stuffed in above the books, protruding just a bit. She immediately felt a pit in her stomach, remembering the last record they'd played in this apartment. Remembering what it had done. The pit grew as she moved closer. She slid it out from atop the books, finding it still sealed, with a $30 price tag on the upper right. Looking at it, Osgood felt her mouth go dry and her migraine throb harder. The bottom half of the album cover showed light to dark blue to nearly black watery depths. Above a whitish line of blue suds was an expanse of water leading to land, showing no human life, just trees. In the trees was the title, in simple uppercase white block letters: *The Shore to the Deep.* Below the waterline, in the same block print, was the name of the band.

"(Rhapsody) In the Shallows," read Osgood aloud. As if from nowhere, she remembered the press release that had been emailed to her. She'd read it just before she'd gone walk-about. "They released it."

Audrey looked up, her eyes moving from the album to Osgood's face and back. "Yeah," she said. "They did."

"Has it—" But Osgood didn't know what to ask. They'd killed The Lord of the Hinterlands, hadn't they? She could still see Audrey stabbing at him with a rebar spear, like Ahab and the whale. Without him, wasn't the band just a band, like any other? Wasn't the music just—

"We scoured the re-release tracks," said Audrey, seeming hesitant. "And those on this album. These digitize now, where the others didn't, if you remember."

"Yeah," said Osgood, recalling when Zack had tried to rip *Ramparts Over the Hinterlands*, the band's final album, and had gotten nothing. Not static, not noise. Nothing.

"We didn't find anything hidden in the tracks. Nothing much has come from it either. Turns out that in 2019 and beyond, Rhapsody in the Shallows isn't as popular as Gloria Mundi Records had hoped." Audrey nodded solemnly. "Didn't stop them from suing us, though."

Osgood looked from the album to Audrey. "Suing you?"

"Yeah," said Audrey. "Turns out, when a company is planning a big re-release of their premier act, they don't want someone talking about how their music got a whole bunch of teenagers killed at the turn of the century."

"Right," said Osgood. "So, they sued. Did they—"

"Win?" Audrey shrugged. "Ongoing litigation," she said, remarkably nonplussed. "The judge told them a few times to come back with a better case than they had, arguing that a 'little podcast' wasn't going to take down one of the most popular bands of the last century."

Osgood laughed. "Little podcast."

"Even at our peak, we still only had ten or twenty thousand," said Audrey. "The judge was right; we were nothing compared to their behemoth."

Flipping the album over, Osgood saw an extensive track listing. "Over twenty-five tracks," she said. "Any good?"

"Remember," said Audrey, "I wasn't a big fan of theirs *before* I found out how involved they were in my sister's death." She said it glibly, but her face noticeably fell when she mentioned her sister. After a moment, she plastered on a fake smile. "It's fine. Zack likes it more than I do."

"I'm sorry, Aud," said Osgood.

Her friend waved away the condolences like shooing a fly.

"Where is Zack?"

"Oh," said Audrey. "He's always in his cave, unless we're actively working on something. Even then, he usually tries to get me down there, instead of coming up to the comfortable seating in here."

Osgood looked around her living room, as though seeing it for the first time. "It is comfy in here."

"It is," agreed Audrey. "It's home."

Osgood met her eyes and felt some unspoken connection there. Some comfort. Some love. "Do you want to," Osgood began but wasn't sure what she wanted to suggest. In the end, she came to, "Get a drink downstairs?"

"I have a headache," said Audrey.

"What a coincidence!"

"I'm going to decline. Another time?" Audrey's fake smile morphed into a slightly more real one.

Osgood nodded. She lifted her coat off the door and pulled it on. "Let me," she looked back at Audrey, who'd returned to her tablet. "Let me know if you change your mind."

"I will," said Audrey. "Let *us* know if you suddenly have an urge to do more street graffiti."

"I will," said Osgood. She closed the door behind her and descended the century-old staircase to the street.

13

"They said I'd find you here. And that you'd have single-handedly opened the bar for the day."

Osgood felt her hackles raise. She knew that voice. She laid her hands flat on the purple bar in the back of Mary's. "Did they also tell you the holy hell that they're going to hear from me for doing that?"

"Oh," he said. "They did."

Terry, a slender man with thinner hair than he'd had last time Osgood had been at this bar, asked his order over her shoulder.

"Tequila sunrise," he said.

She rolled her eyes. "He's not staying."

"You can't decide who's staying or not, honey," said Terry. "Only whether he's drinking with you."

"He's not."

"That's fine," said Goddard. "Can I wait for my drink next to you?"

"I'd prefer you didn't," said Osgood.

"Look," he said, and she did.

Fuck him for getting *more* handsome in the, what, five, six

97

years since she'd seen him last. Perfect scruff, amazing hair. Osgood scowled. "You fucking asshole," she said, shaking her head.

"Guilty." Goddard sat on the stool next to her, then, seeing her expression, raised his hands and stepped down two seats. "Really, I was an asshole to you."

"And to Zack."

"The last time I saw you I—"

She affected a deep voice "'What's it like to be a fraud, Osgood?'"

"I don't think I asked that."

"Close enough," she said. She wasn't certain what he'd said, but the gist was plenty bad. "Especially dickish to say it during my keynote at GhostCon."

"Again," he said, "guilty." He let a smile hit his lips as Terry set a tequila sunrise before him. "Though I recall you then telling everybody how small my penis was."

"Is," said Osgood. She regretted saying it, though. It had taken her off the high road, removed the upper hand. "I regret making my response about your less than impressive —" She closed her eyes and shook her head.

"See the abuse?" he asked.

"You fucking asshole." She stuck her hand in the air and got Terry's attention. "He's not leaving, Terry! Make him! And I need another." She pointed at her bourbon glass, depressingly empty.

Terry took her glass and went about refilling it, ignoring the first half of her request.

"I was worried," said Goddard.

She narrowed her eyes at him. Another glance reignited her fury at his perfect hair and sparkling blue eyes. She felt a rumbling, an irritating rumbling, an *infuriating* rumbling in her jeans. "Okay, Captain fucking America. What on Earth were you worried about?"

"You," he said.

"My alcoholism and addiction are no longer any of your concern. Got it?"

"What?" he asked. She could see true perplexity in his eyes. "I mean you *vanishing*."

Osgood watched the bourbon appear on the bar before her, and she emptied it and returned the glass to Terry before the bartender could turn away. "Again."

Terry frowned. "Are you—"

"I was fucking missing for 15 months, Terry, as Sampson *fucking* Goddard here has just reminded me, so I'd really rather not have my activities policed at the moment."

Terry silently refilled her bourbon, threw his towel on the bar top, and disappeared into the back.

"Looks like I'll have to serve myself next time," observed Osgood.

"Do you know what happened?"

She ignored his question.

"Os?"

She ignored harder.

"The Milwaukee Supernatural Collective was all over—"

She snorted and spit a bit of bourbon out of her mouth. "The *Milwaukee Supernatural Collective*? You fucking hipster!"

"Okay, sure, Spectral Inspector."

She tipped her head in the barest of nods. "Fair."

"I know a group in St. Paul, another in Indianapolis, St. Louis."

"I know cities too," said Osgood. She knew she was rapidly approaching the end of her snappiness.

"Ghost hunters all over the world, in fact. Everybody wanted to help bring back the Spectral Inspector. After all, she solved the Rest Stop Papers Disappearances."

True, thought Osgood. She had. "I had help."

"We all have help," he said. "Once I was yours."

"I think you have that backward."

"We both know that you were the better—"

She turned her body to face him fully. He'd hung his coat on the hooks by the door but still wore his striped scarf around his neck. It led the eye down, down, down... "What do you want?"

"Besides wanting to see you? To express my gladness that you're alive?"

"Yes," said Osgood. "Besides that."

He shrugged. "I want to help."

"You can help by getting the fu—" She snapped her mouth closed. "Sorry."

He shook his head.

"What do you want to help with?"

"Anything I can do."

"Don't you mean anyone?"

He opened his mouth, then closed it. "Do *you* even know what you're insinuating?"

She scowled again. "You fucking around on me while we were dating. You working with other ghost hunters while we were partners."

"Is that cheating?"

"At least one of them is." Her eyes moved from her empty glass to the bottle of bourbon just over the bar's edge, left by Terry when he exited in a huff. Glass, to bottle, to glass, to bottle. She nodded, reached over, and grabbed the bottle, giving herself a full glass before putting it back.

"Same Osgood," said Goddard.

She looked at him, trying to read his face, his eyes. To look beyond the smugness that seemed to be his default and mine deeper for his true intentions. "Very. Different. Osgood."

"Fair enough."

"So," she said. "You heard I was back yesterday, when my,"

she struggled for the word, "overenthusiastic friend posted about it. Then got in your Chevy Malibu and—"

"Been a long while since that car."

"—drove right the fuck down here from Milwaukee?"

"Sorta," he said.

"Sorta," she repeated.

"Well, I did hear that you were back yesterday, and it was from that tweet, by proxy, anyway. One of my associates pointed it out to me. But that's not why I drove down."

She plastered a smile on her face. The one she'd used for school photos long ago. The one she'd used with her prom date when he'd given her that corsage and then later used while telling him that it was okay that he'd splooged half on his pants and half on her dress in the history classroom. Then she'd gone to seek out Audrey for the kind of attention she really wanted.

"Well," she said. "I'm waiting."

"You've used spirit boxes," he said.

She waited. "Is that a question."

"An inference."

"Ah." She nodded. "I have, in the past, occasionally utilized spirit boxes."

"Well," he said. "If it's been a while, you're missing out. Now they have devices specifically for cycling through stations. You can adjust your speed, duration. It's pretty fantastic."

"I have *also*," she added, "been skeptical of the value of having someone repeat random things they hear on random radio frequencies. And have always had to apply a huge level of interpretation to the result."

"Yes, me too." Goddard reached into his pocket and took out his phone. He set it face up on the bar between them, then returned his attention to her without unlocking it.

"Oh, goody," said Osgood. "Are we gonna listen to some spirit box results?"

"If you're willing. I assure you it'll be worth it."

"Oh, Sam, how many times have I heard those words from you before?"

He ignored the comment, just stared at her.

"Well, play it already," she said.

He opened an audio playback app with a large green triangle in the center of the screen. "When we do the spirit box, we record the person listening, as well as audio from the various frequencies being cycled through."

"To see what they heard that they thought was relevant?"

"Yes," he said, "but with less skepticism."

Osgood rolled her eyes.

"I would think, for someone who first traveled to another dimension full of missing teens and then vanished—"

She waved her hand in his face. "You're not the first to make that point today, and it has started to bore me." She slid the phone closer to her, seeing the large play button. "I assume you want me to press this?"

"I'd like it if you would," he said.

Osgood nodded and stared at the phone for a while longer, already rehearsing what she'd say about how the words *could* mean something of value, but no more than clouds that look like dragons are *actually* dragons. She tapped.

A male voice, without cadence or structure, said, "Dork. Has. Open. Ed. The. Harem. Binger. Rises. Odd. Good."

"Dork has opened," repeated Osgood. "Riveting. Also, I'd be up for binging some harems right about now. I didn't know it, but it's been almost fifteen months since I fucked someone."

"That's..." Goddard shook his head. He held his palm out to ask her to wait. "That was our guy saying what he heard."

"Yes."

"Next is—"

The sound of cycling radio stations played, each no more than half a second. Steadily, she could feel the hairs standing up on her neck and arms. Her nipples got hard. The sentence was spoken by multiple voices, multiple stations, songs and news and two-way and short-wave radio communications. Despite its disparate source material, however, what it said was obvious to her. "You're fucking with me."

"I assure you, I am not."

Osgood glared at his stupid, pretty face, looking for any sign of a smirk.

"'Cuz that spirit box just said..." She looked at the phone and shivered.

"I know," he said. "But I don't want to taint what you heard."

She looked at him. "When did you become such a good investigator."

"After you told me I embarrassed you."

"At GhostCon?"

"No, when you dumped me."

"Then some good came out of—"

"Osgood."

"Sam*pson*."

"Please tell me what you heard."

She shook her head. "It's too obvious."

"Too obvious for..." He waited.

"For a fucking spirit box."

"What did you—"

She blurted it out, feeling the heat again in her face and body. "Door has opened. The harbinger rises. Osgood."

"Yep," said Sampson Goddard. "That's what I got, too."

🜨 14 🜨

"**W**hoa, there," said Goddard as she stumbled.

"I'm fine," Osgood insisted, blinking several times to make the marquee sign on the front of Mary's find something resembling focus.

"Clearly," he said and took her arm.

She took it back.

"There's nothing wrong with asking for help."

"I don't *need* your help," she said, throwing the words at him with a quick pitch of her head that she immediately regretted. The old familiar pains had crept back entirely now. Neck movement fed spine pain, which fed pelvic pain, which fed thigh pain. But she wasn't sure she meant it.

"I would never suggest that you *need* my help, Osgood."

"Then what do you want?"

A couple brushed by them, and she realized they were blocking the middle of the sidewalk in the early evening on Clark street. She shivered.

"Do you want this now?" he asked.

She looked at the maroon object in his hand and could not resolve it. Her head swam. After a moment he reconfigured it, and now she saw the armhole. She slid one arm into her coat, then the other, then pulled away from Goddard, as she threw her shoulders into it, all the way on. Again, the pain radiated. "You don't have any oxy, do ya?"

Goddard frowned. "Like OxyContin?"

"Not just *like* OxyContin."

"I, uh." He narrowed his eyes at her. "I do not."

"Don't you fucking judge me."

"Not judging," he said. "I have a pot vape, if that might—"

"Gimme," said Osgood. She held out her hand, then shook it to expedite the transaction. She swayed, and as she watched, her hand separated into two. She squeezed her eyes shut and willed them back together, and when she looked again, they'd converged. She couldn't possibly be this drunk, could she?

"It may be legal, but they still don't like people vaping on the street."

"Then let's go somewhere," she said and shook her head. *C'mon man, think!*

"You do live right..." He pointed at the windows above.

"Not there," she said. "They'd..." What would they do? Audrey knew Sampson Goddard more by reputation, but Zack, Zack knew. He'd been there, at the keynote, when Goddard— "They'd say I need to rest. And I don't want to rest."

"What do you want to do, Osgood?"

She looked at him and cocked her head. His beauty irritated the fuck out of her. His perfectly manicured stubble, all uniform length, shaved to appear unshaven. His hair tousled, like bedhead, but not. Just the right amount of mess to suggest he didn't care about his appearance, when he so definitely did. With his coat open, she could see his pecs right through his tighter-than-necessary shirt. And, yes, those jeans, as snug as they were, very definitely showed the outline of— "Take me somewhere," she said.

"Where?"

"Do I look like I give a fuck?" she asked. "Somewhere I can suck on that."

His eyes widened. "I..."

"The vape, you vain idiot."

"Right," he said. "And I'd really like it if you'd stop—"

She leaned in. "*I'd* really like it if you'd shut your fucking mouth and take me somewhere that I can get high and fucked. Is that *really* too much to ask? I'm still fucking hot. And it's been fifteen months or something."

Goddard opened his mouth then closed it again. She wanted to slap the pretty right off his face. She gritted her teeth.

"Well?" she asked.

"I, uh..." He narrowed his eyes. "I think you may be too dru—"

"You fucking idiot."

"Please stop call—"

She shook her head, looking down at the sidewalk below. She stood on a crack

(break your mama's back)

between slabs. She put her feet heel to toe and walked the line, sticking her arms straight out and alternating touching her nose with her left, then right, then left, then right. "I'm a fully fucking functional alcoholic, *Sampson*." She sneered at him. "I still can't believe—"

"Okay, Osgood."

"So, are you up for it?" Osgood put her hands on her hips and stared at him. "Will you take me somewhere and fuck me?"

"Is this something you really—"

"Oh, for chrissakes, Goddard. It's just sex. I don't want to get into another relationship with you."

He cocked his head.

"The time window on this offer is closing."

He opened his mouth.

"If the next word out of your mouth isn't, 'Yes,' I'm going back in there..." She pointed into Mary's. "...To find someone who *does* want to fuck me. Boy, girl, doesn't matter."

"Yes," said Goddard.

"Good," said Osgood. "The Heartland Motel is less than a mile from here. And you're picking up condoms on the way."

As they drove, Osgood stared at him, leaning against the passenger door. She had to concede that their time together long ago had been nice, if brief. He wasn't stupid-pretty, he was smart-pretty, and she liked that. He'd been often dismissive, though, of her ideas, her plans. If the idea didn't come down from Goddard himself, it was a safe bet their group wouldn't be doing it.

"You were kind," she said, speaking the first words since they'd climbed in.

He side-eyed her. "Today?"

"Yes, but also back then."

"When we were—"

"Yeah." She glanced out the windshield at cars passing. "You were a pretentious asshole—"

"Aha."

"But you were kind about the hoax. The one that blew up Frost and Osgood and *Chicago Haunts*." She adjusted as a sharp bolt of pain radiated up her spine. "Of course, you lost some goodwill when you cheated. And more at GhostCon."

"I do apologize, Spooky," he said. "For both."

"I know," she said. She rolled her eyes at the long-forgotten nickname. He wasn't picking up what she was putting down, was he? "I'm just— Just— You're not *just* someone to fuck."

Again with the side-eye.

"Don't get all cocky now."

"I didn't say anything."

"As we drive around in your black Suburban. What is it with dudes and black SUVs, anyway?"

"This is a very functional vehicle, I—"

She shook her head and waved her hand in his face to get him to stop talking. Another throb had begun in her head. Her left eye hurt, so she closed it to let it rest. She tried to forget the pool of red in that one. Tried to forget the other indicators of— "Something's wrong with me."

He nodded solemnly.

"That's all you've got?"

"I don't know what you want me—"

"I don't either," she said, then leaned her head against the window and looked out.

"Are you sure you don't want me to take you back—"

"So help me, Goddard. If you don't want to fuck me, just say so. But if you do, stop trying to talk *me* out of it."

He flipped on his turn signal and pulled into the Walgreen's parking lot.

"Polyisoprene," she said.

"What?"

"I have a latex allergy."

He nodded and climbed out into falling snow. She watched him pull his collar up and shuffle into the Walgreen's. She wondered, with a last lingering bit of Catholic guilt, if she should be doing this. Not just the sex, but using him this way. She was confident he'd enjoy himself. He always had. And she would, too. He'd had his opportunities to opt out, right? She'd given him off-ramps and he'd gone ahead. His choice. And it would be his choice when they got to the motel and he plunged ahead there, too. The thought made her shudder. The carnal hunger was so strong within her, a primal craving she rarely felt. So often for her, sex had been a distraction, but here and now the desire was real and visceral and consuming.

Returning with a tiny Walgreen's bag in hand, Goddard climbed back into the SUV. He sat for a moment, not starting the engine.

"Something wrong?" asked Osgood.

"I. I just need to say something."

She nodded at him.

"I loved you."

"Okay," she said.

"I know we weren't good together."

She agreed.

"When I heard you were gone, I was worried." He turned to look at her. The concern on his face didn't seem performative. "I did my best to find you."

"Turns out, I just needed to show up," she said.

"Well, I tried."

She frowned. His earnestness gnawed at her. "Sam." She touched his arm. "We were awful together."

"Wow."

"But! You're a good guy." She nodded to reinforce her point. "And I really do appreciate that you cared and were looking." She sat back in the seat and looked through the windshield at the falling snow. "Not everybody gets the opportunity to see what it'd be like if they were just..."

"Gone," he said.

She nodded.

"I don't know what's wrong with me," she said. She picked at a bit of loose cuticle on her index finger. "I don't know what's happening, where I went or why. I don't know what will happen. But I do really, *really* need some release. And it's just not the same by myself. I'm sorry if you feel used."

"I..." He shook his head. "I get it."

"Are you still in?"

He started the engine.

"Good."

Before long, between the swipes of the wiper blades throwing off sticky wet snow, she saw the neon heart of the Heartland Motel. She could remember driving by it as a child and thinking it was the height of luxury, that the massive neon sign proved how much better it was than the Days Inns, Comforts, and other cheapos of the day. It was only upon moving back to Andersonville that she'd realized the truth. This was a no-tell motel, a check-in, check-out same day establishment.

Goddard climbed out, covering his head with his coat, and ran into the office.

Osgood looked at her phone.

Are you ok? asked Audrey.

Yes, Osgood responded.

Were worried, said Zack in his bubble. Osgood wondered if it was meant to say that they had been worried or that they were still.

Fine, just needed to get out, she told them, copying and pasting the message into each bubble.

i know where you are, said Zack.

Osgood stared at the phone, lips pursed. She knew she'd been the one to tell them to track her, to pay attention.

i hpe that wasnt sent with judgement, Osgood tapped out angrily, ignoring the errors.

Ellipses from Zack. Ellipses, ellipses, ellipses. **No,** he returned, finally, **just wanted to let you know I'm on watch.**

"On watch," she grumbled and nodded. She tossed the phone into the cup holder as Goddard returned with the keycard.

15

The motel room felt dim, thin, as if it existed someplace else, where all motel rooms merge into the same room, one with dual beds swaddled in garishly colored duvets below mediocre paintings of mediocre landscapes on patterned wallpapered walls. Osgood stepped back to the door and flipped both switches, revealing that all the lights had, in fact, been on. She squinted and ignored the migraine that had crawled from her left eye across the crown of her brain to the back. She rubbed the spot and thought she felt a bump.

"Maybe when I hit Albrecht's floor," she said to herself. This thought led to another that had been gnawing at the corners of her mind. Not how she'd wound up on Albrecht's floor

(jesus, god, had it just been)

yesterday, but *why* she'd wound up there. Of all the places in the world she could've reappeared, she couldn't fathom why that one was, well, not special, because Albrecht himself was damned special, but why *more* special than the others. Why not her apartment? Or the house she'd grown up in? Or, hell, why not the fucking crossroads, for the sake of symmetry? But no, she'd awoken on her back on the floor in her college advisor's house in the woods of St. Charles.

"Os?"

She looked up from the light switches and turned toward him. Goddard's face held a mixture of anticipation and excitement alongside the concern and curiosity. She supposed that's how she would look, were the circumstances reversed. And she'd still go ahead and chase that sweet release. Before he could again ask again, try to talk her out of it, she slid her coat off her shoulders and followed it with her t-shirt, then bra. She hesitated for only a moment and cocked her head at him, thumbs hooked inside her jeans.

"You..." he said, pointing at her chest.

She looked down and found herself surprised by the blooming bruise, still very much her body's centerpiece. "Not as bad as it looks, I promise."

"Does it hurt?"

"*I* hurt," she said. "Always. Forever." She pointed to the bruise, aiming to poke at it, but hesitating. "This is fleeting."

He appeared to want to say more, but said nothing.

After a silence long enough to irritate her, she asked, "Would you like me to put my shirt back on?"

"No," he said.

"Then shall I continue? Or stop."

When he said nothing, she undid the button. When he still said nothing, she unzipped the fly.

"I—" he said, before stopping himself.

"I hope I've made it clear that I don't expect anything of you," she said.

"You have."

"And that I am of sound mind."

He coughed a laugh.

"Relatively..." She allowed a wicked smile to cross her lips, then she slid her jeans to the floor.

Nude before him, she felt a sense of control that she'd rarely experienced in her life. Always so conscious of the awkward gawkiness, of the unevenness of her tits, of the fact that her pubic hair crawled from her mons in a happy trail to her belly button, and spread onto the tops of her thighs, though she had no interest in shaving and getting combined razor and chafing burns in that spot, of the question of how she represented the concept of *woman*, of *feminine*, when she so rarely felt either of those things. But here she stood, the goddess promised, in front of a genuinely sublime specimen of manhood slowly removing his own clothes.

Then they stood before each other, simplicity in their shared nudity. His growing erection poked down and to the right from a patch of blondish brown curls and rose steadily with every breath he took. She nearly apologized again for calling it small, when it most definitely wasn't, but thought that might sour this tenuous mood. Instead, feeling the hunger growing inside, a yearning so rare, she shoved him to the mattress and swallowed him to the hilt.

Later, as she climbed atop him, ignoring his protestations that she should lie back and relax while he did the work, she was again struck by the room's dimness. She looked at the lamp protruding from the wall as her hand guided him home. She closed her eyes for a moment, experiencing the filling sensation and pushing away the distracting question of when her last time with a man had been. *Who* had it been? But when her eyes re-opened, the room felt even dimmer.

"Everything oka—" he began, but a spasm rocked him as she grabbed hold with her Kegels, and his eyes rolled back.

She pressed a palm to her forehead and noted an odd perspective. She closed her left eye and saw her wrist and the beginning of her arm, then she switched, closing her right, and saw...nothing. *Fuck*, she thought. *Fuck!* She swung her head back to the lamp and tried the same experiment, still seeing nothing from her left eye. She should stop. She should stop and call Audrey and Zack. She should stop and go to the doctor. Possibly the emergency—

The orgasm rolled through her, a forceful clenching tidal wave that made her close her eyes and express a barbaric *yawp* at the ceiling.

"Yeah?" he asked. "C'mon."

Even in her ecstatic convulsions combined with rising panic, she found the orgasmic proclamations of men to be oh so very dull. "Shh." She told him, putting her hand over his mouth.

"Os," he said through her palm. "Your eye is—" She held her palm down and leaned on it, squelching his concern and protestations. She intended to ride this orgasm into the ground. To find her release. It peaked once, then ebbed, and then the wave crashed higher. She felt all her muscles tense and release in their own throbbing synchronous beat. The smells in the room grew in intensity. The generic Lysol scent, the air freshener plugged into the wall outlet, the underlying never-quite-gone smell of stale cigarettes, the musky scent of sweat and sex, of her armpits and his, of the alcohol on their breath, of her pussy, of their juices separate and combined. Below it though, something else.

Below it, fire.

Osgood continued to ride, allowing her movements to grow more spastic. So as not to be distracted by the

(whole going blind thing)

eye issue, she closed both. She threw her head back as she felt another swell.

"Uhgngh," ejaculated Goddard beneath her.

Good, she thought. She wasn't always the most concerned lover, but she appreciated an orgasmic round of applause.

The scent grew. Of fire, of ash, of cherrywood. She could almost hear the crackling and feel the heat. Not almost, she *could*—she felt it, she heard it. The heat was in her chest, building and building. When she opened her eyes and looked down, she saw her hand still on Goddard's mouth, his eyes wide, staring at her. No, staring at her chest.

She tucked her chin to her collarbone, to look straight down at the

(that's not a fucking)

bruise. It bulged outward, only a little, but enough to begin a third mound between her tits. The black and purple had grown a sickly red, and she could see it throbbing in time with her heart, with her breathing. It was of her as much as it was beyond her. When the ripping sound began, she cocked her head, sure she must look comical in her dismay as the bulge grew to a point where the skin could no longer hold and began to split like a membrane pulled taut. The scent of fire poured from the new hole in her chest, still minute, still only—

No longer able to dispassionately observe, Osgood screamed. She pulled her hand away from Goddard's face and put it over her own mouth to stifle another scream.

"Os, I need you to stay ca—" Then Goddard screamed.

She saw it all as though standing in the corner of the room observing a play, albeit a play with a George A. Romero-level of carnage production value. The membrane could no longer hold, and her skin tore along her sternum, yawning open. Her hands went to it and she felt herself grasp at each edge, fingers disappearing within her, pulling, shoving, desperately trying to close the hole. Inside wasn't her body. No heart or lungs. Only darkness.

And in the darkness was...something.

A sharp pain rippled through her body, causing her entire body to clench. She became certain that her pelvic floor held

Goddard with an iron grip, not letting his rapid softening factor in. Again and again, she spasmed, feeling the stark incongruity of ecstatic orgasm and the pain of...whatever the fuck was happening here. The sensations crossed and melded and unmelded. She felt her lips split from dryness as she gasped so heavily for air through them. When she looked back down at her chest, closing her

(please don't let it be)

dead eye, she laughed, dumbfounded, as she saw but could not comprehend the thing between her tits. The thing climbing forth from her bosom. Its head, at first glance, appeared orchid-like, but the slightest turn showed her an insect. It held the edges of the hole in her with calcified stumps, some flat, others ending in jagged points. Goddard screamed again as the monstrosity birthed itself into the world, shoving forward with a slurping grumble, followed by a snap, like a balloon popping. It kicked, or shoved, or pushed at Osgood as it managed to entirely free itself, and she fell backward, tumbling off the bed and landing on her shoulder with a horrible crunch.

She lifted a shaking hand to her chest and felt the hole beginning to close, a new membrane creeping across the gap. She could only see Goddard's feet poking off the edge of the bed. Only Goddard's feet as he screamed. Only Goddard's feet as his toes clenched and his screams turned into the guttural gurgles of someone drowning.

She reached out, managing to raise her hand above the edge of the mattress, all the way toward him. Her fingertips brushed against his toes. Something up there roared, and Goddard's screaming stopped. It roared again. Osgood could feel the sound in her head, surrounding the nerves behind her dark eye. Pain, unlike any she'd felt before, rose up as the sound squeezed her brain. Her vision began to grow jittery, like a poorly received UHF channel on the old black-and-white TV she'd watched over breakfast growing up; the one with tin foil on the antennae. She tried to hold the image together as she saw, one at a time, three digits on the left edge of the mattress, then three on the right. Bone white all of them, calcified and irregular, some sharp, some broken, some dull. Then the thing up top, the thing that had roared, the thing that was born from her chest, peered over the edge of the bed. Its head, if it could even be called that, jittered and shook on its own, pushing at the edges of impossibility. She didn't see eyes but thought she might, in some abstract way, understand where they were. It tilted at her, opened pinscher-laden jaws, and roared a final time, as the squeezing sensation in her head brought Osgood to the brink of nothingness.

🏹 16 🗡

Vibrations in the road. Uneven pavement. Lack of traction, fishtailing.

Osgood didn't rouse fully. She could only see through a hazy point, as when she'd been a child playing explorer with a wrapping paper tube telescope. Far off, she saw windshield wipers. Far off, she saw that the snow fell heavy against the darkened sky. Orange streetlights gave way to the brilliant white LED lights. She could move her head, she knew, but the image didn't seem to change. Just that distance, that far off place. She could feel her brain trying to reboot, to find its way back to a workable state from the squeezing migraine threatening to bring her back down into the watery depths of unconsciousness. It had felt like just a moment there, in the warm purple nothing, before she found herself peering out of her head through some kind of portal, in a vehicle, in the cold night. She felt the movement of the air on her from the vents, but it, too, felt frightfully cold.

Momentarily she forgot who she was, but she'd crawled her way back from that mind-trap before. *Not so easy to do it again, is it?* she asked whatever held her mind with a self-satisfied grunt, then conceded, *Though I probably shouldn't get cocky.*

A heavy brake slam and a swerve. Honks. Another horn blowing by, making a melodic Doppler whine. The rhythmic vibration of the edge of a highway. She wanted to ask where they were going. Wanted to see who was taking her there. She didn't know if she couldn't refocus her sightline or if something internal was preventing her. Did she want to see that thing again? Or what had become of Goddard?

But perhaps Goddard had survived! Beat the devil with some heroic feat and was driving them both to safety. Since she couldn't look, she wondered if she could speak. She could ask the wheres and the whys, and if the SUV were indeed being driven by Sam Goddard, he'd tell her his tale. Her lips moved only slightly. Her words were merely breaths. If she could talk, though, she'd take the same risk as looking over. The driver would see, would know, would understand her mental state. And if the driver wasn't Goddard, who knew what the orchid-headed thing had in mind for her.

I always knew sex would get you killed, Pru, but didn't think it'd be like this! The voice belonged to Audrey, doing an absurd Groucho Marx impression.

She closed her eyes again and breathed, centering, calming herself. In that darkness, interrupted only by the muffled light as they passed beneath streetlamps, she focused. *I am Prudence Osgood.* She repeated it, then once again for good measure. This last one caused the darkness to change. It echoed and swirled before appearing before her. Hazy lettering built from light. **I am Prudence Osgood.**

I'm Prudence Osgood, and I'm losing my mind, she thought. It made sense, of course. She'd just had some sort of flower-insect-man crawl out of a hole in her chest. Either that'd been a part of her craziness, or it was straw that broke her mind's back. The back half of the sentence wrote itself on the nothingness behind her eyelids. **and I'm losing my mind.** A period appeared, like a bit of light stabbed hard into the darkness. She focused on it, and it moved. She chased it around in the dark and thought she might be smiling, not just internally, but externally. **Help,** she wrote, somehow not thinking it, not hearing it in her own mind, just seeing it before her. She knew, though, looking at it, that it wasn't someone asking her for help, it was herself asking for it. Of whom? Of what?

Of me, the benevolent voice from her dreams told her.

My imaginary friend, she thought and rolled her eyes behind their lids, but stopped when it felt like someone was sliding a pulsing knitting needle beneath her left eyeball into her brain.

You know I am not imaginary.

I know, Osgood thought, but then realized, *I know nothing. Also untrue.*

I'm afraid. Admitting it to herself caused her muscles to go limp, as though unclenching her entire body, resigning it to the inevitable.

Nothing is inevitable, the woman told her. *Of course, you are afraid. You want to live.*

I do, she thought.

Then we live.

The stage in her mind went dark, words vanishing. It took multiple attempts, but she finally managed to open her right eye, though her left felt swollen shut. The tunnel vision remained, but the end of the tunnel was closer. She saw trees, powerlines, heavier snow in the dark. She managed to move her point of view slightly and could see, very blurrily, the blue digital clock. After her brain organized the vision, she recognized the number 11.

Hours in the dark, hours unconscious. What had that thing done in the hours?

What is it doing now? she reminded herself of the more

important question. She took a deep breath in answer, feeling the unrelenting ache in her chest and lungs. *Sure! How often do you push a full-grown monster out of there?*

Her vision shifted to the right, then left, then right again. Only little movements, but she realized she was shaking her head disapprovingly at herself. What a waste of energy. During that shake, though, something caught her eye. A reflection of light from LEDs through the windshield, off of—

Her phone. Right where she'd left it in the cupholder before going into the Heartland Motel for some good sex and less-good Cronenbergian body horror.

She wiggled the fingers of her right hand, nails scraping on the thigh it was tucked under, discovering that her leg was bare and now had an angry scratch on it. But she could move. The movement brought the thudding in her head, though, and she closed her eyes again. She growled to herself. She'd fought her way through worse pain than this. She'd fought her way back to walking when even her physical therapists had told her it was pretty iffy.

I'm going to get out of this, she told herself.

First, the phone. This would be the key to any plan of escape. She hoped that Zack's assurances that he was on watch hadn't been just shadow play to keep her from going far. She had to get the phone, because no matter who was in the driver's seat, it'd be better to have it.

You know who's in the driver's seat, someone told her, far away. Some darker voice, but still hers.

She momentarily wondered if the Other Prudence, the one with a grin like a zipper around her entire head, was driving the both of them right to hell. She reasoned that she did know, though, because if her thigh was bare, the rest of her probably was, too, and Goddard wouldn't have taken her out of the motel room, worried about her having a mental breakdown or seizure or stroke, screaming about flower-bug monsters, without first wrapping her in a blanket at least. She pulled her right arm in and slid her elbow along her nude stomach.

Phone first, she reiterated to herself. Then she'd look. She'd grab the phone with her left hand. She could feel the fingers against each other. Her left eye might have gone on holiday, but her left side still functioned. It was riskier than trying with the right because she'd be slightly out of her line of sight. *But essential,* her mind insisted. Yes, the phone would be crucial. If she really intended to do what she thought she might, grab her phone, pull the door handle, and tumble out of the vehicle (which was an incredibly bad idea), then she'd need her phone to get help.

She asked herself if that was *really* her plan, to leap naked from a moving car who knows where.

It's snowing, she told her naysaying brain. *I'm going to jump into a snowbank.*

Perhaps now convinced that she couldn't be reasoned with, her inner naysayer went silent. She flicked the fingers on her left hand. She moved her right back, then up, along her body, feeling no seat belt. She took a mental inventory, the only pressure in her chest was internal, the horrid ache. She was not, in fact, strapped in. One final check as her fingers slid to the door, then up and up. Unlocked.

Alright then, she thought and began to slow her breathing. She wondered as she breathed if this whole plan was just more evidence that she'd gone insane.

"Yes," she said.

Her voice breaking the silence must have startled the driver because the SUV swerved, throwing her onto the center console. She grabbed at her phone, marveling at the luck of that swerve before the correction threw her into the passenger door. The impact sent new shudders of pain through her shoulders and head, and she felt her visual portal to the world closing. She was growing light-headed. She had to look, though; she had to finish the job! Time seemed to slow as she forced her right eye open and swung it across the dash, past the clock, past the blue backlit instrumentation panel, past the dark hands grasping the steering wheel, to something in shadows that was more substantial than a person. Something with its head tilted down to allow it to fit inside. Something with hulking shoulders and protrusions. Something that she only momentarily glimpsed as the SUV passed under another streetlamp. She didn't take time to study it, only noted its inhumanity.

A car in front of them slammed on its brakes, sending a loud screech and the thrumming of anti-lock brakes into the wailing wind, and she felt the SUV slowing, knowing that it would be now or never. After a last deep breath, she reached behind her and pulled the door handle, then shoved her feet against the center console. The door reluctantly opened into the wind and the motion, and she felt her ass slide off the leather seat of the SUV into nothingness, followed by her legs. Time slowed even further for her as she saw the thing lean out of the shadows, reaching out one limb to grasp at her ankle. But it didn't hold.

The SUV swerved to the left, aiding in her exit, and the thing's broken finger slid along the length of her foot. Then she dropped for what seemed an eternity. The door slammed shut again, clipping her toe as it did, sending new shockwaves of pain through her. She could see the sky, the muddled grays and blues of a snowstorm lit from below. The snow fell on her face in heavy wet gusts as she descended.

She braced as best she could for impact, knowing that however it went, it wouldn't be easy or pretty. Crossing her arms over her chest felt, at that moment, like the right move.

When she hit, she hit hard. The surface of the road

slammed her with a double fist of solid asphalt and icy snow. She felt the wind leave her chest and she began to tumble forward. The pain intensified as she rolled, hitting a wall of snow, then another larger one. She felt needles of cold jabbed into her entire body. She screamed into the void of the snow-storm and her mouth filled with dirty slush. She continued to tumble, now down an incline.

Momentarily she recognized that she'd fallen off the road and rolled into the gully beside it. When she finally came to a stop, everything hurt, more than in all her years of needing oxy to quell the pain. More than when her broken body had been pulled from the wreckage of her Buick Skylark at the crossroads.

She raised a shaking left hand, the phone still grasped in it, *thank christ*, and pressed her right finger to the fingerprint reader.

Nothing.

Again.

Nothing.

Again!

Sobs erupted from her mouth.

Nothing.

Again.

A click and the home screen opened. She moved her finger to the phone app but saw another icon, a red button labeled only **emergency**. She pressed it, then her hand could hold no longer. The phone fell out of her hand and bounced off her stomach before disappearing.

"So long, world," she whispered, lying back in the snow. "It's been a real hoot." Her words were lost in the wailing wind.

Osgood closed her eyes and waited for death. Surely death would be warmer.

17

Darkness falls.

Not simple darkness but deep velvety black.

The void.

Osgood sits in nothingness on a floor that she either cannot see or isn't there. She looks down at herself. "Jesus Christ," she says. "Why am I always fucking naked?"

We all come to this as we came in.

"Thank you for that incredibly vague and unhelpful comment." She stands and, by instinct, wraps her arms around her chest to keep warm before realizing that it is unnecessary. She is warm. Perfectly warm. That realization carries with it another one, one that she tries to dismiss but cannot, one that blurs her vision with tears. "I died, didn't I?"

No response.

She wipes at her eyes, realizing that her left eye can see her hand. On the tail of that comes the realization that the pain from behind that eye has ceased. She breathes a sigh of relief. "But why am I relieved?" she asks the darkness. "Dead people don't feel pain." She scowls, but the scowl hesitates. "Do they?"

Still nothing from the peanut gallery.

"Not talking to me anymore?" Osgood asks. "Fine. I don't need more voices in my fucking head. Especially ones that I *know* aren't just my projections of my mother or friends." She sneers at the dark and, for good measure, turns around to sneer in the other direction. After a moment, though, her sneer falters. This new voice had been different. Kind. Helpful. Loving.

But where is it now? she wonders as she stands on nothing in this void while no doubt her body is freezing in a mound of snow, god only knows where.

"I came back to die? Seems rather shitty."

A flash catches her attention, either incredibly far away or very tiny. The flash burns like the embers on a sparkler on a balmy Fourth of July. She squints at it, and it seems to focus itself. At first, it's merely a dot, but then it begins to expand, bright, swirling, seeming to grow with every rotation. At a point, it stops growing but continues to swirl like some eddy far away. Whites and yellows and pale blues mingle and split and mingle and split as it goes. In the center, just white.

"Go into the light, Carol Anne," says Osgood. She scowls again and begins to walk toward the swirl, growing more and more sullen with every step. "It's not fucking fair!" she screams at it and stops. "I already did this. I already died when I was only 19. Life already fucking broke me, and I'm absolutely sick of it!"

You didn't.

She whips her head in the direction of the voice, but there's nothing behind her. "I didn't what?"

You didn't die.

Osgood shakes her head. "Fine. I didn't die. I—" What had the Lord told her? "Sidestepped between worlds."

That is far more impressive than merely dying.

"And it has gotten me jack shit, so who cares?" She looks

around her in a full 180-degree arc, then turns back to the quietly swirling light.

Will me to you.

"What does *that* mean?"

Would you like me to be there?

"As opposed to a voice in my head?" Osgood shouts. "Does it fucking matter? I'm walking the last mile here."

The voice is silent.

"Fine. I want you here. I *will* you here." When nothing happens, Osgood closes her eyes and imagines a woman, her figure vague and unformed.

"Thank you," the woman says, her voice no longer in Osgood's head. "You had to do that."

Osgood opens her eyes and flinches at the sudden appearance of another person in the dark. The woman is nearly as tall as herself, with curly brown hair flowing over her shoulders. The white she wears is at once a hippie dress and what she'd always imagined an angel might wear when, as a child, she paged through her parents' bible.

"Alright, so—" Osgood stops, and a flush crosses her cheeks. She covers herself as best she can.

"Modesty is unimportant, but you can change it if you'd like."

Osgood narrows her eyes. "How?"

"How did you bring me here?"

"I have no fucking idea."

The woman smiles, and in that crooked smile, Osgood sees something familiar she cannot place. "You use that word a lot."

"Yes, I fucking do."

The woman shrugs. "Your world."

"Hey, ghost lady, can—"

"I am not a ghost."

"—you refrain from speaking in riddles for a bit, and just tell me some shit?"

"My knowledge is at your disposal," the woman says. "Though I warn you it may be limited."

"I am dead."

"Is that a question?"

Osgood feels her frustration rapidly ripening to rage but holds it back. "Am I dead?"

"Nearly," says the woman.

"From falling out of the SUV?"

"I do not know."

"But I'm dy*ing?*"

"Yes."

Osgood nods and considers that. It's one thing to assume it, another thing entirely to have your imminent death confirmed by a spectral being. She looks over her shoulder at the quietly swirling maelstrom. "And is that 'The Light?' With a capital L and everything?"

"That is the passage."

"To?"

The woman shrugs. "I have not yet been there. But it is where most of us go."

"Most?" Osgood shakes her head. "Does that mean there are multiple passages?" She wonders where that passage leads for her. Prudence Osgood, who never gave much mind to religion beyond scoffing at it. Prudence Osgood, who broke most of the deadly sins regularly. Prudence Osgood; no saint.

"It is not heaven," says the woman.

"Is—" Osgood stops and swallows hard, realizing the gravity of her question. "Is there a heaven?"

"There is existence, and then there is another existence."

"And this is?"

"The space between."

"The margins," says Osgood.

"So you have said."

Osgood puts her hands to her face, feeling far more tears on her cheeks than she'd have thought. In doing so, she realizes she's exposed herself fully to the woman and turns away in embarrassment.

"Again, you do not have to be modest."

She wishes she had her coat, her clothes, some semblance of normalcy here. Something that could ground her in the reality of this. Something that would make her not feel like these were just the last neurons firing their final charges in her brain.

"There." The woman points at her.

When Osgood looks down again, she's wearing her jeans and Chucks, a *Ghostbusters* t-shirt, and over it all, her maroon leather trench coat. "Well," she says, gobsmacked. She hadn't even felt the clothing settle on her body. "You did that?"

"*You* did that."

The words of the Lord of the Hinterlands disguised as a much younger Prudence Osgood flow back to her. *As I built my kingdom, so have you built yours.*

"Indeed," says the woman.

"If I go that way," Osgood points at the swirl, "I die."

"Eh," says the woman, raising her shoulders and cocking her head. "If you go that way, your essence, this..." she circles her palm at Osgood, "this moves on. Your body, yes, your body dies."

Osgood chews on that for a moment. "Can I go back?"

"Yes."

"How?"

"You did it once before."

She scowls at the woman. "Let's pretend I've forgotten how that works."

"Your earthly tether is damaged," the woman tells her. "I

don't know how badly, but it is likely severe, to have brought you here."

Osgood thinks about her daring and incredibly foolish escape from the SUV. Leaping naked, backward, into a snowbank on the side of a road. She nods. Of course, her body is damaged. She's about to insist again on being told how to go back when she realizes the big question and asks it. "Who are you?"

"Lil."

She stares at Lil. "I thought there might be more."

"There is," says Lil. "And you are Prudence."

"I prefer Osgood."

"So did I, which is why I kept it even after the scandals." Lil smiles, radiating that benevolent energy Osgood has felt since the first time hearing her voice. "Although Prudence is a lovely name. My sister's."

"It's my great-great-aunt's—" Osgood stops and stares at the woman, at Lil, smiling back at her. The crooked smile looks familiar. So do the eyes, brown, like hers. But it's more than just the eyes, it's the face, the hair, the freckles, her height. "Lilian."

"I prefer Lil," says her great-grandmother.

"We're..." Osgood points between them.

Lil nods. "I am afraid that we do not have much time."

"What do you mean?" Osgood throws a furtive glance at the swirling abyss over her shoulder.

"When the essence escapes the body, it comes here. From here, it can go forward or back, but if it cannot or will not choose, it remains here."

"I want to go back," says Osgood.

"And that is why we do not have much time." Lil moves forward and puts her hand on Osgood's shoulder.

Osgood flinches as she does it, nearly pulling back.

Lil removes her hand quickly.

"Sorry," Osgood says.

"Are you—"

"Since we're—" Osgood can't say it aloud but points between them. "I was worried one of us would disappear or —" She laughs. "Shatter or something."

"It does not work that way," says Lil.

"Whew!" says Osgood, miming a theatrical brow wipe.

"Going forward will take you to the next world. Going back will return you to the last. Remaining here is dangerous, even for one as powerful as you."

"Power..." Osgood shakes her head. "The Lord said that too, I don't know what—"

"The ability to step between worlds is a gift. I, too, have gifts. As did my daughter, and my granddaughter. And then you." Lil's smile grows stern. "But there are those who would take advantage. Which is why you cannot remain."

"I—"

"The passage is closing." Lil points behind her, and Osgood sees that the swirling light is collapsing in on itself. "When it closes, your body will die."

"Shit! No, I—" Osgood whirls back around to Lil. "Help me go back."

"There will be pain."

"I understand pain," Osgood tells her.

"There will be suffering."

"How do you know all of this?" asks Osgood. "How are you even here?"

"We will speak of that at some point. But not this one."

"I'm afraid," says Osgood.

"There are things in your world worth fearing. One beacon has already been activated. Once three—" A roaring of wind drowns Lil out.

Osgood throws a look over her shoulder and sees that the

path of light is nearly gone, and wind seems to be whipping through it. "Oh, God."

"No," says Lil, "Just us. Be good, Prudence."

She looks back at Lil, seeing the woman raise her left hand. Osgood looks at it just long enough to be distracted as Lil shoves her with her right.

Osgood leaves her feet, nearly folding in half with the strength of the shove. She sees Lil recede shockingly fast into darkness, then pain consumes her. Her body is on fire. A scraping sound. A wet and sticky sound. Then a pop.

The light is blinding and Osgood screams.

18

linded by the light, Osgood wondered if she would ever stop screaming into it, daring it to consume her, ready to let all this go and fall into the next world. But the light wasn't swirling any longer and after a while it resolved into fluorescent tubes. Commotion around her, hands on her. Talking. Strange voices. She couldn't understand.

A sharp pain as she bumped her right arm against—

"Pru!" was the first word she understood, but she didn't know from where or whom it came.

She shook her head and blinked, hoping to focus, hoping for something resembling cohesion in front of her. The left side of her vision remained dark and she tried several times to open that eye before realizing that...it was open.

"Pru, they took your—"

She attempted to swing her left arm at the source of the voice, a shape of hazy khaki, but couldn't move it more than a little, something held her down.

"Please, stop struggling, let me—"

Osgood opened her mouth and loosed a wail from her burning throat.

"Can I get some help in here?!"

More hands, more forms holding her down. Warmth in her left arm, traveling up and up and then, slowly, calm fell over her. She sank into it, growing calmer with every breath.

"Thank you."

"I'm going to let the doctor know that she's awake."

"Thank you."

A figure close to her face, right in front, coming closer and closer, broke her calm. Even with her growing relaxation, she felt another scream rising. Maybe this scream would alert some

(Lil)

one who could help her.

The figure came into focus as hands slid her glasses onto her face. She blinked a few times. She heard a sigh and a flop, perhaps into a chair near her.

Above her was white tiled ceiling punctuated by white fluorescent lights. She lifted her head, feeling it swim as she moved it off its cushion. She closed her eyes and rested it once more. After a moment she looked again, this time down her body, and she found herself lying prone in a hospital bed.

"I'm—" she said, then cut off when a powerful spell of coughing hit her. A hand pressed a mask over her mouth and nose, and she felt the convulsions stop as cold oxygen fed into her. She breathed as deeply as she could with her burning lungs, then she nodded to the form that had brought her the mask, silhouetted by the lights.

She turned her head and saw her father. His thinning hair was a mess atop his head, and his face had the light beard of three or four days. The circles under his eyes gave his face a hollow look, almost like the shriveled apple faces he'd taught her to make, once upon a time.

"Bas— Dad?" she asked.

"Honey," he said. "You, uh... You almost..."

"Died?" she asked.

He nodded, his eyes wide. He removed his wire-rimmed glasses and pinched the bridge of his nose.

"Harder to kill than that, apparently." Osgood looked at herself as far as she could lift her head. Her right arm wore a cast, and a sling strapped it to her chest. Her left hand had a taped-down IV. They never could find her veins in her arm. Always had to use the hand.

"They gave you something to help with the pain."

"This is *with* pain relief," Osgood mused, feeling the aches, the bruising, the burning. The ongoing pains of living.

"The doctor," he began, then looked away from her.

"Yes."

"Pru, the do—" He stopped talking and blinked at her for a moment. "Os."

Osgood felt a swell of regret joining the pain in her chest. Her years of rebellion, the Queerification of Prudence Osgood, had been a time of turmoil and judgment from her parents. When looking back, she'd always lumped both of them together in that, and often she was right, but her father...well, sometimes he tried. "Thanks, Dad."

"The doctors are worried about your eye."

"I am, too!" She laughed dryly and regretted it as it turned to coughing again.

"Well, it's more than—"

"Miss Osgood?"

Osgood turned to the door and saw a slender, dark-skinned woman in light blue scrubs and a white coat. "Just Osgood, please."

"Osgood, then." The woman nodded. "I'm Dr. Laghari." She sat in a rolling chair and slid up next to the bed. "We thought we might lose you there."

"So did I."

The doctor looked from her to her father and back. "Okay, so, now that you're awake, can you look at this please?" She held up her pen in front of Osgood's face. "Follow it with your eyes."

Osgood did her best, but the pen completely disappeared when it went to her left. She sighed. "I can't see—"

"With your left eye?"

Osgood nodded.

"I'm not surprised." Dr. Laghari slid her chair over to a large TV screen with a keyboard below it. She lifted the keyboard, then turned to them. "I need you to..." She paused and frowned. "Before you react—"

"I was dead, Dr. Laghari," said Osgood. "Now, I'm not. Do you really think you can tell me anything worse than that?" Osgood saw the doctor's eyes dart to her father and then back to her. "I can handle it. Give it to me straight."

The doctor hesitated for another moment, then nodded. She tapped on the keyboard and woke up the screen. For a moment she poked around on the screen with a touch pad, then an X-Ray appeared. "Alright, first, your arm. It's broken, but it is a simple fracture."

Osgood saw the stark split of her bones on the screen and rapidly inhaled.

"Your right ankle was twisted, but not broken, so rest will take care of that."

"So far this isn't frightening me," said Osgood, allowing a wry smile. She looked at her father, who was pale and wide-eyed, then back at the doctor, frowning with pursed lips. "Alright, just...Please tell me."

"Before I do that, I have a question for you. That bruising on your chest and back...What caused that?"

"It's a long story. Is it fucking up my insides?"

"P— Os," said her father, admonishing her for the profanity.

"Well, no. Your chest X-rays surprised us." Dr. Laghari tapped a few keys and brought up another X-ray, this one of Osgood's chest.

"It looks fine," said Osgood. "Or...am I missing something?"

"No." Dr. Laghari shook her head. "No, you're not missing anything. It is fine. Which is understandably a surprise, considering the—"

"Bruising."

"Yes." The doctor held her eyes on Osgood's, waiting for more explanation.

What could Osgood tell her? *Oh, that bruising? It's from the time an interdimensional demigod shoved his hand into my chest. More recently, it opened into a rift, out of which climbed some weirdo bug-flower-man.* Doctors tend not to enjoy that sort of talk.

Finally, Dr. Laghari turned away, tapping a few more keys and bringing up a two-paneled view of Osgood's brain.

At this image, Osgood lost her breath. Just behind her eyes was a massive clump of darkness, radiating another shadow directly backward. The surrounding brain tissue seemed squished up against her skull. Osgood's mouth dropped open. She intended to ask what the fuck that was but instead laughed at the absurdity of it. "I guess that's why I've been having migraines."

Dr. Laghari opened her mouth then closed it again, looking back at the screen. "Well," she said. "Yes, that would..."

"Humor is Prudence's defense mechanism," her father told the doctor.

"Don't forget cutting remarks and pushing away those I love," said Osgood, distractedly. She couldn't take her eyes away from the thing in her head. It seemed enormous, the kind of thing that would make a doctor look at a chart and then shake their head and apologize that there was just nothing they could do. Inoperable. Stage four cancer. Cancer ran in the family, after all. Another thing she'd inherited in the Osgood line. She'd expected breast cancer, or cervical for chrissakes, but not— "Brain cancer," she whispered.

"Oh," said Dr. Laghari. "Let's not use the C-word yet."

"But it's my favorite," said Osgood, wishing her mother was here so she could use that *other* C-word. "I'm sorry."

"No, please," the doctor replied. "If humor helps you—"

"It might not be cancer?" Osgood hoped aloud.

"We..." Dr. Laghari looked up at the screen again. "We won't know until we go in."

"Brain surgery."

"Yes."

Osgood felt her father's hand on her shoulder. Under other circumstances, she might have pulled away. But just now, right here, it was exactly what she needed. "When?" she asked, hearing a tremor in her voice.

"With a mass this size," said the doctor, "we'd like to do it immediately."

"Immediately," repeated Osgood.

"Tomorrow morning." She looked at her watch. "Six-ish hours?"

Osgood wondered about her voice going up at the end of the sentence. "Are you asking for my permission?"

"Of course," said the doctor. "Surgery isn't mandatory for anyone. But our oncology department thinks, cancerous or not, if this is allowed to grow, you will likely lose vision in your right eye as well."

Blind, thought Osgood. *Hard to see ghosts when you're blind.* "Yeah," she said to the doctor. "Yeah. Okay. Tomorrow. Sure."

Dr. Laghari seemed relieved that she wouldn't have to

convince Osgood. "As with any surgery, there are risks involved that—"

"Yeah, just do it, Doc."

She nodded. "We already have the surgery scheduled. Your father gave consent, but with you awake, we needed yours."

"Sure," Osgood said again.

"We have some of the best surgeons in—"

"I'm sure every hospital says that," interrupted Osgood.

Dr. Laghari nodded. "We will deal with this."

"And if it's cancer?"

"We will deal with that." She stood again. "Do you have any ques—"

"No. Thank you."

The young doctor nodded again, clutched a folder to her chest, and left the room through a pink and gray patterned curtain.

"You could've been nicer to—" her father began, but he stopped when Osgood turned to look at him. "Oh, honey," he said instead.

"I need you to do something for me," she said.

"Absolutely."

"My friends. The ones from—" She stopped. "Well, you listen to the podcast."

"Audrey and Zack."

"Yes."

"Can you call them for—"

"They're in the waiting area," he said, pointing at the door. "They brought you in. Called me."

Osgood recalled the moment her finger had hit that emergency button on the phone, the moment before the collapse. How much she'd hoped that the action would do something, would bring the cavalry. Apparently, it had. "Can I have time alone with them?"

"Oh," her father said. "Yes. Sure." He stood, grabbing his coat. "I. I love you, Os."

Osgood looked at him. His eyes were red and watery. She tried to remember the last time he'd said that, but she couldn't. Conflicting emotions, her anger at that time span clashing with relief that he was saying it now. Then the relief won, and she told him she loved him, too.

He left the room.

In her haste to leave, Dr. Laghari had left the dual images of her brain on the screen. Osgood stared at the mass, then squinted at the hazy line behind it, the shadow trailing to the back of her head. She reached back, pulling on the IV bag and sending a small wave of pain through her hand, and felt the bump on the back of her head. She'd felt it earlier at the motel before she and Goddard had

(conjured a creature)

had sex. The lump had grown.

Could be from when she'd hit the ground, of course. Could be a perfectly rational explanation.

"Or could be the tumor trying to poke its way out of my head," she said to the empty room.

19

"If I die," began Osgood.

"You're not going to die," insisted Zack.

Audrey, perhaps sensing this was a moment better suited for quiet comfort than verbal reassurance, put her hand on Zack's arm and leaned forward. The three of them sat in silence for a while, leaving only the sounds of the various machines and the background hospital noise from the hall.

In that silence, Osgood thought about what she wanted to say. She'd been sure she could wing it here, could speak from the heart, or whatever organ it was from which she usually spoke, but now she was grateful for Zack's interruption. The beginning of her sentence, "If I die," had been enough to leave her speechless. So she turned to other things. "You must've found me quick."

Zack looked to Audrey, then nodded. "I got nervous when you didn't answer our texts and were on the move." He looked back at Audrey.

She nodded and took the lead. "We decided to follow when we saw the vehicle was going to go right past Mary's."

"Well," said Osgood. "While I normally would grouse at you about being a bit too on-watch, I think it's safe to say here that you both saved my life."

"You were in the snow for about ten minutes," said Zack. "We got stuck behind a freight train."

"Where were we headed?" Osgood asked.

"South," said Zack. "Beyond that, we don't really know."

"Do you..." Audrey looked down at her shoes, then at what seemed to be a particularly interesting fingernail, then back up at Osgood. "Want to tell us what happened?"

"I fucked Goddard."

"I assumed that much," said Audrey.

Zack glanced up at the ceiling.

Osgood narrowed her eyes. So blasé. *Be blasé about this,* she thought. "Then, while I was riding him, my chest split open, and a literal fucking monster came out, kicked me off the bed, did *something* to Goddard that made him scream holy hell, and then I passed out. When I came to, I was in Goddard's SUV, being driven by, I think, that same *monster.* When I was able to move, I grabbed my phone from the cupholder, opened the door, and shoved myself out into a snowbank on the side of the road, where I promptly died."

"Wait, what?" Audrey cocked her head.

"Which part?"

"All of it," conceded Audrey. "But the death part especially."

"Oh yeah," said Osgood, nodding. "I died. Met my great-grandmother in the margins and was given a choice whether to go forward or come back. I chose to come back." She held her hands up, palms to the ceiling. "Tadaaa!"

Zack exhaled a long breath.

"There's a lot to," began Audrey, but she didn't finish. "You're sure you died?"

"No," said Osgood. "May have been a fucking hallucination because of my fucking *brain tumor* that has made me go blind in my left eye." She swung her arm wildly in the direction of the screen that still showed her brain scans.

Her two companions looked at the screen. Audrey swallowed hard.

Even with only one good eye, Osgood could see the redness in Audrey's and the flush in her cheeks. Maybe her own blasé attitude wasn't a good tack here. Maybe she should step back from ironic detachment, just this once.

Zack walked over to the screens, then stood, his hands in his pockets, examining them.

"So, if I die," said Osgood.

"You're not going to die," said Zack, though his confidence had certainly waned.

"Still think so, with the new information you've received?" Osgood asked him. He didn't respond, just lifted the small keyboard and began to type. She turned her attention back to Audrey, who had covered her face in her hand. "Aud."

"I don't—" said Audrey beneath her hand, but she stopped herself, sniffed deeply, and looked at Osgood. "You're not going to die." Her confidence was admirable.

"Maybe not," said Osgood, "But the fact remains that something is happening here, and in six-ish hours, I'm getting my skull opened."

"Right," said Audrey.

"And right now, no matter how any of us may feel about that surgery, I need your focus on the other thing."

Zack turned from the screen. "The, uh," he hesitated at the word. Osgood didn't blame him, because when he did say it, it sounded just as silly as when she had. "Monster... What did it look like?"

Osgood nodded at him, thankful for the excuse to turn the conversation away from the countdown to people fiddling in her brain. "It looked like an orchid... and an insect. It had hands, but they seemed bone-like, broken and jagged. I saw its face and I saw its hands, but I didn't really get a look at much else." She saw it in her mind, crouched in the driver's seat of the SUV, so incongruous in that place, so not-belonging. "Big, though. Eight feet, maybe."

"And it...came out of your chest," said Audrey, her voice wan and quiet.

"Right through the," Osgood used air quotes, "'Bruise.'"

"You said you turned inside out," said Zack.

"What?" Osgood shook her head. "No, opened up."

"Before," he said, returning to the seat next to her bed. "When you disappeared."

"Yes," Osgood agreed, hearing the bone scraping sound of it in her mind.

"What if the Lord of the Hinterlands punched...a hole..." He looked around, trying to figure out his thought as he was saying it. "A hole through you, out of reality into the margins."

"That I got pulled into."

He nodded. "And that something else could come through, into our world."

Osgood stared at him, wanting to dismiss the idea, wanting so desperately, so entirely to just reject it as absurd. That wasn't how the real world worked. That wasn't how dimensions worked. That wasn't— "That makes a disturbing amount of sense, and I would rather it not."

"Us too," said Audrey. Zack nodded.

"If I die," said Osgood under her breath, speaking the thought as it came to her, "the gate will be closed."

"Let's not martyr ourselves just yet," said Audrey, reaching out and taking Osgood's hand, flinching as she realized she'd tugged the IV.

"It's true."

"I think we're a bit beyond the spectrum of truth," said Audrey.

"Fair enough." Osgood closed her eyes and thought for a moment. "It would probably be a good idea to check out the Heartland Motel."

"Already on that. A buddy of a friend works the office on the overnight shift. He said you were in room eight. He's keeping staff away from it in exchange for bitcoins."

"That's...a disturbing invasion of privacy for something that purports to be a no-tell motel."

Zack cocked his head. "Skeezy guests, skeezy employees?"

"Makes sense."

"Os," said Audrey, her voice firm, causing both Osgood and Zack to turn to her immediately. "What do you need?"

"Please tell Albrecht," she stopped, uncertain, "something." Osgood turned to Zack. "And do your internet Boolean thing for this..." she shook her head. "I feel like a loon calling it a monster."

"From your description, it sounds monstrous," said Zack.

Osgood nodded slowly.

"Absolutely," said Audrey. "Both of those things, yes. But seriously, what do *you* need?"

Their eyes met. Osgood's single good one to Audrey's weepy ice-blue pair.

"I'm afraid," said Osgood.

Her friends nodded.

"At some point, I'll be too broken to fix. Not even all of the king's women..." She sniffed and wiped at her nose with the back of her hand, causing the IV to tug just enough to ache again. "Would've been better if I hadn't come back."

"Are you asking if that's true?" asked Audrey.

"No, I'm saying it is," said Osgood.

"Not so," said Zack.

"Zack," Osgood began to protest.

"No!" Zack snapped. "You think people don't care about you. But they do. *We* do." He pointed at himself and Audrey.

"I know that you—"

"Your parents do," he said. "Your mom may have absolutely no idea how to show it and the worst possible instincts when trying, but she does."

"Zack," said Audrey.

He held up his hand. "Our listeners care. They've showed it with their outpouring of concern, their offers of help. Everyone wanted to see if they could do anything. Offering connections. Offering money. They paid for us to keep the apartment, the car... Your student loans."

"You paid my student loans?" asked Osgood, shocked.

He nodded. "When you speak into the microphone, Os, people listen, and people care. When we told your story, people listened, and people cared. When we told them what you went through to help Audrey find closure, to help all those families have some kind of answer, even if it wasn't the one they expected."

"Or wanted," snapped Osgood.

"Or understood," said Audrey with a shrug.

"People care," said Zack. "We care."

"I never doubted that—"

"I'm telling you this because we need you to fight," he said, "to not go into tomorrow's surgery with your typical 'if I die' mindset."

"My typical..." Osgood nodded. "Okay."

"I'm also telling you this because it's better than the other thing I want— No, need to tell you about." His eyes darted between them.

Audrey narrowed her eyes at him.

"Okay," said Osgood again, dragging out the *y* this time.

"What did the doctor tell you about the tumor?"

Surprised by the question, Osgood stammered. "That they won't know if it's cancerous until—"

"Anything unusual?"

"Besides that it's a brain tumor?" Osgood laughed a strained, high-pitched laugh.

"How about the shadow going to the back..."

Osgood instinctively moved her hand toward the bump on the back of her head.

"Did they show you any imaging other than this one?" He pointed to the screen.

"No."

"Okay," said Zack. "You know how you have a perplexing bruise that's not a bruise, and no one can understand why there's no damage beneath it?"

"Or how a monster would be able to crawl out of it and not mess up the internals," offered Osgood, the humorous tone in her own voice beginning to scare her.

"Yeah," said Zack, his tone serious. "It could be cancer."

"Great," said Osgood.

"It could be the radiation that we all got dosed with while in the...other..."

"Hinterlands," said Osgood.

"Yeah," he said. "Or it could be—" He cut himself off, rubbing his face with his hands.

"What, Zack?"

He sighed. "If I were where you are, I wouldn't want you to be telling me this."

"I don't want any of this shit, Zack," said Osgood. "We're so far beyond want. Why don't we just try for honesty."

He didn't look back up. "So, look," he said. "My dad wanted me to go to med school and insisted I take all these electives one summer."

"Alright."

"Have you heard of a teratoma?" he asked, seemingly uncomfortable with the question itself.

Osgood looked to Audrey, then back to Zack. "No."

"It's..." He stood and walked back the screen, lifting the keyboard and tapping a few keys. The image changed to another view, this one from the front. "It's a rare type of tumor where all sorts of cells that don't belong can grow."

"Alright?" Osgood hoping her tone would encourage him not to continue dragging this out.

"Well," he shuffled. Then he noticed something on his shoe and leaned down to look at it.

"Zack," said Osgood. "So help me, if you don't get to the point, I'll get out of this bed and choke you with my IV cord."

Silence.

"That's a tooth," he said, poking his finger at a bright bit in the middle of the hazy dark clump on the screen. "I guess they didn't show you this view, figuring just a tumor was enough to make you agree to the surgery. Teratomas are—"

"That's a *tooth?*" asked Osgood, loudly enough she was sure the nurses' station and the waiting room could hear.

"—often filled with things like teeth, and hair, and even eyes."

Osgood stared at him with her mouth agape. "I don't even know what to say to that."

Audrey shook her head. "This is all great trivia, Zack, but—"

"What if it's not a real tumor?" asked Zack.

"That would be—" Osgood snapped her mouth closed. "What?"

"That's not a real bruise," he said, pointing at her chest through the hospital gown.

She looked down at it, then back at him. "Alright?"

"You keep touching the back of your head," he said.

"I touched it once!"

"No," said Audrey. "He's right, you keep touching it."

"I have a bump," she said. "From when I—"

"Right here?" Zack asked, hitting two keys and switching to a closer image of the back of her skull, one that showed a more vivid shadowy line poking right through the curve of the skull.

She looked at it. The confusion, the anger, the fear, all tumbled together into one emotion that she felt was beginning to approach good old-fashioned hysteria. But no doctor with a wind-up vibrator was coming to cure it. "Do tera— do they grow arms?" she asked, finally.

"Teratomas. No," he said. "They're pretty much balls of horror. This is something...different."

"You have *terrible* bedside manner," she exclaimed.

"I'm going to have to agree with Osgood on this," said Audrey.

Zack threw up his hands. "There's no way to tell you this without it being awful!"

"Well then," said Osgood taking a few deep breaths to calm herself. "Do it quick."

"Cordyceps," he said.

"Quicker than that, Zack."

"It's a fungus that turns ants into zombies."

"I did *not* expect you to say that," said Osgood.

"After it bends the ants to its will, it makes them climb to a high peak, where it grows a stalk out of their head to spread its spores."

Osgood realized her hand was on the bump again. "You're right, there's no good way to suggest that to someone." The hysteria rose. "So, you think—"

"I am not a doctor."

"No, you're fucking *not*," Osgood snapped.

"I don't think this is what's happening, I'm just—"

"What am I supposed to do with this information?"

"Nothing," said Zack, deflated. "I just... You woke up in the middle of the night, drawing symbols all over the place. Including ones for opening a door or something. You said you birthed a monster from your chest." He sat on the floor below the monitor, turning his head away from them. "What if something came back with you? A hitchhiker

(there are those)

"entity, of sorts. And it's been

(who would take advantage)

"calling the shots." Without looking, he pointed at the screen above him. "It's not so crazy."

"No." Osgood felt a strange calm settle over her. "No, it's not."

Zack turned his face to hers.

"I'm not going to die," said Osgood.

"No," said Zack.

"And that thing is coming out tomorrow."

"Yes," said Zack.

"And then we are going to find the creature that came out of me, find out what it's trying to do, and stop it."

"You," said Zack. "Um, you will probably need to stay in the hospital for a few—"

"I'll stay until I leave," insisted Osgood.

"That's—" began Zack, in the tone he'd always used to correct her. He seemed to rethink it, though. "Yes," he said, instead. "Yes."

Osgood turned her face to the screen. "Show me the teratoma again?"

He switched back to the front view of the cloud of hazy dark in the center of her brain. *A fucking tooth,* she thought with a shudder. But it was nothing compared to—

She moved her hand away from the back of her head.

20

"You've certainly looked better," Osgood told her reflection. It seemed to agree. Her left eye, despite being sightless, was open and filled with blood around the iris and pupil. She found it disconcerting to look at, yet couldn't look away. There was a long scrape of road rash (*Or ice rash*, she thought.) along her right cheek. Her hair had become even more of a tangled mess, to the point where she couldn't even run her fingers through it. "They'll have to shave it," she told her reflection. "How else will they get into your brain?" She'd known that, of course, but reminding herself of it made it real. She'd only done the full buzz once and had thought her head looked entirely too big for it. When she'd finished it up, using the old dog grooming clippers in her parent's basement, her first thought had been how much she looked like that alien on the cover of *Communion*, an image that had terrified her when her mother of all people had brought it home to read. She'd decided at that moment to never again go that short. And she'd certainly never gone down to the skin. But this time wouldn't be her choice, would it?

"None of this is my choice," she grumbled and splashed water on her face, gently rubbing the coldness in, taking solace in the chosen dark of two closed eyes rather than the forced darkness of the left one, imposed by whatever had set up shop in her head.

In her own darkness, she considered the next several hours, the next few days. Despite Zack and Audrey's insistence, despite her own protestations, there was definitely a chance she would die during this surgery. It might not be a huge chance, no, but it was there. And short of dying, the fear of significant damage to other parts of her brain swam before her: her speech center, her ability to recognize people. Her identity.

Her memory.

("I've just arrived at Mars this morning, Aud.")

She'd just barely figured things out. Who she was, what she wanted, what she liked and didn't. In one night, that could all be taken from her. She could be turned into some docile zombie, of the kind 1950s asylums had in droves. "Just an ice pick to the brain'll do ya. Go right under the eye."

The echo of her voice, with her eyes closed, gave her the willies, and she opened them. The faucet dripped, sending its own ominous echo through the room. She could hear her blood rushing through her ears, along with a faint ringing, due to years of listening to the loudest possible music at the loudest possible volume. But beneath those, the echoing drip. She hit the cold-water paddle with the back of her hand, feeling the slight tug from the IV tube attached to the wheeled stand beside her. She could do this, right? It's not like it'd be the first time, if she died.

Ah, but three strikes, and you're out! She snorted at her thought and took a deep breath, allowing herself to hang there, head down over the sink. The coolness radiating from the porcelain was lovely. She could just stay here if she wanted. Stand here until they needed her.

"I'm sure they'd like it if I got some—" The word "sleep" caught in her mouth as she looked up. "Jesus." In the mirror, she saw the back of her head. She reached her hand around to the back to feel that knobby bump and yelped when she saw her hand crawling in the mirror. She closed her eyes, really squeezed them shut, hoping it would expel this vision, this horror. When she opened them again, though, she still only saw the back of her head. She turned to the left so that her good eye could still see the mirror. The image in the mirror turned, too, but it remained the back of her head. That lump, just on the edge of her short hairs before they turned into long, tangled curls, protruded more than she'd thought, more than she could feel. She reached back and touched it again, leaning forward toward the mirror. After all, if your horrors help you see something better, why not indulge them?

Her fingers pressed at the nub that looked like she'd been knocked in the head with

(Maxwell's silver hammer)

something blunt. But no bruising surrounded it. She could feel her skull beneath her scalp on either side of the lump, but the lump felt hard as a rock. Her throat burned as panic began to rise, and she closed her eyes again. Wouldn't do to get all panicky and screamy over something in her mind. After all, there really was something in her mind, wasn't there? Something that shouldn't be. Something fucking with her vision. So why shouldn't she hallucinate? Why should she—

Osgood yelped in pain, feeling like she'd been stabbed in that very spot on the back of her head. She resisted the urge to slap at the place, to get whatever was on her off, whatever was biting to stop, whatever was trying to come out— That was it, wasn't it? Something was coming out, not going in. She

COOPER S. BECKETT

nodded and experienced brief vertigo as the image in the mirror nodded in the opposite direction. She closed her eyes to let it pass, to shake it off, to be...something that would approximate well again.

The skittering sound drew her back. Something like a wet click, the kind of sound from movies involving large bugs. The lump on the back of her head began to throb, and a crackling accompanied the click. She howled at the pain but kept her eyes open. It was with a wide eye that she saw the skin above the lump split in a crimson X.

The kind you'd use to suck out the poison, she thought loopily, recalling way back when she'd gotten along with her parents, watching something on PBS something that included sucking the venom out of—

She screamed as something white and chalky emerged, shoving its way forward. She heard it scraping against her skull, inside and out, as it grew longer and longer. It was uneven and jagged and sloughed off like shale when she touched it behind

(in front of)

her head. It continued to slide its way out, longer and longer, backward from her head and forward toward the mirror. How could it be moving in both directions at once? She wondered it because it was the only question that made sense to her. She couldn't think about what it was. Why it was here. What it was doing in her head.

She felt and heard a *thunk*. Focusing her eyes on the mirror in front of her, she saw the glass crack and begin to fall away as the bony tendril shoved directly through the mirror and out through it toward her. Toward her dead eye. It continued to grow in both directions, shoving open the bathroom door behind her and pushing through the mirror until it touched her glasses.

She wanted to leap back, wanted to run, wanted to

scream, but was held in place by the stalk behind and before her head. The left lens of her glasses plinked down onto the tile floor beneath her, and then the stalk continued on, into her dead eye. A spatter of blood hit the mirror, and something snapped in her, allowing her the freedom of one thing, the freedom to scream.

She opened her mouth as wide as she could and loosed a plaintive wail, the likes of which she'd never produced before. But if anything was worth a true and proper scream, it was this.

21

"**O**s!"
     Osgood didn't listen, wouldn't look up, just
     covered her head with her arm and hoped this all
would end, or would turn out to be a dream, or a prank from
the margins. Some bored entity had recreated her world and
sent her back, just to fuck with her. The hand grabbed at her,
and she yanked away.

"Osgood!"

She swung wildly, hoping to smack away whatever was
trying to get to her. She followed it with a kick, and another
swing, and felt a rip of pain as the tape and IV pulled out of
the back of her hand. She opened her mouth to scream again,
but nothing more came out, so instead she opened her eyes.
Time to face the music. Time to look upon the demon and
despair.

Osgood found herself in the corner of her hospital room's
bathroom, wedged between the toilet and the wall. Her
glasses were gone, so the world was blurry. She searched on
her chest and stomach and came up empty. The blurry form

in front of her came nearer, nearer, aiming for her eyes, casting a dark shadow.

She struck out again with her damaged hand and made contact, but with a hand; it grasped hers, held it tight.

"Os, let me put your glasses back on."

Osgood slumped, and her adrenaline began to ebb. "Audrey."

"Audrey, yes."

She didn't move as Audrey slid her glasses onto her face, and the world came into hazy monocular focus. Crouched before her was her friend. "It came out of my head."

"What did?" asked Audrey.

"And broke my eye—" But when she touched her glasses, she found the lens still in place. "Is my eye there?" she pleaded with Audrey.

"Your—"

"The bloody one!"

"Yes, your bloody eye is still—"

"Iris? Pupil? Intact?"

"Yes?" asked Audrey, uncertain. Her voice changed as she stood and reached out her hands. "Let me help you up?"

Osgood reached a shaky hand behind her head and felt the lump, as it had been, slightly raised but nothing more. The skin was intact. She began to nod and found she couldn't stop, so she reached her arm toward Audrey, who grasped her hand and her elbow and slowly helped her stand.

"Okay," said Audrey. If she was concerned, she was doing a fucking great job not letting on. "Do you need to do anything in here?"

"What would I—"

"Pee?"

"Oh," said Osgood. "No. I'm—" she stopped herself with a laugh. "I was about to say good."

Audrey allowed for a small smile, then led Osgood back

into the hospital room and slid her back into bed. "You didn't pull out the needle," she told Osgood, pointing to a white bit of plastic on her hand. "Though I'm not sure how you managed not to."

Osgood stared at it.

Audrey disappeared back into the bathroom and returned with the IV stand. "I can put it back, if you want. Or I can get a nurse."

"You can put it back?" asked Osgood.

Audrey nodded.

"You," said Osgood. "Please."

"I'm sorry if this hurts," Audrey said. "I haven't done it in a while." Her hands moved quickly, and Osgood was reattached to the IV tube.

"What are you doing here?" asked Osgood after a while.

"Do you not want me here?"

"No!" Osgood insisted, then realized how that sounded. "I mean, I do. I just didn't know that... Sometimes it's family—"

"Your father told them I was your married sister."

Osgood snorted.

"Seemed to work." Audrey smiled, but it wasn't genuine. It was the smile you give the dying. The smile you give the already dead. "I asked them if they were going to shave your head."

"And?"

Audrey nodded.

"Thought so," said Osgood.

"I offered to do the first pass," she said, holding up a black plastic case. "I thought it might feel less invasive if—"

Osgood's heart could barely take it, and she felt the tears fall from her eyes. She just nodded, then again more emphatically.

Audrey went to a cabinet and removed another hospital gown, then helped Osgood sit up in her bed and slide down, climbing on behind her. She leaned Osgood into her lap, soft in fleece pajama pants. Then she tucked the extra gown around Osgood's head. "So we don't get hair everywhere."

"They probably would want you to do it in the bathroom," said Osgood.

"They do," said Audrey. "But I feel like you deserve a more calming experience than that would allow."

"Boy howdy," said Osgood.

Audrey slid her fingers into the tangled nest of curls and gently ran her nails along Osgood's scalp. She slid her fingers back out, then in again, shaking them slightly to help loosen the tangles. Osgood began to ask, why untangle it if you're just going to cut it off, but instead closed her eyes to be present in the sensation. It felt, at once, both intimate and not. Both romantic and friendly. Both sexual and not; enough though, even with all that had happened, Osgood began to feel a slight tingle between her legs.

She looked up at Audrey, seeing that her friend was looking away, and her cheeks were wet as well. They stayed like that for quite a while, Audrey's fingers running small circles along Osgood's scalp and loosening the tangles.

"Not having you there this past year has been so strange," Audrey said, after a long silence. "But what was weirdest was that you'd been out of my life for so long, then back ever so briefly before you vanished, and somehow that collapsed the timeline, so the time without you before felt so short and our time together vast. Only to have you disappear again. Like Caroline."

"I—"

"I'm not asking you to apologize for it. I know you didn't choose it or do it on purpose. I know that something happened." Audrey's fingers paused as she sniffled. "I missed you so much. And every fucking time we got one of those videos or saw one of those *things*—"

Osgood felt a bit of ire raise within her. She wasn't sure what the doppelgängers had been—Tulpas, something else? But she felt akin to them, connected. She said nothing.

"The projections. We saw one in Mary's once, at the bar. But it was gone by the time we went in."

"Oh," said Osgood, then realized she had no follow up.

"Every time it wasn't you, I felt further away. Like our connection was breaking again."

"It never broke," said Osgood.

Audrey just sniffled.

"I'm not going to die."

Audrey nodded. "Every time one of us says that; it sounds more like wishful thinking."

Osgood had to concede the point.

"I don't want to do this without you," said Audrey. "Neither does Zack."

"You two have managed to—"

"Keep up." Audrey wiped her eyes and put a hand to her cheek. "That's all we did. Survived."

"Thrived," said Osgood. "I never could make the podcast profitable."

"But you did," said Audrey.

Osgood stayed silent.

"After fifteen months, here we are again, and in less than three days, we're already worrying about another split. Another gap."

"A big one," agreed Osgood.

"Seems like," said Audrey. She was quiet again for a while. "We should do this." She held the big electric clippers above Osgood's face.

Osgood nodded. "Bye, hair," she whispered.

Audrey began to cut, and the plastic blade guard sliding along her scalp almost felt like a massage. Occasionally she felt a wispy touch, as a lock of curls drifted by her ear or down her cheek. She couldn't imagine having this done by the staff. She was sure they were lovely people, but to lose her hair and not have this...love. This spot, such comfort she'd not felt in... She couldn't remember, in fact. Lying here, with her head in Audrey's lap, Audrey taking care of her. It felt like...home.

"Bye, hair," Audrey whispered back, then snapped off the clippers. She leaned down and kissed Osgood's forehead.

"I love you," said Osgood.

"I love you, too," said Audrey. They stared at each other, eye to eye, as best as Osgood could manage. After a while Audrey nodded. "Okay, need to get this hair to the garbage."

Osgood nodded back and leaned forward, lifting herself up on her elbow. Audrey slid out from below her, wiping at her scalp and face with the hospital gown, then took the bundle to the garbage can near the door. The love Osgood felt for her at that moment was stronger than any she'd felt before. She'd only been in real love a couple of times, differentiating real love from confused adolescent feels, and one of those times, even if it hadn't been truly reciprocated, was with Audrey. What she wouldn't give to come together with her, with wild carnal abandon, with the adult senses of their bodies, their needs, their wants. But now wasn't the time, she knew, though that little voice in her head suggested, *If not now, when?*

"We can't fuck in the hospital," Osgood told the little voice, in a voice she thought was small enough to not be heard.

"We can't?" asked Audrey, turning back, eyes wide, wearing a slight smirk.

"I'm sorry." Osgood turned away.

"Sorry for what?"

"Objectifying. Wanting. Needing, probably."

"You shouldn't be sorry for any of that," said Audrey. "But you're right, we can't fuck in the hospital."

"Sigh," said Osgood.

"Sigh," repeated Audrey.

"You know the moment I knew I wanted more than to be friends with you?"

Audrey smiled and shook her head. "Just now?"

"The first moment," said Osgood.

"Those halcyon days of junior high and our confusing bodies."

"Yes, that time."

"I don't know," said Audrey. "When was it?"

"*The Wicker Man*," said Osgood.

"Excuse me?"

"Remember? Dad told us that we should watch it, since it was May Day. But he'd only ever seen the TV cut, so he didn't know about—"

"The dance," said Audrey, nodding.

"Britt Ekland's naughty naked dance."

"He couldn't have turned it off faster, I don't think."

"I saw plenty before he looked up from his magazine," said Osgood. "Saw plenty and felt plenty. Felt it in a way I hadn't before. And when he turned it off, we both groused about it. But he told us it was time for bed. And we lay on my bed together talking, looking at each other. And you looked different to me. That moment was different. You went from being friend Audrey who is a girl, and I like boys, to potential girlfriend Audrey, and maybe I don't like boys as much as I thought."

"I remember that night," said Audrey. "I thought you were just jazzed about seeing nudity. Aroused or not, Britt Ekland's ass was amazing."

"Actually, wasn't hers. Body double."

"Well, that's disappointing."

"Look," said Osgood, her tone serious. "I could be dead in —" she glanced at the clock. "Any time after three hours and some."

"You're—"

"Let's not do that anymore," said Osgood. "If I die, I couldn't *not* have told you that you were the love of my life."

"Oh, Os," said Audrey.

"And that I missed you as a friend, for that crazy long time we weren't speaking. But I also missed everything else. You as a girlfriend. You as a lover and confidant and..." Osgood looked away. "You as everything."

"I don't..."

"You don't have to say anything. You don't have to respond or consider or anything." Now Osgood looked back. "I just needed you to know."

Audrey's cheeks were wet again. "I'm going to get us some more water," she said.

Osgood nodded and watched as she went to the door but paused with her hand on the doorframe.

"Pru," said Audrey, without turning back around.

"When you call me that, it sounds completely different than when my parents do."

Audrey looked over her shoulder and directly into Osgood's good eye. "What you said? Me too. Me too."

2 2

"Okay, Prudence, we're going to have you count back from 10."

Osgood watched the nurse slide a needle into her IV and pump in a new liquid. She felt it reach her bloodstream. "Osgood," she said.

"What?"

"Osgood, not Prudence."

"Okay, Osgood. Count please."

Lying back on her pillow, feeling the chill of the waiting area, Osgood turned her attention to the ceiling above her. Soon they'd be here to bring her to surgery. Soon there'd be nothing else to—

Her father squeezed her shoulder. Some comfort came from that, but she wished it'd been Audrey instead. He was trying to be supportive, but all she wanted was—

"10," she began.

—to live. To live the way she used to. When things were good, simpler. When her podcast had thirty followers. When her gigs amounted to identifying, with Zack's help, that the cold spot ancient Emily Langston had thought was her eight-years-gone husband was, in fact, the faulty air conditioner in the room. The mixture of triumph (debunked!) and deflation ('I'm sorry your husband isn't trying to communicate.") was easier than the things that had come afterward. When she could still come home after a long day and not have anyone monitoring her. Not have anyone staring at her, as though she were living on the edge of a razor blade. Playing fast and loose with risk. Drinking her liver dead. Taking bootleg drugs like they were going out of fashion, just to quell the pain, to force the reality of existence into remission.

If you run fast enough, the real world can't catch up, can it? Or is this that catch up?

The brain tumor, the blindness, the vanishing from the world, and before that the chronic pain that had remained with her. The chronic pain in her body and the chronic pain in her mind was mostly self-inflicted, wasn't it? So much of this could be traced to her own choices.

But even so, did this punishment fit the crime? Was there any way that this could be just? That Prudence Osgood, for crimes against friends and lovers, for using and discarding sexual partners, for not taking care of the body she'd been given (a dubious honor, that), for not honoring her mother and father, should be sentenced to contend with all of this?

Seemed dreadfully unfair.

"9," she continued

But if one tallied up unfairness, wasn't it Audrey who won handily? Sure, she wasn't saddled with chronic pain, monsters emerging from her chest, or a baseball-sized tumor in her head. But her twin sister had vanished, been taken as the property of a spectral entity, and she'd shouldered the blame for it, or, if not the blame, the responsibility. And that responsibility was endless, decades of searching and wishing and mental floggings for her inability to progress.

She'd had a partner in Osgood who'd willfully tricked her,

someone she trusted, who'd straight up lied to her face and said, "There's a ghost," when it was nothing but fishing line and fancy lights and sounds.

Osgood wondered how she could've done that. What had caused her to think that'd be a good plan? She'd blamed their producers, sure, but she'd gone along without too much pushing. Is it kind to show someone fake proof of something, if proof is what they desperately want?

Maybe.

That was what her ancestors, the Psychic Osgoods, had thought. Along with turning a possibly dishonest buck, they could bring comfort to those who needed it. But nothing stopped that comfort quite like learning it'd all been a lie. And thus, the gift that Osgood had given her partner, her first love, was a horror show. The gift of betrayal.

Maybe that's why Audrey seemed to be thriving now. She'd turned The Spectral Inspector podcast into a hit, something that Osgood had never been able to figure out how to do. She'd rallied a community and shown spectral proof to the world, whether they chose to acknowledge it or not. And now she held the dubious honor of getting her friend back. The one who'd betrayed her, so long ago.

Such an honor.

"8."

From the looks of it all, Zack and Audrey were working as peers. The kind of partnership he'd always wanted from Osgood, but she'd never wholly given him. Sure, he was essential, but always at arm's length, placed in a separate category. Because who knew if or when her *real* partner would return.

Audrey, always Audrey.

Now Zack had a command station, had moved out of his family garage and into digs that he himself controlled. She still had no concept of where his own money came from, and she imagined if she were to ask him, he'd suggest that she didn't want to know. Once, she'd noticed a printing press in the corner of his garage space, and he'd hastily covered it with a tarp.

He also thrived in her absence. Moving to full-on producer of The Spectral Inspector, not just an in-name-only producer who really did the job of an intern, catering to the increasingly drunken, demanding "talent's" every whim.

She'd taken him for granted; she saw that clear as day. She'd never seen him for the value he was, at least not until he'd been shot and offered up as a sacrifice to the Lord of the Hinterlands.

What would she have done, if he'd died that night? Would she have cried? She thought so but couldn't be sure. Would she have immediately tried to take on the burden of his death, telling his family, trying to explain the unexplainable to his father? Looking at herself honestly, she was sure she would've drunk herself into the sort of alcohol coma Zack had always been concerned about. Just kick the ladder right out from under herself, despite what would surely have been heavy protestations from Audrey, and shuffle off into the glorious stupor.

But he hadn't died. In fact, he'd emerged better than she had from the Hinterlands. He'd thrived, indeed.

Better off without her.

"7."

Osgood lifted a hand to her shoulder, to place atop her father's, and in that motion, she saw time slow and blur. He was here for her. Was it duty? His English sensibilities, his ideas of right and wrong, were much more committed than those of the vulgar American he'd produced with his American wife. That wasn't fair, though, was it? Any of it? Her father had never once lorded his heritage over her or her mother. And short of some linguistic quirks, an outright hatred of using pronouns when talking about people present and a John Cleese accent, he didn't seem to bring that much British to the table at all. Duty or not, he stood by her here, now, as she walked into the darkness before surgery. Darkness, so they could peel up her scalp like old carpeting and drill into her skull. Darkness, so they could split open the sack containing her brain. Darkness, until they were ready to dig through the gray matter in search of the conqueror worm.

Because she'd have to be awake for that. Twilight, sure. But alert, so they could tell if they broke her. If they broke her brain. The better to fix any problems quickly. Or to just admit defeat. Because the problem might be too large, too vast. With its tendril reaching back, so that the entire mass could climb out of her head at any moment. What would they make of that?

And, beyond that, what if it was cancerous?

"6."

Admittedly the idea of a tumor with teeth, in her brain, was terrible enough, but the fact that it could also be cancer from spending too much time in an apparently irradiated world, well, that just made her spin out. If that were true, she wanted to die on the table. Shuffle off to Buffalo by choice, rather than curtsey later to a hostile invader.

Would that just make her selfish? Would she just be taking the easy way out?

Audrey would weep, were Osgood to die. And she was reasonably sure her father would as well, stiff upper-mustachioed-lip and all. Zack would be crushed.

She still had so much to make amends for. So much life to live, that she'd just forgotten in the last decade and change, as she'd descended into the madness of oxy plus copious alcohol, to quell the pain and the dreams. To silence her demons.

She may have silenced them, but they'd crept in anyway. Stealthily, angry at being hamstrung.

Or were these all new demons, not manifestations of...

She took a slow breath.

Not manifestations of her pain, of her self-loathing, of her self-destructiveness. But really-for-real monsters, hell-bent on...something.

Surely, they wanted...

Something.

That thing driving around in Sam Goddard's SUV wanted something, must've had a goal, and a destination, and a plan, and everything. It hadn't needed her, beyond its birth. Did that make her its mother or its midwife? Was it born from her or through her?

It needed...

It needed.

Stopping.

And she needed to be a part of that. Because it was here for something specific, or it would've just gone from room to room at The Heartland Motel, tearing shit up. Ripping its way through those...

What am I trying to say?

Through the people cheating on their spouses, through the hookups with sex workers, through the teenagers who couldn't get a moment's privacy in their own spaces...

She'd been...

There...

After all.

When she'd been young and exploring.

When she'd been...

Her parents hadn't fathomed that they shouldn't allow Audrey to sleep over. Had it been a boy whom little Pru had wanted to camp with in the yard, or snuggle up with in a shared sleeping bag, surely, they would've objected.

But instead, she'd had her first taste...

Her first...

The first...

The...only
who mattered. Who *matters*
more
than
anything
more than me.

23

Z ack turned the corner into the kitchen and dropped the stack of plates and cups he was carrying. Several shattered when they hit the floor. "The *fuck?!*"

Osgood didn't know what to tell him, since she wondered the same. "The fuck," she said, as if to explain.

"How did you get here?" he asked, then pointed. "Your eye."

"What about it?"

"It's fine!" He held his arm out, pointing long past the time proper etiquette would have suggested appropriate.

Osgood closed her right eye and, sure enough, she could see from her left. She reached her hand up quickly to the back of her head and found no lumps. Sliding her fingers up further, she encountered her curls. Loose, springing, not matted. "The fuck," she said again.

"How did you get here?" His arms hung at his sides now, but he made no effort to clean up the shattered dishes on the floor. "And why? You're supposed to be in surgery."

It was only then that Osgood noticed her friend's lack of clothing. His body was slender and largely hairless, with a small paunch above a light patch of black hair. She looked back up to his eyes when she saw his penis. "Why are you naked?"

"There's no one here!"

"But why are you naked?"

"Oh, like you weren't *always* naked when people weren't here." Zack grabbed a hanging apron off the wall and put it on, to hide his apparent shame. "And you're still not supposed to be here."

Osgood nodded. As much as her brain wanted her to focus on other things like the broken plates and the nudity, this current situation deserved analysis. "I was waiting for surgery and counted down after they injected me with the first dose of anest— They shaved my hair!" She put her hand back into the mess of curls on her head. "What color is it?"

"It's, uh—"

"Not a hard question, Zack!" She noticed her arm was clad in the maroon leather of her coat. "The fuck?"

"It's purple, Os. The way it was—" He stopped, also seeming to notice her coat. "Um," he said. "You should go and look on the coffee table in the living room."

"Why?"

"Just. Yeah. You should." He nodded. "And I'm going to put clothes on. And text Audrey."

"Where's Audrey?"

"She's at the hospital with—" He nodded again. "Go look. I'll be quick."

Osgood didn't move, but when Zack turned to leave, exposing his tiny butt to her, she looked away, then started down the hall. She made a stop at the bathroom and gazed into the mirror. Sure enough, her left eye matched her right. Her hair was still the reasonably-vivid shade of Manic Panic's Purple Haze it had been before...well, before they'd traveled to another world, the Hinterlands. Before she'd lit off for the territories herself for fifteen months. She wore a shirt with the *Ghostbusters* logo on it, under her coat.

"The fuck," she said again, allowing it to move beyond question to mantra.

She walked to the living room and stopped at the end of the hall. She felt a swell of hot, sharp panic rising in her chest and throat. On the table was a loosely folded pile of maroon leather. Her coat. Along with a pair of jeans and a t-shirt. She felt her breath begin to quicken as her mind rapidly cycled through possible explanations, no matter how wildly speculative or improbable. As she walked into the room toward the table, she realized another important thing: her pain was gone. Standing here, she felt no aches in her body, none in her head. Her chest felt...well, she could hardly say normal, because she couldn't remember a time when she'd been pain-free, only pain dialed-way-back with drugs. She shed the coat and tugged at the neck hole of her shirt. She couldn't see straight down through it, so she yanked it up over her head and looked down. She wore an old black bra, earning its strained keep holding her tits at bay. Between them, though, was nothing. No bruise, no red-purple-black and blueness. Nothing.

"Oh, uh."

Osgood turned back to the hall leading where a now-dressed Zack, clad in jeans and a black t-shirt, leaned on the frame, looking away.

"We're not past this yet, Zack?" asked Osgood.

"I just..."

"I *just* saw your dick."

"I wasn't crazy about that either," he said.

"Fair enough," she said. "But look."

He didn't.

"Zack, it's important."

Finally, he turned his head toward her.

"No bruise," she said, pointing to her chest.

"No—" he began, stopping himself. "Right! No bruise."

"No bruise, no pain. Duplicate coats!" She reached out both of her arms, pointing simultaneously at the coat on the table and the one she'd tossed on the floor near the doorway.

Zack looked down at it for a moment, then knelt and picked it up. He smelled it.

"Weirdo," she said.

"It's real," said Zack.

"Of course it's—" she began, indignant. "Oh."

"Oh," he repeated.

"You think I'm a ghost."

"The thought had crossed my mind. Yours?"

She had to concede that, didn't she? Among the many things she thought this pain-free and seemingly healthy version of herself might be, the most logical explanation was, "I died in surgery."

"That was my thought, yes," said Zack. "But Audrey says all is well at the hospital. She didn't know if she should come here or stay...with you."

Osgood didn't know what to suggest. "But it's possible I died. That I'm a ghost."

"Sure," said Zack. He walked over to her in such a curious way that she leaned back, then further, then further, almost falling over. When he was close enough, he poked her shoulder.

"Well, weirdo?"

"You're solid," he said.

"I figured I was, once you picked up the coat."

"Ghosts aren't solid," he said.

"Well, we've never really dealt with a—"

"Audrey and I did." He looked away sheepishly. "Last year."

"Ahh. So now you know all the things about all the

ghosts?"

"Well, no, but—"

"If I'm not a ghost, and I'm solid, how am I here? Astral projection isn't usually—"

"Tulpa?" asked Zack.

"Tulpa," said Osgood, feeling a strange relief by simply speaking the word.

"It's possible that you formed a Tulpa while under, to continue investigating." Zack gave her a nod, satisfied that he'd at least come to a maybe-sorta answer.

"But I thought Tulpas were independent."

"This isn't science, Os," said Zack. "It's ancient Buddhist spirituality and mysticism. Even avid practitioners disagree with what it means and how it works." His phone buzzed in his hand. "Audrey's coming home," he said after a glance.

Osgood's mind raced as she tried to put together all the possibilities, all the avenues, including the potential that this was just a very vivid dream. Her dreams were always vivid, so why wouldn't anesthesia dreams be vivid, too? And she wouldn't remember after, but here, now, she could explore. She pointed at the clothes on the table. "You got those from the Heartland Motel?"

Zack nodded. "My buddy's friend let me in."

She hesitated, unsure if she really wanted to know. "What did the room look like?"

Zack frowned. "Like *something* had happened, but it wasn't at all clear what that something had been." He swiped on his phone and walked over to her, holding it up.

On the screen was the motel room she'd been in so very recently. The room where she'd hoped she could put these things behind her, or at least out of mind for a few minutes, and just experience something pure and carnal. "Instead, I made a monster..."

"Hmm?"

"Residue?"

He nodded. "The bed was goopy."

"Some of that could be from..." she began but stopped when she saw the distaste on Zack's face. "Such a prude."

"It wasn't jizz," he said. "Goopy. Like snot."

"Lovely," she reached out and swiped her finger across the screen. It did nothing. She tried again. "Really?"

"Huh," said Zack, an expression of wonder on his face.

"Anything else?" she asked, clipped.

He nodded and swiped. He turned his phone vertically, and the screen showed the pillow, headboard, and cheap art above. Across the wall and art, in a flowing arc from the bottom left to the upper right, was a dark spatter of something.

"Blood?"

"I don't think so," said Zack. "The color here isn't quite accurate. In person, it was brownish green."

Osgood frowned. "And you took my clothes."

"Yeah," he said. "Also found a three-pack box of condoms with one missing. That condom was in the trash, un..." he looked away. "Soiled. Along with the wrapper."

"His clothes?"

Zack shook his head.

Osgood frowned.

"There's also this," he said. He swiped once more, and a black and white security video appeared on the screen, showing the parking lot in grainy night vision. After a few moments, the door to their room opened, and a man emerged, carrying a nude woman. He shuffled her into a black SUV parked in front of the room door.

Osgood opened and closed her mouth. "Play it again?"

Zack obliged.

"That's Goddard," she said.

Zack nodded.

"I thought it was the..." Osgood shook her head. "Again?" She spread her fingers on the screen to zoom in on the image. She saw blooming darkness on the pale woman's chest. "It's me."

"Did you think it was someone else?" asked Zack. "You said—"

"I didn't think it was him."

Zack looked from the phone, to her, and back. "I mean, it may not be—"

Osgood put her hand to her face. "I don't understand what's happening, Zack."

He nodded and looked at his phone once more before turning it off and putting it in his pocket. "I know."

"I mean, any of it."

"Why don't we sit down?"

Osgood nodded and followed him to the couch in front of the coffee table.

"Look," said Zack. "I was able to get this segment removed from the security cameras at the motel."

"How?"

"I... Ways?" He didn't offer more.

"Okay."

"I've got a trace on his license plate, so if his vehicle pops up anywhere, I'll get a ping."

"Okay," she said again, but she could hear the hollow sound of panic in her voice, the sound of confusion, of desperation.

"And..." he said, seeming to search for an *and*. "And! Audrey's on her way back now. So soon she'll be home, and we can figure out what's next, together."

"Don't forget," said Osgood. "I'm also in the hospital undergoing brain surgery."

"I. No, you're right. Yes."

She nodded

24

"Okay," said Audrey. She looked from Zack back to Osgood. "I cut your hair."

Osgood nodded.

"And..."

"Yeah, Aud," said Osgood impatiently. "We already got there."

"Well, I'm going to need some—" Audrey stopped herself and looked to Zack. "Tulpa?"

"Maybe?" Zack responded with a shrug.

"And...*not*...a ghost," said Audrey, with some hesitance. She moved toward Osgood and reached out her hand slowly. She extended her index finger to—

Osgood shook her head and took Audrey's hand. She felt her friend rapidly inhale and tug on her hand slightly. Osgood held firm. "I don't know why," she told Audrey. "But I'm here."

"Alright," said Audrey.

Beep beeep!

Zack looked at his phone. "Yes!" He darted out of the living room and down the hall.

Osgood frowned. "Do you think he wants us to follow—"

"Yes!" called Zack from the hall. "Yes, follow!"

She followed, tugging Audrey, still bundled in her coat and scarf, still bewildered, along behind her. They followed him down the new back stairs and into the darkened cavern behind the red door.

"Jarvis," said Zack. "Work mode."

Lights above snapped on one after another after another, and Osgood blinked back surprise, first at the brightness, then at the vastness of the space. "How on earth can you afford this?"

"Well, we," said Zack.

"Technically, The Spectral Inspector, Incorporated owns it," said Audrey.

"Spectral—" Osgood shook her head at that and marveled at the rows and rows of metal shelving, piled high with equipment new and old, some fully dissected, others still mint in the box. All the shelving seemed to narrow to Zack's command center, which she'd glimpsed briefly in dim lighting, now lit by stark bright LED light. "How does The Spectral In—"

"Lucrative advertising opportunities," said Audrey, sounding uninterested in talking about the money. "You remember me shaving your head."

"Yes."

"And when you said…"

"I remember it all, Aud," said Osgood. "I'm me."

"Well…" Zack wobbled his hand back and forth.

"Would you like to add something to that?" asked Osgood, putting her hands on her hips. She blew a purple curl out of her eyeline.

"I mean…" He shrunk back into the over-sized leather desk chair, then seemed to hem and haw about what to say next. "You said you're not in pain."

"Right."

"And you don't appear to need your glasses."

Osgood flicked her eyes back and forth. Everything in the room was sharp without them. Contacts, though, surely. She reached up and put her finger to her eye, provoking surprised yelps from her friends. "What? I'm checking if I have contacts in." She felt her finger touch her eye. No sliding. Nothing. "Alright."

"So," said Zack, holding his hand out.

Osgood waited.

"If you are actually a Tulpa, you're a thought-form, a projection." Zack shook his mouse, then clicked through several folders before selecting a video thumbnail. The six screens, two rows of three each, were filled by a full frame video. A theatre. Red curtains. A shadowy woman standing at the end of an aisle. Osgood hadn't seen this one, but it felt very familiar. As before, the person filming approached...well, her. And when they reached her, they walked around and saw her face. "Dressed exactly like..." he pointed. "You."

Osgood looked from the screen to her current clothing. Identical. "I mean," she said. "That's not a huge surprise. I'm almost always wearing some variant of..." She trailed off, watching the lips of the projection move, watching the unfocused eyes. "But those couldn't communicate."

"We don't know how it works," said Zack.

"That's..." said Osgood. "*Very* frustrating."

"Yeah." He gave her an emphatic nod. "But we should move beyond this."

Audrey cocked her head at him. "Move beyond the Osgood doppelgänger that showed—"

"Tulpa," corrected Osgood.

"Yes, both," said Zack. "Because I got pinged."

"Someone swiped right?" asked Osgood.

"Cute," said Zack.

"I'm funny when I'm not in pain," said Osgood.

"See, you're not you," said Zack.

Osgood scowled.

Zack clicked several times, opening first a browser, then condensing the six screens down to the one directly in front of him to surreptitiously type in his password, then bouncing the image back to the full array.

"Really?" asked Audrey. "You don't trust us?"

"She's not her!" he exclaimed.

"I." Osgood shook her head. She didn't really have a follow-up.

A video filled the screens. Bathed in the blue light of morning, a woman in a knit cap and scarf stood before a backdrop of trees. "Hi, Spectral Inspectors," said the woman. "It's Hedges."

"She's cute," said Osgood.

"Saundra Hedges," said Zack. "Of Chicago's Southside GhostHunters."

"Southside GhostHunters," Osgood repeated.

Onscreen, Saundra began, "As you have hopefully read in my previous emails—

Audrey leaned over. "She emails us constantly."

"—my group is conducting a long-term study of Bachelor's Grove Cemetery that includes strategically placed instrumentation, including a seismograph, long-range electromagnetic field detectors, and hidden cameras."

"Wow!" Osgood laughed. "Does the Midlothian police department know about her?"

Audrey shrugged.

"Remember the time we got kicked out of Bachelor's—"

"Shush!" said Zack.

"At 9:52 last night, our proximity sensors showed movement in the cemetery, and our cameras began recording.

Unfortunately, as soon as the motion woke the cameras, they promptly began to capture roughly ten hours of snow."

"Helpful," said Osgood.

"Seriously?" asked Zack. "Awfully glib attitude from a projection of a woman undergoing brain surgery."

Osgood said nothing. Then, just to get a word in, any word, she said, "Person."

"With the blizzard, and no further pings from our system, we assumed that it was an animal tripping the alarm, and I decided to check on the equipment in the morning." The video image moved away from Hedges' face and pointed at a small instrument, covered in plexiglass, snow pushed away from it. "The seismograph registered a 3.2 event at 11:12."

"An earthquake," said Osgood.

"Yeah, a decent sized one for our area," said Audrey.

"Huh," said Osgood.

"But there's more," enthused Hedges, clearly relishing her opportunity to show them something. She pointed the camera at her face again and, while walking, slightly out of breath, backward down the path, continued to narrate. "Our EMF detectors all registered spikes of 11 milligauss just before the earthquake and have maintained a steady 6.8 ever since."

"Huh," said Osgood again. "That's high."

"Yeah," said Audrey. She put her hand on the back of Zack's chair and leaned in.

"The big thing, though, is this." She turned the video around once more, and now it showed the entrance to the small cemetery. Osgood felt transported through time, back to her earliest memories of ghost hunting, when everybody had said that Bachelor's Grove, a cemetery in the south suburbs of Chicago, off the old Midlothian Turnpike that had been closed and forgotten by its town, was the most haunted place in the Midwest. Then she saw the writing. "What the fuck?" she asked, a sentiment both Audrey and Zack seemed to share.

"As you can see," said Hedges, "nearly the entire cemetery has been covered with dark red or maroon spray-painted symbols on the snow."

The video panned across the blanket of snow covered in lines of crimson. Osgood felt the gnawing concern growing within her and didn't need to look long to recognize symbols she'd drawn at the crossroads. "That's the same shit I—"

"Yeah," said Zack. He moved the video to only the upper left four monitors, and on the remaining ones, with several keyboard taps and mouse clicks, put up a stitched-together image of the shots that Osgood had taken at the crossroads.

"We're going to document this fully," continued Hedges. "I've got both Marty and Jess coming out with their DSLRs and wide-angle lenses. They'll be here shortly. I would have more for you but didn't want to disturb it." She panned down. "As you can see, despite all the writing, there are no footprints in the snow."

"Fuck, yes!" exclaimed Osgood, her vague concern given form. "I wondered what looked so weird about the footage. I mean, other than the symbols drawn in the snow."

"Jesus," said Audrey. She pointed to one of the monitors showing Osgood's chalk drawings. "This symbol," she said, then pointed at the main screen, which bobbed and weaved a bit as they heard Hedges breathing heavily in the cold. "Same."

Zack tapped the space bar. Sure enough, drawn almost identically in both chalk on pavement and spray paint on snow was a spiral with three lines bisecting it at different depths.

Did you hear me, Prudence?

Osgood flicked her head over her shoulder. There was no one behind them. Who the hell had that been?

"Pictures are already coming into our cloud folder," said Zack. He closed the video and opened a folder.

"Why did they send it to you?" asked Osgood, still squinting toward the back of the cavernous room.

"What?" asked Audrey.

"The Southside GhostHunters," said Osgood. "Why are they so excited to send this to you?" She turned back to Zack and Audrey, both looking at her. "I mean, us."

"Contact fame?" suggested Zack.

Audrey cocked her head. "I wouldn't use the word fame. But notoriety, sure. And if they find something cool enough for us to ask them to come on The Spectral Inspectors, then..."

"Aha," said Osgood. "You've become The Guardian for these—"

Prudence, we really need your confirmation here.

She swung her head back again and squinted at the back wall of the room, suddenly shimmery.

"Well," said Audrey. "I wouldn't put it *that* way. It's more like when you were on *This American*—"

"Something's happening," said Osgood, just before the wall broke and light overwhelmed her.

25

"I've got response."

"Wuh?" asked Osgood, continuing to squint at the blinding light.

"Prudence," said the voice she recognized but wasn't sure from where.

"Osgood," she said.

"That takes care of the 'can you tell me your name' question."

"My name," said Osgood.

"Can you follow my finger for me?"

The silhouetted shape of a finger appeared in front of Osgood's face. It moved to the left, then right. Osgood felt her eyes rolling in her head as she followed it.

"We have movement in both eyes."

"Excellent."

She knew that one too, female, the barest trace of an accent.

"What's going on?" asked Osgood, distressed that her voice seemed to have dropped several octaves and slowed to nearly half-speed. She wondered if that was real or just a result of the swimmy feeling she was experiencing.

"We lost you for a little while."

"I died," said Osgood. Then she snorted a laugh. "See?"

"No," said the woman. "No, you didn't die."

"I didn't?" asked Osgood.

"No, you just drifted deeper into the twilight than we wanted."

"I don't like those books," said Osgood. She squinted again at the light.

"Is it too bright? Would you like me to get some sunglasses?"

"My future is so bright," said Osgood with another snort. "I gotta wear shades."

"She sounds drunk," mumbled a third person.

"Drunk is better 'n dead," Osgood told the mumbler, then tried to point in the direction of the person but couldn't move her arms. "Paralyzed maybe?"

"Oh, no. Just confined."

"Unhand me, woman!" said Osgood.

"You're doing great, Prudence," said the first voice. "We've got almost all of it."

"Osgood," said Osgood.

"You'd like to be called Osgood?"

"I. *Am*. Osgood." She tried to nod but again only pushed against restraints. "Close only counts in horseshoes and hand grenades."

The first voice, which she was now reasonably sure was behind her, chuckled and agreed.

"Will you tell me what's happening?" Osgood asked. "Pretty please?"

"You don't remember why you're here?"

Osgood considered the question. Why *was* she here? And

where was here? "Because I can sidestep between worlds," she said finally. That should cover it.

"Alright," said the first voice.

"Osgood, do you remember why you're at the hospital?"

Hospital? Yes. Right. "Teratoma."

"Did she say what I—"

"Teratoma?" asked the woman. "Where did you get that—"

"You don't lock down your computers when you leave the room," said Osgood, to silence from the invisible peanut gallery. "Hah!" she said instead of laughing. "Zack was inside you before he even had to buy you a drink."

More silence, then some mumbling between all three voices. "Yes, well," said the first voice. "You're correct. A teratoma tumor is why you're in this room now. Do you remember what brought you in—"

"Show me its teeth," said Osgood, plastering a toothy grin on her own face.

Again she silenced them.

"Osgood," said the woman, now close. A very hazy, dark shape, a head, swam before her. "We are working on removing the teratoma now. We roused you to twilight again to see if you were cogent."

"Five by five," said Osgood. "Did I salute?"

"No, you are still confined."

"No, I'm fine," said Osgood.

"I'd like you to close your right eye." The voice waited patiently. "No, just your right eye. Though that's good, that you can close your left—"

Darkness. Osgood felt instantly relieved. Maybe she could just stay here in the dark. So comfortable. Without pain. Maybe Lil would come, and they could just—

"Now open your left eye."

Osgood did, and the brightness flooded back in.

"Pupillary movement."

"Bright lights," said Osgood.

"I've got her...'shades,'" said the man with attitude.

"I've had enough out of that guy," said Osgood. "He's acting like he's the one with fingers in his brain." She felt sunglasses sliding onto her face, and the light dimmed immediately.

"Darker. Still blurry," she said.

"Can we—? Thank you."

She felt another pair of glasses sliding on. "You already put them on!"

A face came into focus before hers.

"Dr. Laghari," said Osgood.

"Hello, Osgood."

"You didn't want to tell me it was a teratoma, did you?" Osgood asked the doctor. "You didn't want to tell me about its teeth."

Dr. Laghari hesitated. "We have found most patients do better when they learn any unsettling specifics of their tumor afterward. They stress less during the—"

"Does it have eyes?" asked Osgood, unsure why she thought it might.

The doctor didn't respond, but a shift in her eyes confirmed Osgood's sudden suspicion.

"And its outgrowth, the one moving toward the back of my skull..."

"How did you—"

"I'd shake my head and wag my finger at you were I not...*confined*."

"We are..." began Dr. Laghari. She stopped, then smiled at Osgood. "We are completely confident that we will be able to remove all of that, as well."

"You do you, Doc," said Osgood. "I'm giving you a thumb's up. Wish you could see it."

"I can see it, Osgood," said Dr. Laghari. "You're not paralyzed."

"Just confined."

"Just confined," repeated the doctor.

"And not dead," said Osgood.

"Absolutely not dead," confirmed the doctor.

"Whew!" exclaimed Osgood. "'Cuz when I showed up at home, I thought for sure that I was a ghost."

"When you—"

"Have you ever heard of a Tulpa, Dr. Laghari?"

Dr. Laghari shook her head slowly. "No, I haven't."

"I hadn't either," said Osgood. She felt her eyelids growing heavy. "I'm a little woozy, Doc."

"That's to be expected," said the voice behind her.

"You can hear him too, right?" Osgood whispered to Dr. Laghari.

"Yes, Osgood," said Dr. Laghari, with what seemed like a genuine laugh. "That's your surgeon."

"Hello, Osgood," said the surgeon. "Dr. Hayward, at your service."

"Doc Hayward?" Osgood snickered. She felt her eyes flutter closed and then open. "That's the guy from..."

"Osgood?"

"I don't feel..." began Osgood, but she couldn't come up with the word she wanted, just an image of a brick-lined tunnel. "Spooky."

"You don't feel spooky?" asked Dr. Hayward.

"That's." Osgood frowned.

"Should I do some cognitive tests?" Dr. Laghari asked someone behind Osgood.

"A big one," said Osgood. "Big...cog."

"Do you know what year it is?"

"2019," said Osgood.

"It's 2020, Osgood."

"Right. Fifteen months, right."

"What about—"

Dr. Laghari didn't stop talking, but her words seemed to have been replaced by a muffled throbbing sound.

"Like...heartbeat," said Osgood. "Womb."

The brightness dimmed further, and Osgood wondered if they'd placed another set of shades on her. Then the darkness filled all the empty spaces.

She hung in darkness a while.

I need to go back, she thought, surprising herself with a thought she could hear. *They need my*—

26

"——onfirmed two other earthquakes, one two nights ago, then another last night."

"When Osgood— Fuck!" Audrey jumped backward away from Osgood, who found herself standing very close to the two of them in Zack's command center.

"Welcome back," said Zack.

"Sorry to, uh, scare you," said Osgood.

"It's...Jesus." Audrey crouched and put her hands on her knees, breathing through the surprise.

"Not sure I could do this as effectively were my..." she thought about it. "Main processing system not hobbled in such a manner."

Zack nodded. "You were talking to someone else before you disappeared."

"I could hear the doctors," Osgood said.

"That's," he smiled and shook his head in awe. "That's something."

"Like her consciousness is actually leaving—"

"Her, me, Os," said Osgood. "*Not* an experiment."

"Yes," said Audrey. "Sorry."

Osgood shook her head and shrugged. "S'okay," she told them, suddenly understanding a little bit of her father's annoyance, from back in the diner. "Sounds a lot like astral projection."

"Usually people can't see those projections," said Zack.

"Is this a known fact?" asked Audrey.

He looked uncomfortable. "I read..."

"Read what, Zack?" asked Osgood.

"The Time-Life book on—"

"*Mysteries of the Unknown?*" asked Osgood, recalling the commercials that played endlessly on Saturdays while she was watching TV growing up.

"Yeah," agreed Zack.

"Okay, as I've no idea how much time I have here before they draw me back, do you have any updates?"

"As I was saying when you..."

"Came in?"

"Yes," said Zack.

"Must've been a door there in the wall," said Osgood.

"What?"

"Nothing," said Osgood.

"Right, well, as I was saying, there seems to have been a minor earthquake around 4 am on the morning you returned, centered around St. Charles, and then another not far from the crossroads the following night."

"Blowing holes through reality everywhere, aren't I?" Osgood grinned, but neither returned it. The grin faltered and vanished. "I don't know what to say, folks. Or what to do."

"We know," said Audrey. "Neither of us expect you to have all the answers."

"It'd be nice to have a few," said Osgood. The three of them were silent for a while. "I should ask my father if he has any pictures of Great-grandmother Lillian."

"To confirm if you saw—"

"Her, right," said Osgood. "Anything more on Goddard's whereabouts? Or Goddard's monster?"

"Nothing," said Zack. He perked up suddenly and swirled to face the computers. "We did get some very high-resolution images from the South Side GhostHunters, though." He clicked through a seemingly endless series of folders before double-clicking an image that filled the primary monitor. Then he blew it up to fill all of them.

"That's the whole fucking cemetery," said Osgood, recognizing Bachelor's Grove's bisecting road and obelisk monument.

"Yeah," said Zack. "And then the crossroads." He tapped some more, opening another program, then he dragged two files into it. "Bachelor's Grove," he said as that image reappeared. "And the crossroads." A smaller image, grainy and not as clear, appeared atop the white cemetery image. This one was hers, chalk drawings on black pavement. Zack tapped a few more keys, and the top image faded, still visible, but transparent enough to show the one below it as well. Zack filled the six monitors with the images. "You see it?"

"Yeah," said Osgood. How could she not? Her crossroads drawings weren't just similar, the same symbols or sigils, almost two-thirds of them aligned directly with the spray-painted symbols and sigils from Bachelor's Grove Cemetery. From last night. Where the Goddardmonster had tried to take her. "Okay, that's...a lot to take in."

"Do you want a theory?" asked Zack.

"Probably not," said Osgood.

Zack nodded and turned back to his computer.

"Obviously, I want to hear your theory, Zack," said Osgood. "I just don't *want* it to be— You know what I'm trying to say."

"Probably not," said Zack.

Osgood snickered and nodded.

"Cordyceps," said Zack.

"I like that word even less this time," said Osgood.

"Something controlled you, got you to make these drawings," he told them, pointing up at the smaller collection of symbols. "You didn't just do it."

"Okay," said Osgood. "I'll concede that. But a fungus wasn't what made me do it."

"Not *actually* cordyceps!" Zack wiped his face, his go-to gesture for *Catch up, Osgood.* "Let's call the cordyceps fungi a… principle, an idea."

"Let's," agreed Osgood, with an edge in her voice.

"Os," said Audrey quietly.

"Audrey had some abnormal cell growth after just ten real-world minutes in the…Hinterlands. You came back with what seems like a spectral bruise; doctors can't even tell it's real when they examine you."

Osgood took a deep breath. "Yes."

"What if you encountered something in the margins, and it…" he trailed off, looking away.

"Go on, Zack," said Osgood. She leaned forward until her face was right next to his. "And it mindfucked me? Put something in my brain?"

"I see no reason I should be getting shit," said Zack without looking at her.

She nodded and backed off, sitting in a chair against one of Zack's many metal shelving units.

"Do *you* have a theory, Os?" Zack demanded, the edge now strong in his own voice.

"No," Osgood admitted.

"Audrey?" His edge softened for her.

"I'm honestly just trying to wrap my head around everything happening." Audrey turned to Osgood. "Three days ago, you were still…gone, Os."

Osgood nodded. "Did we keep our roof access in the remodel."

"It's still difficult," said Audrey. "But yeah."

"I need to...be elsewhere...for a bit."

"How long before you're elsewhere again?" Zack seemed like he was trying to sound concerned but came across as desperate.

"I don't fucking know, Zack," said Osgood, turning and walking out of his warehouse office. As she climbed the stairs to her apartment, she chided herself. Neither of them deserved her ire. But right now, maybe she could be forgiven for high tension. Existing in two places, without any seeming rhyme or reason. Undergoing literal brain surgery.

Osgood opened a closet door off the kitchen and pulled a ladder away from the wall of the small storage space. Leaning it against the shelves, she climbed up and shoved the ceiling panel to the side. Light burst into the closet, and Osgood rose to meet it. Wishing she'd put gloves on before she'd done this, Osgood boosted herself out of the square opening and onto the roof of her apartment and Mary's. Where once it'd been her lone chair up here on the flat tarpaper roof, now there were two camping chairs and a small table. She kicked one forward to dump the snow from it, then righted it and sat. From here, she could see the lake, a bar of deep blue-gray beneath a stark white sky. She wondered if it was frozen. Didn't feel cold enough now, but sometimes the deep-freeze crept into Chicago early. She remembered a year where it'd gotten down to zero at Thanksgiving. To the right, she saw the middles of Chicago's downtown skyscrapers, their heads in the clouds, bodies obscured by closer buildings.

She closed her eyes, breathing in and out, marveling that there wasn't even the barest stab of pain. She'd felt the pain of that accident at the crossroads for almost twenty years— over twenty, in fact. The constant reminder that her body had been broken, and life had wanted her to stay down. Somehow, she'd managed to get back up but couldn't shake the pain. From her thighs and back and neck's near-constant reminders, to the light pinprick in her chest whenever she took a deep breath, the accident was and likely always would be a part of her. But not now. Not this.

Not I, thought Osgood. *The projection, the doppelgänger, the double, the Tulpa.* Whatever she was now seemed to be able to live free from the unfair pain of simply being alive. She knew it was naive to think she could possibly remain in this form. She had a body, not far away. She looked over her shoulder in the direction of Swedish Covenant Hospital, where she was undergoing surgery. It was too far away to see, of course, and obscured by other buildings, but she could feel that she was there, strapped down and confined, as Dr. Hayward poked around in her brain to remove the teratoma. To remove the cordyceps.

Fungus or not, something had shoved itself through her brain, to the back of her head. And she had a sense that if it were allowed to grow much longer, that bathroom dream would assert itself into a horrifying reality. She regretted the way she'd smacked Zack down. He'd seen the teratoma. He'd noticed the—

"Fuck," said Osgood. "He really is fucking essential." She nodded to herself. "And I should go tell him that, shouldn't I?"

The wind was the only response, but she knew the answer. This was the downside of being the mystery, wasn't it? The answers might not be great for you. She stood and walked back to the square panel, realizing that she'd left it open and surely the kitchen was freezing now.

Something is happening. Lil's voice appeared in her head, layered over her own. It felt like she'd been absent for ages, but it hadn't even been a day.

"What's happening, Lil?" asked Osgood to the frozen day. The wind was again her only response. "If you know, I think we'd all be thrilled to get some insight. Don't worry about us feeling bad we couldn't solve this shit ourselves. We'd much rather know what's—" Osgood stopped and cocked her head. She could feel it. Lil was right. "Something *is* happening."

What that something was, Osgood didn't know, but she could feel herself vibrating, her innards rattling around most disquietingly. She looked down and saw the snow at her feet bouncing and shaking. "Not in my head then," said Osgood, feeling a wealth of relief. As the vibration grew, the shaking of the snow became more violent. She planted her feet harder to keep from falling over. She looked around at the trees that seemed only to be disturbed by the lazy wind. The snow at her feet bounced and tumbled, then rose. She felt her hair rise as well, the way it had when she'd visited the Wisconsin Dells when she was eight and touched a massive Van de Graaff generator. She held out her hands, feeling only slightly steadier, and watched as the snow rose past her ankles and approached her knee. A whirring sound began to build, like the hum of that Van de Graaff so long ago. Electricity, static buildup. The snow continued to climb.

When the blare came, it knocked Osgood on her ass. The sound of a tuba playing its lowest note, but a tuba the size of Chicago. The sound felt as though it was accompanied by wind. Wind that blew...south. The sound ceased, and the snow dropped back to the roof with a light poof.

Osgood turned her face north, where the buildings of Chicago gave way to Evanston and the ritzy North Side suburbs. Beyond those suburbs, though, beyond all of it, she saw...a glitch in the sky. Like a shimmering bar of azure glass had been dropped in front of it. The shimmer felt so close, but so very far, and Osgood knew that if it was as far as it seemed, it'd have to be enormous.

"Os," called Audrey from the closet below.

"Audrey, please tell me you heard that!"

"I didn't hear any—"

"That sound!" pleaded Osgood. "That loud blaring sound! Or felt the vibrations."

"I—"

"Fuck," said Osgood.

Audrey popped her head out of the hatch in the roof and looked at Osgood. "What's going on?"

"Do you see that?" asked Osgood, pointing north toward the shimmery blue.

From the hatch, Audrey squinted into the wind, then looked back to Osgood. "I— Lemme climb up." Audrey rose and stood on the roof, helping Osgood back to a standing position.

Osgood pointed again, and Audrey leaned over to follow down her arm and finger like a rifle sight.

"I don't. What am I looking for?"

"The blue...thing."

"I don't see it, Os," said Audrey, after seeming to give it a real try.

"Probably didn't feel the earthquake, either," said Osgood, forlorn.

"Another one?" asked Audrey. "Must've happened as I was coming up the back stairs. They feel shaky to me by themselves." Audrey put her hand to the side of Osgood's face.

Osgood jumped.

"You're shaking," said Audrey. "You should come back inside."

"Yes," Osgood agreed, still feeling the vibration within her, a phantom sensory shadow, like when she'd used her Hitachi for too long. As she turned toward the hatch to climb back down at Audrey's beckoning, she saw another bar of azure. "It's there. There, too!" She pointed, assuming Audrey wouldn't see this one either. She didn't, and Osgood nodded. "North and west," said Osgood to herself. She paused with her feet on the top ladder rung and looked up at Audrey. "North and west," she repeated.

Audrey nodded, but her face showed confusion. She held Osgood's hand to aid her descent.

Osgood stopped. "Wait."

"What?"

She climbed back onto the roof. "North." She aimed her finger at the azure glitch in the north, then turned to the left and found the one to the west. She gave herself another 90-degree rotation and found, just to the southwest of downtown, sure enough, the barest sliver of blue shimmering haze. "South."

"What, um," began Audrey, uncertain. "What do you think it means?"

"Triangulation," said Osgood. She was uncertain why she knew that, or how, but she knew something else as well. Knew it with startling certainty. With such confidence that she found it frightening. She pointed south again. "Bachelor's Grove Cemetery." Then west. "The crossroads." Then north. "Whatever just happened there, the vibration, the sound...he caused it."

"How do you know?"

Osgood shook her head. She stared at the shimmery glitch to the north, seeming to float out over the coast of the lake. Maybe beyond the northern suburbs, all the way up into Wisconsin. "I know."

27

When Osgood stepped off the ladder to the floor, she felt the backs of her legs bump against a chair. Odd as this closet didn't have room for a chair. She went off balance and fell into it. Like a light-switch being flipped, everything changed. One moment, she saw the organizer unit in the storage closet, overflowing with miscellaneous things she'd never known where to put, and then a TV mounted on a wall above her, tuned to Fox News, making her eyes roll. Below the TV was a row of mostly empty identical chairs, set against vaguely floral print wallpaper. The chair directly below the TV, though, was in use by her father, sitting with his eyes closed and his chin on his chest. His face seemed worn, with days of stubble on his cheeks and chin. His hands clutched a magazine rolled into a tube. She wondered how she'd wound up here. Was there some sort of control happening within her exposed brain? Or was she independent of...the real Osgood?

She grimaced at the phrase and stood. More important things were happening just now, weren't they? She could have an identity crisis later. Just now, Zack and Audrey needed her.

She reached into her trench coat pocket for a phone that wasn't there. "Of course," she grumbled. Maybe she could take her father's phone and call them. She stared at the phone, which had slipped between the armrest and his thigh. *You don't know their numbers,* she reminded herself. She blinked at the phone and man before her. She wasn't sure she knew any phone numbers, in fact. Any except her parents' landline. But that wouldn't be helpful, would it?

Osgood turned her head to the desk, where a nurse typed slowly on a computer. Maybe she could use the computer to look them up. Or look up the Spectral Inspector's website, find a phone number? She knew that was folly, that there was no way the hospital would allow her to do that. She might be stuck here. With a sigh, she moved to the chair next to her father, facing the desk and the door leading...back.

He stirred, bumping her with his elbow. He mumbled, "Apologies," and wiped at his eyes, following it with a long and challenging-to-stifle yawn.

"S'okay," said Osgood.

He gave her a squinty smile and nod and then looked back down at the magazine he held so tightly. Slowly, his face changed, and he turned it back up to meet hers.

"Hi, Dad."

"Pru! What on Earth? You're alright!"

"I—" Osgood was cut off by the most intense hug that could be given over two armrests. She wanted to tell him to wait, that her appearance here wasn't indicative of the way the surgery was going, that she wasn't...what? Her? Instead, she wrapped her arms around him and patted his back.

"I've been so worried," he said into her shoulder. "How did— I mean..." His pause was accompanied by a stiffening of his shoulders. When he unclenched from the hug and leaned back, his face had changed again, now suspicious. "Wait. How did you get—"

"Dad," said Osgood, again buying time to figure out how to explain this to him.

"Nurse!" her father exclaimed toward the woman at the desk.

"Yes, sir."

"Would you..." He seemed uncertain what he wanted to ask, then looked from the nurse to Osgood and back. "Could you ask someone to update me on the surgery?"

"Prudence Osgood," said the nurse, bringing the final syllable up as a question.

"That's right," said her father.

"Certainly." The nurse picked up the phone and spoke quietly into it.

Basil Osgood turned his attention back to her. "This is a dream?" He seemed to have meant it as a statement but turned it into a question at the last moment.

"I don't think so, Dad," said Osgood. What could she tell him? How could she reassure him? "I'm okay."

"How can you be okay?"

She nodded. "Fair question."

"Did..." He looked down at his lap. When he continued, his voice was so low she could barely hear the question. "Did you die?"

"Not yet," she said.

When his eyes returned to hers, they were full and horrified.

"No! Sorry!" she said, chiding herself for her own gallows humor. "I. That. Look." *Whatcha got, Pru?* she asked herself.

Ask him about Eliza, the voice of Lil in her head suggested so loudly that she thought she heard it in the room.

"Eliza!" she exclaimed.

"What?"

"I'm supposed to ask you about Eliza."

Her father shook his head. "Excuse me. I need you to

explain who you are and what is— Why you would ask about my sis—" He shook his head again and slammed his hand down on the armrest, hard enough that the nurse looked up. He smiled at her, trying to play it cool, then told Osgood out of the side of his mouth, "You aren't my daughter."

"I am," said Osgood, trying to counter his exclamations with calm. "I could explain how, or more, but I don't really know for certain."

"Try."

"Okay." Osgood frowned. "I *think* I have..." *What? Powers?* "The ability to do certain things." *Well, that explains everything, doesn't it, Pru?*

"Continue trying," he said.

"Right." She nodded and looked at her hands. "Okay," she said. "Remember when we used to go to see the Bears play? And we'd park out by the planetarium and barbecue, and sometimes we wouldn't even get to the game because we were enjoying hanging out on the planetarium peninsula so much?"

"Yes," he allowed, still skeptical. "How does that explain things?"

"Oh, I. I thought that telling you something that only I would know about—"

He leaned over and pointed at the door to the back. "My daughter is in there having brain surgery. And I *just* got her back..."

"None of it makes sense, does it, Dad?"

"I don't want to lose you—*her*—again."

She took a deep breath. She wanted to reassure him that she was okay, or maybe she just wanted to reassure herself. Instead, she told him how she really felt. "You should've stood up for me."

He looked at her, eyes wide like he'd been slapped.

"When Cynthia—"

"Your mother," he said, almost reflexively.

Osgood held her tongue for a moment. "When *my mother* called me a dyke. When *my mother* told me that I embarrassed her. When *my mother* told me—"

"Yes." He looked away again. "Yes."

"You should've defended me then. Not sent me notes over the years about how you wish I'd—"

"I'm sorry," he said.

"Yeah, well." She sighed. This hadn't been her intent. Not now. Though she wondered if it was why her mind had put her here. Was it to tell him how she felt, for real, without sitting in a hospital bed with the specter of death over her head? "I needed support. After my accident. Not money. I needed *support*."

"I regret that I was unable—"

"*Chose* not to."

"You didn't make it easy," he said with an edge. "I should have supported you, yes. I should have defended you, yes. But maybe you didn't have to be so antagonistic to your mother. To us."

Osgood felt the old familiar rage rising. The fight they always had. But she quelled it. "Maybe it's the fact that my body is in surgery right now, and I'm not..."

"Again, if you could tell me—"

"I don't know," she insisted. "But yes, I could've done things better as well."

"Thank you for saying so. I apologize again." He reached over and, for a moment, his hand hovered over her knee. He was questioning putting it down, wasn't he? Then he did. She heard his breath flow out.

"I'm real," she said. "Whatever that means."

He squeezed her knee and held it for a while. Then he wiped tears from his eyes and squeezed again. "I want to be your father again. I want to be a family again."

She nodded. "I love you, Dad. I'm just not there yet with Cyn— My mother."

"Alright." They sat in silence.

"Mr. Osgood?" called the nurse, hanging up the phone.

"Yes!" he looked up quickly.

"They tell me that surgery is going well. I'm sorry that I don't have more information."

"No," he said. "No apologies. Thank you. That's plenty." He looked back to Osgood. "You're really still in there. And really here."

"Somehow, yes," said Osgood.

"Why did you ask about Eliza?"

"What?"

"You said you were supposed to ask about—"

"Right!" Osgood nodded. "Who is Eliza?"

"Eliza is your aunt. My sister."

Osgood frowned. "But I don't...you don't." She realized the folly of these statements. "Clearly, I've been misinformed."

"Eliza and I—" He sighed. "There are things about this family that—" He looked at Osgood and shook his head. "It's hard to suggest that supernatural ideas are problematic while sitting next to—"

"A supernatural idea?" Osgood suggested.

He nodded, mouth open with words unsaid. "You are a remarkable woman, Prudence."

"I am a remarkable *person*, Dad."

"Do you have to do that now?"

"No," said Osgood. "No, I don't."

"The women in the Osgood family..." He seemed very uncertain what to say beyond that. "...are also said to be remarkable."

"Said to be—"

"If the supernatural is real," he began.

Osgood stopped him with, "Can confirm."

"Well. Then I guess saying she *is* some sort of witch, instead of saying she *thinks* she's—"

Miss Osgood?

Osgood turned her head away from her father and saw, blurrily, a heart monitor. She heard its beeping grow louder. *Fuck,* she thought. *Not yet!* "Dad!"

He stopped, eyes widening again.

"Can you call her?"

"I haven't spoken to her in—"

"You didn't speak to me in, either. Can you call her?"

"I." He instinctively reached for his phone. "I guess I—"

"Do it, please! Now! It's important!"

"I have to find her number!" He dropped his phone in his scramble to unlock it.

Miss Osgood, can you hear me?

"Listen to me, Dad." Osgood grabbed his wrist. "I *think* you're about to see me disappear."

"I'm— What?"

"Which, in many circles, would be considered a rather obvious confirmation of—" She saw a blinding light in first one of her eyes, then the other.

Pupilary response is—

She closed her eyes and ignored the rest, the other, the outside. "Supernatural activity. As if talking to your daughter's doppelgänger while she is in surgery isn't enough."

"Pru—"

"Call Eliza and tell her that I need to speak with her as soon as we can possibly talk," said Osgood. She felt pressure in her head, a sort of overall constriction. The vision began to fade in her left eye. "I'm about to go," she told him, grabbing his hand. "Call her and tell her Lil told me to reach out to her."

"Who is Lil?"

"Jesus!" exclaimed Osgood, as the entire world shifted. She went from sitting to lying prone, from looking at her father to looking at the ceiling, from being in the waiting room to being in a hospital room.

A young man with sandy blond hair had his hand on her wrist. She pulled it away.

"Well," he said. "I'd say you're awake."

"Yeah," said Osgood in a weak and raspy voice. "It would appear that I am."

🜋 28 🜋

As Dr. Laghari explained the results of the surgery to her father, Osgood let her mind wander. It felt like only a couple of weeks ago she had been barely keeping up with rent by writing obituaries, wondering if this would be the month she'd give sex work a try, then lamenting that she'd waited until her body was old and broken before going that route. She'd been a hot number back in the day.

Not too bad, just now, she thought. *Hot enough to bed Goddard.*

But was a cheat, wasn't it? He was a former— Her mind said *lover* and she blanched at that. "Boyfriend" didn't feel much better. Especially considering Osgood's newer trend. Four on the Kinsey Scale and all that. Not a lesbian, no, but far enough from straight that she could no longer see brake lights.

She thought about that time before the gap, before the Hinterlands, before the Lord...fuck, before Audrey's return. She'd been back in Osgood's life for what felt like only days. Could still be spoken of in hours. So frightfully brief. And then Osgood had gone and disappeared. And then she had gone and almost died. She reached up to her head and felt nothing but gauze. She winced as she touched a bit too hard, then pulled her fingers back to lightly trace over her newly bald dome, wrapped in bandages. As her fingers found her ear, then cheek, she had a discordant feeling of the fingers and the cheek not belonging to her. Both felt disconnected.

Osgood felt untethered to her body.

She supposed that anesthesia—and fucking *brain surgery*—would do that.

But also, she felt the sense memory of her hair, the locks falling as Audrey slid clippers across her scalp, giving her the *GI Jane* cut before they shaved her completely.

If I die, I couldn't not have told you that you were the love of my life.

She'd said that. Opened her chest for the second time that day to release something just as dangerous, if not as monstrous, as the first.

She wanted to ask Dr. Laghari and her father if Zack and Audrey had come, if she could see them. She wanted to know if it had all been real. She looked at Basil Osgood. She should ask him, too. Had she spoken to him in the waiting room or had that all been a dream? Had she been home? Had she seen the shimmery azure bars?

Shit, thought Osgood. Those shimmers. The triangle around Chicago. She didn't know what they meant. Hadn't even a guess. Just knew that they posed a problem and were connected to her. "The crossroads, the cemetery, and..." she said under her breath, trailing off because she had no idea what was to the north, besides Goddard's home base.

Osgood wondered if he was heading home. Why send up these flares if he was just going to go—

"Prudence?"

"Osgood," said Osgood, without a thought.

"Right, yes," said Dr. Laghari. "Sorry."

This snapped Osgood's attention to them. They both stood at the end of the bed, looking expectantly at her. Waiting, maybe? Waiting for— "What?"

Dr. Laghari laughed a bit. "Do you have any questions for me?"

Osgood only had one. "When can I leave?"

"We want to watch you tonight," said Dr. Laghari. "And probably tomorrow, but if you remain stable—"

She snorted a laugh at that. Surely they were only speaking of physically stable, not mental.

"Funny?"

"Just thinking of something else," said Osgood, waving them away from that line of inquiry.

Dr. Laghari stared at her, uncertain for a moment. "Well. Yes. If you remain stable, then tomorrow or the next day, we should be able to release you. You won't be able to drive or do anything strenuous—"

"Like hunting monsters?" Osgood thought, then widened her eyes when she realized she'd said it aloud.

But the doctor laughed. "Well, no, let's leave monster hunting to the monster hunters and instead focus on brain surgery recovery."

"The teratoma," said Osgood.

Dr. Laghari paused before nodding, clearly uncomfortable.

"Did it have eyes."

"You shouldn't worry—"

"Am I tumor-free?" Osgood could hear her natural tone of defiance returning to her voice.

Dr. Laghari looked from her father back to her. "Well, I cannot definitively state that you are—"

"How about this one?" Osgood asked, pointing to her head.

"We believe," the doctor began, slowly, "yes."

"And when you removed it, was it a teratoma?"

Again, she hesitated. "Yes."

"And did it have eyes?" asked Osgood.

"It had—" She sighed. "Most patients are very uncomfortable with the concept of—"

"I, personally," said Osgood, "am not most patients. And what makes *me* very uncomfortable is my doctor not answering my questions about the thing they removed from my head."

"Pru," said her father.

"No, this is important!" Osgood pulled her arm across her chest, making sure to go lightly against her other one in its cast. She felt the starchy, over-washed fabric of her hospital gown scratch against her tits and the bruise surrounding them.

"Yes," said Dr. Laghari.

"Yes?" asked Osgood.

"It did."

"Hah!" exclaimed Osgood, immediately wondering why she'd said that. She felt hot in the chest and face, a bit woozy. "It had eyes," she said quietly to herself.

"It had a single *very* underdeveloped ocular—"

"Eyeball," said Osgood.

"Eyeball," repeated Dr. Laghari.

"I assume someone photographed it," said Osgood.

"We don't—"

"Oh, c'mon!" Osgood attempted to lean forward before again feeling the wooziness and falling back against her pillows. "I'm sure it's hospital policy to document any weirdo thing that shows up. When was the last time you removed a teratoma?"

"I— I've never removed a teratoma," admitted Dr. Laghari.

"So, I'm sure someone whipped out their phone and snapped a pic."

"We don't—"

"Maybe a selfie?"

"Osgood, really," said her father. He came around to the side of her bed and took her hand.

"No, Dad!" She yanked it back. "My tumor had a face, and I want to see it."

Dr. Laghari stared at her defiantly and said nothing.

Osgood cocked her head to the side because of what she saw beneath the professionalism, confidence, and double-speak in the doctor's dark brown eyes. Osgood knew what fear looked like and was all out of fucks to give. "I think you should tell me."

The doctor held her stare for a moment longer and then turned her attention to Osgood's father. "If either of you have any other questions, please feel free to have me paged; otherwise Nurse Morgan will be taking care of you for the rest of—"

"Creepy, wasn't it?" asked Osgood.

The doctor hesitated. "For the rest of the evening until—"

"An eye. Teeth. In my brain."

"The night—" She shook her head. "I'm sorry. I have to get to my next patient." With that, Dr. Laghari turned and shuffled out of the room as quickly as she could.

"What the hell is the matter with you?" her father asked, and in his raised voice she heard their endless arguments of yore. Thankfully he stopped short of adding, "Young lady."

"Um!" She pointed at her head. "Brain tumor! Blind in one eye! Apparently able to somehow create duplicates of myself. Pick one."

"You're not blind, Prudence."

She waved her hand in front of her face, watching her

hand disappear into darkness when it crossed her left side. "Sure seems it,"

"Did you miss everything the doctor said?" he asked. "Or were you too busy wanting a photograph of your tumor?"

"You don't want to see a tumor with a face?" demanded Osgood.

"I should say not!" exclaimed her father. "You have a patch over your eye. It was injured by the tumor, yes, but she said your vision should return in a few weeks."

"Well, that's—"

"But you're right," he continued. "Let's talk about your duplicate."

"My Tulpa," said Osgood without further explanation, then changed the subject. "Did you call your sister?"

"I left a message," he said, blowing past the question. "You remember appearing in the waiting room, then?"

"Yes," she said. "And at home."

"How did you—"

"If I knew, Dad," said Osgood, "believe me, I'd tell you."

He slumped into the seat next to her bed and put his face in his hands. "This has been a lot to process in a few days."

"You think *you've* had a lot to process? Try being gone for fifteen months!"

"I want to know what happened then, too," he said.

"So do I!"

He looked at her with tight lips and a tense brow. He smoothed down his mustache with his index finger. "Is there anything that you can tell me?"

"You listened to the podcast, right?"

He nodded. "But that can't be..."

"Real?"

He said nothing.

"Did it say we discovered a portal to another world and killed an interdimensional being?"

He waved the question away, averting his eyes. "That's just nonsense."

"Sure," said Osgood. "Just like your daughter talking to you in the waiting room while she's having brain surgery. Tell me, Dad, are you crazy or am I?"

"Look, no," he insisted. "You're not crazy. It's just..."

"Can you take it on faith?" she asked.

He considered that.

"To help aid in the repair of our relationship."

He nodded slowly.

"It's all true," said Osgood. "Everything that happened last year."

"Okay." He said it but clearly didn't believe it. That was okay. She didn't need him to believe, just needed him to not be actively defiant or shut her down.

"I need to talk to Zack and Audrey and Eliza."

"I left a message for Eliza," he repeated. "Your friends are —" He looked into her eye. His face was pale, paler than the traditional Osgood family skin tone. "I'll get them."

"Dad," she asked as he stood and walked toward the door. "You okay?"

He shook his head.

"We okay?" she asked, a trifle more hesitant.

He looked at her for a long while, then nodded, allowing a small smile to cross his lips.

"Good," said Osgood.

"I'll tell your friends that you're awake." His hand lingered on the door frame for an extra moment, then he left Osgood alone in the room.

She closed her eyes, now able to feel her lashes brush against the inside of the tape and gauze patch. "Dr. Laghari," she said to herself. "And..." she racked her brain. It was a familiar name, one that made her laugh. What had it been? "Doctor," she said, giving herself a head start. "Hawthorn?

Hawkins? Hopper?" No. Close, but none of those. It'd made her laugh and afforded her a warm feeling. One of comfort, one of— "Hayward!" she exclaimed, recalling the other doctor's name.

"Laghari and Hayward," she said to Zack and Audrey as they walked into the room.

"That's," said Audrey. "Great?"

29

"Hey, Os."

Osgood snapped her eyes open, disoriented. When had she fallen asleep? Hadn't her dad just... Audrey was standing right next to her, hand on her shoulder, smiling down. Osgood sighed, contented. "Home," she said.

"Not yet," said Audrey.

With a blink, Osgood realized what she'd said. *Home*, not because that's where she wanted to be, but because home was where Audrey was.

"How're you feeling?" asked Zack, stepping up next to her. He seemed to be bobbing around, and Osgood realized he was standing on his tiptoes.

"I'm..." Osgood began, realizing her head was swimmy. "Did they give me anything?"

"I, uh, don't know." Audrey looked at the IV next to Osgood and the various machines, then looked back with a shrug. "Probably?"

"Brain surgery recovery will make you tire very easily," offered Zack. "Even just emotional excitement can exhaust you."

"Yes!" She poked her finger at Zack, remembering the particular emotional excitement. "Hayward and Laghari."

"I'm going to need more than that," said Zack.

"I need you to hack into their phones."

"Alright." Zack laughed. "But who are they?"

"My doctors."

"Your doctors," said Audrey.

"Why are we hacking into their phones?" asked Zack.

"They took a picture of my tumor and won't show me. It had an eye." Osgood nodded at Audrey's grimace. Then she turned her head back to Zack and waved her hand at him.

"Now?" he asked.

"Yes, please!"

Zack snorted and mumbled something but dropped his messenger bag off his shoulder and flopped into a chair at the foot of the bed. He removed his laptop and set it on the table. Before long, he was typing away.

"How are you feeling?" Audrey asked. "Besides swimmy."

"Migraine," said Osgood.

"Unsurprising," said Audrey.

"So, I—" Osgood began, then looked away. "Tulpa?"

"Yes," said Audrey.

Osgood turned back to her. "I don't know how I did that."

"However you did," said Audrey. "It was something else."

Zack affirmed this with a grunt, not lifting his eyes from the computer.

"What's the plan?" asked Osgood.

"Well, Zack has found some information on the symbols at the crossroads and the cemetery." Audrey turned to Zack to give him the floor. "Zack?"

He looked up from his computer to find them staring at him. "What?"

"The symbols," said Audrey.

"She's got me trying to..." Zack shoved the rolling table

with his laptop away, wearing a petulant sulk. He removed a tablet from his bag and walked to the bedside opposite Audrey. He tapped the screen several times, then lay the tablet on Osgood's lap.

On the screen, she saw a close-up of a chalk symbol on pavement. Osgood tilted her head at it, trying to discern some meaning on her own. She was somehow sure she'd drawn it, but she hadn't been driving her own body at that moment.

"I've found several of the symbols via image searches, many in very old texts." As he spoke, he swiped through an image gallery. The photos shifted between her pavement drawings, the spray paint on snow, and images and sketches from textbooks, some heavily pixelated. "Fifteenth and sixteenth century. Some older. Nothing is identical to those I've found in searches, except for the Tulpa sigil, which is everywhere. Many, though, are close enough that they could indicate either a new stylistic choice or an evolved runic language." Zack pinched the screen and it changed to a grid of images. He pinched again to get folders, then jumped into a new folder with a tap. "These four are the most common, repeated multiple times at each location, and appearing in several books over the years."

"What kind of books?" asked Osgood.

"Witchcraft?" His inflection indicated uncertainty, as though he didn't quite believe what he was telling her. "Also, some texts purporting to be books of the dead. Not the exciting evil-dead-raising kind, but the normal common religious texts."

"Witchcraft," repeated Osgood, hearing her father's words in her head: *Then I guess saying she is some sort of witch...*

"Most books of the type tend to just be omnibuses or collections of those that came before," offered Audrey.

Zack concurred with a nod. "Anyway. The symbols are a combination of fire, water, and blood."

"They're..." Osgood began but shook her head.

"Like, literally, within them are symbols for fire, water, and blood." He pointed out different aspects of the complicated symbols before her.

"Okay," said Osgood.

Audrey put her hand on Zack's shoulder. "They seem to be either meant for summoning or for opening."

"Opening." Osgood's hand went to her chest.

"Yeah," said Audrey.

"The recurring idea I've found is that these symbols are used for rituals designed to open portals to the spirit world."

"The margins," said Osgood. "They're trying to open a door to the margins."

"Or from," said Zack. He pointed at her hand on her chest.

Osgood looked down and saw that her hand was shaking. She pulled it away and reached to Audrey, who took and held it. She'd drawn those symbols and, very shortly after that, something had come out of her chest. Then early this morning, something else had drawn those symbols, most likely Goddard. What would, or had, come out of him? "Um, yeah," she said, shaking the nervous sounds out of her voice. "Have we heard from any...ghostbuster friends up north?"

"No," said Zack with a dismissive tone. "We have not heard from any northern ghostbuster friends."

"Gimme a break, Zack," said Osgood. "I've just had brain surgery."

"Sorry," he said. "There's unfortunately nothing new to report. I mean, except the symbols. Nothing *new* new." He pressed the button on the bottom of the tablet, bringing up the home screen.

Osgood saw the time. "9:55? PM?"

They nodded.

"Feels like I just saw you in the morning, and almost immediately after, I was here with dad."

"You were?" asked Audrey.

She nodded. "I seemed to zip directly from coming down the ladder at home to being in the waiting room. Then they were waking me up from anesthesia."

"Oh, wow," said Audrey. "There was like an eight-hour gap between when you vanished at home to when you were done with surgery."

Osgood thought about that. "I wonder if I went anywhere else."

"Oh," said Zack. "Nothing I read about Tulpas suggested they are a form of astral projection."

"I was physically there," said Osgood.

"Yeah," he said. "That, too, is unique."

"Throughout history, there are countless variations on that," said Audrey. "Maybe doppelgängers, Tulpas, and astral projection are different cultures' ways of describing essentially the same thing that they cannot explain."

Zack frowned at her. "But astral projection is the only conscious one. Doppelgängers are independent and, usually, bad. Tulpas are—"

"I said maybe!" snapped Audrey.

"Calm down, everybody," said Osgood. Both turned to her, clearly surprised to find her the calm and reasonable one. In the quiet, they heard a *plink* from Zack's laptop in the corner.

He went to it, tapped some keys, typed for a while, then looked up. "I have Dr. Hayward's cloud storage password."

"Dr. Hayward?" asked Audrey. "That sounds familiar."

"*Twin Peaks*," said Osgood.

"Oh," said Audrey.

"Password is Donna."

Osgood snorted.

"What?" asked Zack.

"Donna was his daughter on *Twin*...Nevermind." Osgood pointed to the computer, then again more emphatically.

"Okay," Zack said, drawing out both vowels.

"I'm in his cloud photo backup," said Zack. He tapped, then again, then again. "Well, he sure saves a lot of porn gifs to his phone."

Osgood grew impatient. "Anything from—"

"I'm looking! The only photo from today is a thumbs up selfie in what looks like a very sad hospital break room."

Osgood scowled.

"Laghari?"

"Still waiting; her password doesn't seem to be a regular word or name."

"Why does it matter, Os?" asked Audrey.

Osgood looked at her. "If your brain tumor had a face, wouldn't you want to see it?"

"Well," said Audrey. But that was it.

"How about Goddard's SUV?" Osgood asked.

"What about it?" asked Zack.

"Has it been spotted?"

Zack frowned. "Generally, people don't just mention spotting a car until it's been involved in a cri—"

"A cry?"

"Wait," said Zack.

"Wait for what?"

"For me to finish what I'm doing!"

Osgood scrunched her lips at him as he smacked a key on his laptop and then leaned back in the chair.

"Yes?" asked Audrey.

"Running his license plate through the toll camera network."

"Not bad," said Osgood. "See! Sometimes you just need to be shoved toward your good ideas."

"Yeah, yeah," said Zack. His laptop *plinked* again. "Oof, looks like Dr. Laghari utilizes best practices for password selection. I could break it myself, but it'll take longer than..." he looked up at Osgood. "You clearly want. Let me farm it out to a couple friends."

"Do what you need to, Zack," said Audrey.

Osgood turned to her. "The voice I hear..."

"The voice you hear?" Audrey repeated.

"Told me to ask my father about 'Eliza,'" said Osgood.

"Who is that?" asked Audrey.

"Well, apparently she's my aunt."

"I didn't know you had an aunt."

"*I* didn't know I had an aunt!"

"Huh," said Audrey.

"Dad said she's some sort of witch."

"Your father?" Audrey snorted a laugh. "Basil Osgood used the word 'witch?'"

"I, too, was shocked," said Osgood.

"You have an aunt that's a witch?" asked Zack.

"I honestly don't know, Zack! But he also said that I was remarkable..."

"You are," said Audrey.

For a moment, Osgood thought she saw the love in Audrey's eyes that she felt in her own heart. She lost herself in that thought.

"Go on," said Zack.

"Right," Osgood broke the eye contact off but still felt the flutter in her chest. *That was something,* she thought. "He said it about my...super...natural...ity."

"Your supernaturality."

"Are you being skeptical or a dick, Zack?" asked Osgood.

"Both?" he returned.

"He said that the Osgood women are also remarkable."

"Like your great-grandmother?" asked Audrey. "The Psychic Osgoods?"

"I thought you said they were grifters," said Zack.

"I was only repeating what I'd been told."

"Do you think your family..." Audrey looked for the word but seemed not to find it on the ceiling. "Suppressed their true natures?"

"Hopefully I can connect with my aunt and find out," said Osgood.

"I hope so, too," said Audrey.

"Got it!" Zack exclaimed.

"Got..."

"Dr. Laghari's photo account."

"That was *disturbingly* quick for someone with a complex password," said Audrey.

"I know, right?" Zack's face was gleeful as he nodded enthusiastically. He tapped a few keys. "Well, she has no issue whatsoever with taking naked selfies."

"Lemme see!" said Osgood, but then she thought better of it. "No, we shouldn't— Those aren't for us."

"Good, Os," said Audrey. "Though she was cute."

"Yes!" said Osgood. "If annoying."

"Yeah, well," said Zack. "She *did* take several photos of your—" He abruptly stopped and closed his eyes, head swaying slightly.

"Zack?" asked Audrey.

"Yeah," he said, taking some deep breaths. He tapped some more keys, clicked several times, then closed the laptop. He stood, tablet in hand, took some more deep breaths, and seemed to center himself.

"You okay?" asked Osgood.

"It's not...pleasant," said Zack.

"Well, let me see, please!"

Zack nodded and handed over the tablet. He thumbed his password, then opened a folder. The thumbnails were graphic enough themselves. Once the folder was open, he walked away and sat back down, looking at his hands in his lap.

"Jesus." Audrey put her hand to her mouth.

Osgood tapped to open one of the pictures to full screen and lifted the tablet closer to her face. With fascination and repulsion, she regarded the thing on the screen. It sat on a bright blue piece of fabric or paper, atop a shining chrome tray. The blue was tinted a dark purple-crimson in an uneven spatter pattern around the thing. The teratoma itself, the thing that had been in her head, looked enormous. She recognized the lack of scale in the image, but she recalled the MRI photos that had showed the shadow in her brain, and it had been plenty big. She thought at first that it looked a bit like a meatball, but that idea immediately caused her to dry heave. The teratoma, a mass of pinks and purples and browns and reds, did indeed have a tooth, a canine, jutting out of it. And above that, a semi-formed eye stared wildly upward. The iris was a cloudy orange, leading to a jagged and imperfect circle of a pupil. It seemed to have rolled back into the ball of the tumor itself, it but looked like the eye of someone having a seizure, or one of those paintings of martyrs, where their heads were lolling and their eyes rolling wildly in the sockets. That thing had been in her head, a part of her. That thing had—

"It saw me, when I was gone," she said under her breath, feeling tears pour down her cheeks. She dropped the tablet to her lap, seeing herself alone in the darkness. A great eye opening and focusing on her. Its iris brilliant orange, streaked with yellows and reds. The white crisscrossed by throbbing crimson veins. "It saw me and knew what I was." She looked at Zack, who still looked sick to his stomach at the foot of her bed. Audrey had also gone pale, but hadn't flinched, hadn't left her. She grabbed Audrey's hand. "It saw me and knew what I was and how it could use me to get out!"

"What saw you?" asked Zack, cautiously.

"I don't know!" Osgood pointed at the tablet. "But I think it was that!"

30

"Absolutely not," said night nurse Morgan.

"Really," insisted Osgood, standing next to her hanging IV, holding onto the pole for uncertain balance. "I'm feeling *much* better, and I'd just like to go home now."

Morgan, an imposingly tall woman even compared to Osgood, stepped from the doorway into the room and folded her arms over her patterned scrubs. "Well, Miss Osgood..."

"Just Osgood," said Osgood.

"Fine," said Morgan. "Osgood, I need you to climb back into bed, as we don't just let people who had brain surgery walk out the door after their doctors have gone home."

"I have rights!" insisted Osgood as Morgan took her shoulder and good arm and guided her back to the bed. She tried to pull away, but the nurse had a good solid grip on her that tightened to a painful hold until she ceased her struggles. Osgood stopped resisting and climbed back into the bed.

"You do have rights," Morgan agreed. "And we have hospital policy."

"Then can you send in my friends?"

"Visiting hours are very much—"

"So, you just want me in here alone all night?"

Morgan narrowed her eyes at Osgood. "Are you unable to spend an entire night alone, ma'am?"

"Don't call me ma'am," snarled Osgood. "Yes, I *can* spend an entire night—"

"Well, then, you ought to be fine. It's already 2:00."

"2:00?" asked Osgood incredulously. How could it be 2:00? Where were had the hours gone? It'd just been...well, she wasn't sure when Zack and Audrey had left. She remembered talking to them about the

(eye in the sky)

brain tumor and then—

"Yes, 2:00 in the morning and other patients are trying to sleep. If you're not going to be quiet and calm for yourself, maybe you can for them."

"Did *they* have a brain tumor with a face removed this morning?"

Morgan put her hands on her hips and said nothing, fixing Osgood with a stare.

"Fuck it," said Osgood. "Fine. I'd put my hands on *my* hips in defiance if one of my arms wasn't *broken!*"

"Is there anything else, Miss—"

"Osgood."

"Yes."

"Tell Dr. Laghari I'd like to see her as soon as she gets in."

"I'll make sure she rushes to your side," Morgan said, her tone suggesting she wouldn't concern herself with anything of the kind. Without another word, the nurse left, closing the door behind her.

Osgood stared at the light coming from the small rectangle of glass in the door. She shook her head. "Such bullshit." But was it? She was losing time on the regular, wasn't she? She probably *should* stay for observation. But to stay with the people who'd hid that...thing...from her? She reminded herself that they were also the people that had removed that thing from her head, possibly saving her life, certainly saving her eye. That was the right call, wasn't it? Trust them to do their thing, including keeping her here, making sure she was safe, calm? "Making sure I don't die," she said with resignation, lying back on her pillow and turning her face to the window. Outside, snow fell in enormous flakes, the kind she'd always hoped for when she was a child, the kind that stuck and stayed if the night was cool enough. The kind that turned the world white and piled up and canceled everything in the morning. There was something intensely comforting about snow like this, reminding her of those simpler times when she'd watch the snow fall out the bay windows from over the back of the couch at her house, their house. The three of them. Cynthia, Basil, and little Prudence. A trio against the world. Long before the rift had begun, before the move to the suburbs, before Osgood had any aberrational inklings, before the accident.

Had life really been simpler then? Or had it just seemed so since she'd known less? Now she might have more defenses, more coping strategies, more cop-out strategies, but the world had been just as complex then, even if her own small sphere wasn't. After all, that was the era just before the first Gulf War. During the Cold War, Reaganomics, bombs just moments from flying at nuclear midnight. Osgood sighed dramatically, an affected move even with no one to watch. "Who are you if no one is watching?" she asked herself with a weak laugh.

But someone was watching.

She saw him as she followed the snow down to the pavement of the parking lot two floors below, from the dark brick to the orange-lit cars topped with a sparkling, pristine blanket. She saw *it*. It was just a silhouette and stood completely still, out in the snow. For a moment she mistook it for a tree, wondering wildly how on earth a tree had been planted there, of all places. Even when she noted how foolish that idea was, how it couldn't possibly be a tree because there was a car parked behind it, she still didn't quite comprehend what she was looking at.

"What the fuck is that?" she asked under her breath, lifting her head off the pillow. As she sat up and the image of the thing rotated to the correct orientation, she realized why she'd thought it was a tree. The silhouette in the parking lot was enormous, hulking. Its oddly shaped head twitched and tilted, making it so there was no question that even though she couldn't see its eyes, it was looking at her.

Osgood moved toward the window, sliding her butt along the bed until she could boot-scoot her way into one of the chairs next to the glass. She put her good hand up against the window, feeling its exquisite coldness as she looked at the dark form in the snow. As much as she didn't want to, she knew what it was and where she'd last seen it. That was her monster, of course. The thing that had crawled from the gaping hole in her chest, birthed into the world as a yowling orchid-headed monstrosity.

But it also was not.

Because as she looked at it, it was indeed the huge creature that she might as well just go ahead and continue calling a "monster," but it was also a human, changing with just the slightest variation of her head's position, like the old lenticular cards that showed a normal portrait, until you tilted it and it became something horrifying. Her mother had hated those cards and thrown them in the trash, along with her Garbage Pail Kids, while she was at Welles Park day camp, the last summer they'd lived in the city.

The human form's arms and shoulders and chest all moved exaggeratedly as it breathed, seeming to throw its entire body into each breath. She had no doubt, either, that this human form was Sam Goddard, and she felt relief flood in.

Why the relief, Pru? He's also apparently a monster.

Yeah, she had to concede that point. Looking at him now, then tilting her head only slightly until the monstrous form returned, she wondered why he'd come. "Well, duh," she whispered. "He's coming to get me, Barbara."

She felt the tug of an alternate possibility, that Goddard and the monster might not actually pose a threat to her, that the only reason they seemed like they did was... But that was where it fell apart, and she pressed her thumb to the spot just above the bridge of her nose but yanked it away again when she yelped in pain. She watched it for a moment longer, switching it with her head from Goddard to the orchid creature and back, again and again. How long had it been there, she wondered? Was it watching? Why? To make sure she didn't leave?

"An even better question," she suggested louder, but not loud enough for Morgan to hear. "Is how did it know that it could find me here?"

It answered one of her questions by raising its stump of an arm, with those jagged digits, and pointing directly at her. As much as she tried to reason that it might be pointing at another window on her floor, she knew it wanted her. It backed that suggestion up by producing a wailing roar. She could see the falling snow knocked asunder by a shockwave emitting from the horrid sound. Snow fell off cars in the lot, and she heard several alarms go off. The noise-proofing in her room kept the sound to a minimum, but the cacophony was too loud to be ignored. Too loud for others to ignore as well, it seemed, as a blonde in pink scrubs rushed from a dark doorway, pointing her key fob at a car. Osgood looked back, between the blonde and the car, to where the Goddardmonster had been but was no longer. The blonde made more and more elaborate gestures with the key fob, moving closer and closer to her car until it finally stopped. The other alarms still wailed.

Osgood wanted to shout at her, to bang on the window and tell her to run from the Goddardmonster! But she knew that any attempt to alert the nurse downstairs wouldn't be loud enough and would only draw the ire of the grumpy night shift at her nurses' station. She looked back to the doorway just in time to see the silhouette of the Goddardmonster disappear from a yellow fluorescent beam of light into the cavernous dark.

It was in the hospital.

She nodded. She knew it, could feel it. It was coming for her.

And visiting hours were over.

𝕩 31 𝕩

Chased by a monster through a hospital, thought Osgood. *Really not where I expected to be at 40.* She had to concede, though, that being chased by something all the time did feel on-brand.

The back staircase was lit only intermittently by harsh blue-white fluorescent bulbs and the red glow of EXIT signs. Before her were two flights of stairs, one going back down to three and one going up to four. She crouched in the corner to catch her breath. She'd only traveled down one hall and up one flight of stairs and was already out of breath.

"You had surgery today, Pru. No, yesterday," she told herself, then regretted speaking, as she heard it echo back to her. She really ought to cut herself some fucking slack, though. After all, here she was crouched on bare feet, her ass in the breeze under her hospital gown. Her hand ached from the IV she'd yanked out before recognizing that she could've just disconnected the tube. But now was not the time for regrets. Not when Goddardmonster was somewhere inside the hospital walls.

Surely Nurse Morgan Ratched would be searching for her

soon as well, if she wasn't already. Then hospital security, perhaps?

She took deep breaths, trying to stabilize her breathing, and held up her phone. The screen only showed one signal bar, but that should be enough for texting. Of the three apps on the home screen of Zack's makeshift burner, she recognized the private texting app and opened it. Her contacts were sparse, but there were more than she'd ever had in this app on her own phone. Here was Audrey and Zack and a group text message thread labeled SI. She opened that one and typed out, **need an extraction,** but then thought it too glib and deleted the letters one at a time. Her revised message was, **need a hospital pickup, goddardmonster is here.** Before sending, she backtracked and added a slash between Goddard and monster. She hoped that slash was accurate as she watched the phone, waiting for the ellipses to indicate typing. Waiting for confirmation.

She heard a *slam* several floors above her and froze. That couldn't be the Goddardmonster, but it really wouldn't be great to see anybody at this moment besides Zack and Audrey. She did her best to quiet her panting breaths and waited. After a while, she allowed the tension out of her shoulders and looked back at her phone. Still nothing.

She knew that if she left the stairwell, she'd probably be able to find signs directing her to an exit. Any exit. But she'd also certainly come up against other people and staff who would wonder what on earth she was doing wandering around out of bed. Then it'd be restraints, wouldn't it? Three working limbs, three restraints. She'd been there before, hadn't she? In the darkest times. In dimly lit dorm-style cinderblock hospital rooms, restrained with leg and wrist cuffs and an additional Velcro strap across her abdomen, digging into her underboobs, restricting her breathing to whatever extent the staff thought a good idea that night. Osgood felt her breath catch at the thought and closed her eyes to shake it out. She needed to focus, be here, be present, as difficult as that might be. Her institutional time was hardly relevant to the current—

A loud *pling!* rang out, echoing through the stairwell.

"Fuck," she said and slammed her thumb onto the phone's volume-down button. Then she heard her word echo back and said it again, but much quieter.

On our way, from Audrey. Then, **just give us your location.**

Stairwell now, Osgood thumbed back, **going to find exit.**

Be careful!

Osgood felt her usual gut reaction to platitudes like that. Of *course,* she would be careful! Didn't that go without saying? She knew what it really was, though. One of those things that people say when they know they can't offer anything helpful. *My condolences. Get well soon. Feel better.* Meaningless, ultimately, but showing care.

Love u booth, thumbed Osgood. She tucked the phone into her sling and pulled herself back to a standing position.

Below, a door banged open. This was followed by unusual footsteps, uneven and wet. That was her cue to move. She climbed the stairs on shaky legs, making it to the fourth-floor landing far slower than she wanted. Behind her came slow and deliberate footsteps, along with a scraping sound. Why wasn't it coming up faster, she wondered? Why was it—

"I know you're here, Osgood." The voice was Goddard's but not. It was guttural, broken, almost as though being piped through a voice modulator. It seemed so unbelievably calm in this heightened moment.

Osgood pressed herself against the wall.

"You can't hide from me."

"Really?" Osgood asked with a strained laugh, then immediately regretted it. The steps stopped and the stairwell fell silent. As the silence drew out, longer and longer, Osgood couldn't hold it back. "'Cuz it seems like it took a long fucking time for you to find me."

The Goddardmonster choked out a juicy chortle, emphasizing that the thing down there was *not* Goddard. "The other beacons needed to be lit, and it became clear you weren't going to do it, Spooky!" This time the nickname felt as though it slapped her in the face. The tone was the one Goddard had used when they were fighting, not when they were loving.

"Fuck you," she said and moved again, climbing two more flights of stairs as quickly as she could. She stopped and listened over the oblong shaft that wound to the bottom between the railings. Nothing. Or at least... As she slowed her breathing, stopping momentarily to help create real silence, she could hear it down there, breathing, waiting.

The vibration almost caused her to scream, but she stifled it by shoving her hand in front of her mouth. Pulling out the phone, she saw the notification, **Ten minutes, tell us where asap!** She nodded at the message from Audrey. She needed to do this part, find her way to an extraction point. Any exit would do. But to find one, she needed to get back to the first floor.

"Well," she called down to the Goddardmonster. "Are you coming?"

It laughed, first low, then louder and louder, edging more and more into performative. It wanted her scared, didn't it? It wanted her to panic, to lose hope.

"I helped destroy the Lord of the Hinterlands, motherfucker!" Osgood screamed down to it. "You. Don't. Scare. Me," she lied, then tucked her phone away and climbed another flight.

Below her, the Goddardmonster began to advance, first in

slow plodding steps, then gaining speed. She heard it round one landing, then another. She'd need to make her move soon, she knew, and she wouldn't be given much leeway to do it. She leaned against the bar and opened the door to the fifth floor, just a smidge. The hall lights were dimmed and about thirty feet from her was a nurses' station. A man in dark blue scrubs, with a day's growth of beard and a douchey smile, leaned over, flirting with a blonde nurse who needed to purchase her scrubs top in the next size up.

Osgood looked back into the stairwell. She couldn't see the Goddardmonster yet, but she knew it had reached the floor beneath her. She peeked back out, toward the elevator bank across the hall. Above each elevator were displays showing floor numbers and all were settled on 1. She took several breaths, preparing, asking something, the heavens, the occult, Lil, she didn't know what, "Just give me this." She ducked out of the door.

As she moved across the hall, she didn't take her eyes off the man in blue. He laughed and then laughed again, louder. She pressed the down button on the elevator panel and watched the numbers above. It felt like an eternity before 1 changed, first to 2, then 3. On the other side of the hall, the door rattled. The Goddardmonster had arrived.

The elevator stopped at 3 and held. "Fuck." Osgood threw another look at the man in blue, then back to the stairway door.

When the door opened and the Goddardmonster emerged, Osgood had tucked herself into a small alcove behind a plant. She felt a tingling in the flesh between her tits, like static electricity, as it drew near. It flickered between Goddard and the creature with the orchid head. She saw it look in her direction but not see her. She looked away, feeling a new migraine beginning from trying to coalesce the Goddardmonster into one or the other.

"Excuse me?" The voice was firm yet friendly, and Osgood looked back in time to see the Goddardmonster turn toward the man in blue, who strode up to it as the blonde nurse watched.

The flickering lessened, and Osgood thought that the thing inside Goddard might be focusing on presenting the human face. Sure enough, when it spoke, it was almost entirely Goddard's voice. "I'm so sorry, but I've lost my fiancée."

Osgood rolled her eye, then flicked it over to the elevator bank, seeing the 3 become a 4.

"Visiting hours ended long—"

"No," laughed Goddard. "I know, I came in with her just a bit ago, and I can't—"

"Can I ask what you're here for?" asked the man in blue.

"Yes," Goddard leaned forward and then back. "Nurse Pollack."

"So?" Nurse Pollack said, crossing his arms over his chest, his biceps squeezed by the short sleeves of his scrubs.

"Who bought tickets to the gun show?" Osgood asked herself, then blinked back the haze that had descended. Wouldn't do to drift off again. "Jesus."

The elevator chimed and the door slid open. Goddard whipped his head toward the door, and flickering became a jitter, back and forth, both the creature and Goddard replacing each other in flashes.

"Sir," said Pollack.

"Yes!" exclaimed Goddard, turning his attention back to the nurse in blue.

Osgood knew that her window, like the elevator doors, was closing. She moved around the plant and wondered if she could make it. *Ten feet, maybe fifteen?* she thought. She looked back at the small confrontation between the nurse and the *thing* that he didn't see.

"She broke her arm," said Goddard. "And got some frost-bite. They took her for an X-ray and never returned."

"Well," said Pollack, walking toward the nurses' station. "Why don't you come to the desk, and we can—"

"Certainly!" Goddard looked over his shoulder and scanned the area, just missing Osgood in the alcove. Then he turned and followed the nurse.

Now or never, Pru, she thought and, in her crouch, moved to the now-closed elevator, whose number above said 5. She pressed the down button, not taking her eyes off Goddard-monster, Pollack, and the blonde.

"What is her name?" asked the blonde.

The elevator chimed, and Osgood felt the world shift into slow motion. She stood and at the same time saw all three at the desk look in her direction.

"Miss, are you alright?" Pollack asked.

"I see you!" roared Goddardmonster in a horrible deep, guttural voice.

Osgood leaped into the elevator, hitting the first-floor button, then pounding "Door Close" over and over as she watched in horror. The Goddardmonster reached up and grabbed Pollack's right hand, then twisted it around, snapping his wrist with a horrible crunch.

The blonde at the desk gasped. "Security!" she screamed.

Scuffling footsteps approached.

As the door closed, the Goddardmonster looked into Osgood's eyes. He reached around and, without looking back, twisted Pollack's neck until it too made a horrendous crunching snap.

The doors closed and the elevator descended.

With a shaking hand, Osgood retrieved her phone and tried, desperately, to type to the group chat. **In lvator. Gddm,onstar killed nurse. B reddy.** Hitting send far too hard caused her to drop the phone, and she slumped against the corner of the descending elevator.

She heard the snaps, two in quick succession, again and again in her head. She'd gotten that man killed. Because of her. Because she'd chosen to go up instead of down. Because she'd led that thing there. The throbbing migraine in her head grew exponentially, each throb louder than the last, shooting through her. She closed her eye and put her head against the elevator wall. Breathing through the pain, she waited as the elevator descended, almost certain that Goddardmonster was on his way down as well, likely after killing that pretty blonde nurse.

She'd have to beat him out. Out of the elevator. Out of the hospital.

Out into the night.

32

When Osgood stepped off the elevator, she saw the one next to hers had begun its own descent, and she knew without question that what would emerge from those doors would be the flickering fury of the Goddardmonster. Even thinking about it, and how it shuffled between forms, caused her headache's throbbing to grow more insistent. To her left, as had been four floors above, was a nurses' station, and beyond that, the double doors leading to a waiting room. Above those doors was also the word EXIT. To her right, the hallway turned right again almost immediately. She asked herself if she could manage to stand and run through anyone who tried to stop her as she barreled past the nurses' station and through those exit doors. And how much further would the actual exit would be, beyond those doors? When she saw the elevator next to her hit 2, she took off to the right.

Her hands trembled as the headache pulsed, joined by a chorus of others aches and throbs, until her entire body hurt in that way it had before, in that way that had called her, siren-like, to the tincture of oxycodone. In that way that could nearly make her pass out.

Nearly, nothing, thought Osgood, throwing a look over her shoulder before shoving herself through an emergency exit door. Lights began to flash, and an alarm blared. The gust of wind that whipped through the opening blew right through her hospital gown and into her soul. She shuddered from head to toe, and it *hurt*. The door hit its fully opened point and then slowly began to shut. She felt woozy enough now that she wasn't sure if she had minutes or seconds until she did pass out.

Her feet hit the snow and pavement beneath. She felt something sharp rip into the sole of her foot and went down to her knees, which screamed from the cold. She reached into her sling and grabbed the phone, dropping it from her shaking hand into the snow. She wailed "No!" as she dug around in the inches of powder before her, her hand growing numb.

Wasn't it just yesterday you tried to die in the snow, Pru? Had it been yesterday, she wondered. It felt like so much longer. But here she again found herself nearly naked in the snow.

Her hand got purchase on the phone, and she lifted it, the screen seeming way too bright. **Pulling up**, read the notification. It had arrived 30 seconds ago.

Osgood thumbed gibberish into the shaking white box, then tapped the microphone. "I don't know where I am, but I'm outside. Come quick." She hit send and tried to stand. Her shaky legs didn't support her the first or the second time. Trying once more, pressing her palm into the painfully cold snow, she managed to bring herself to a crouch.

Got you on GPS, trying to find an inlet.

She squinted into the snow, growing into a blizzard before her eye. She was in a corridor around a single lane street. She assumed it led back to the staff parking lot. She looked toward the sounds of cars passing and suddenly saw two rows of brilliant halogen lamps. She held her hand before her face to hide from the light.

Something banged against the closed door behind her, and she knew that this would be close.

Zack's Jeep Cherokee skidded to a stop in front of her, and both the front and back doors opened. In a flash, Zack and Audrey had lifted her to the open back seat, shoved her up and in, and slammed the door behind her.

Osgood lay with her face against the heated leather of the back seat. She heard two more doors slam, and the lights in the Jeep went off.

Almost immediately, Osgood was thrown forward into the well between the back seat and the front, as Zack skidded backward away from the hospital.

"Jesus Christ, Zack!"

She wanted to concur with Audrey's assessment but shoved herself back up onto the seat. She took a deep breath.

"Zack!" Audrey exclaimed.

"I'm doing it!"

"No, look!"

He hit the brakes.

After two tries, Osgood was able to lift her head enough to see the Goddardmonster, illuminated by headlamps, standing, staring, breathing heavily.

"It *is* Goddard," said Zack.

"You didn't believe me?" asked Osgood, weakly.

"Well, you said it's a monst—"

"I see the monster."

"Okay," said Zack.

"So let's go!" Audrey turned in her seat, putting her hand on Osgood's shoulder.

Zack resumed their speedy exit, reversing down the length of the corridor until he reached a cross street. As he left the hospital complex on Foster Avenue, he pulled into traffic and slowed to a more reasonable speed. "Home?"

"No," said Osgood. "Goddard knows where home is."

"Right."

Audrey climbed over the center console to reach behind Osgood and pull a blanket over her. After laying the blanket atop her, Audrey leaned down and kissed the back of Osgood's neck.

"I realize that this is an inappropriate time," mumbled Osgood, her face still pressed against the leather. "But I love it when you do that. All tingly."

Audrey gave her a surprised laugh and nodded. "I'm glad." She sat back in her seat and suggested, "How about Albrecht's? Does he know Albrecht?"

"I think they may have met," said Osgood. "But not enough for him to know— Also," she said, interrupting herself. "It occurs to me that he may not need to *know* where anyone lives, if the thing inside him can home in on me."

"You think it can do that?" asked Audrey.

"How the fuck do I know what it can do?" asked Osgood. "It did find me at the hospital. My chest-baby monster."

Neither Zack nor Audrey seemed to know what to say to that, and, for a long while, the car went silent.

Osgood felt herself drifting in and out. For moments, she'd see the orangey-pink fluorescent glow of streetlamps passing overhead, then darkness. More than once, she caught the middle of some sentence or question and was unsure if they were talking to her or each other. Their silences didn't clarify. She thought about the nurses on the fifth floor. She'd seen Goddardmonster kill someone, hadn't she? If it hadn't killed him, it'd certainly broken his neck. What had it done to the blonde nurse afterward? What had it done to the people who surely rushed toward the emergency exit, once the alarm began to sound? That bang against the closed door, it hadn't been someone trying to get out, had it? Because it was easy to get out through that door, all you had to do was hit the large red metal panel that said Emergency Exit. Couldn't miss it. The only reason for the bang was if, before opening the door, maybe you hurled someone into it.

"People died tonight," she whispered.

"A nurse?" asked Audrey.

Osgood nodded, her cheek rubbing against the leather. "My fault."

"Not your fault," assured Audrey.

"If I hadn't—"

"If *we* hadn't gone into the Hinterlands," said Zack as a counter.

Osgood considered that. "Well, yeah, if we hadn't done that, things would be different."

"We do what we can, Os," he said. "We can only ever do that much. And we help people if we're able."

"But I killed people!" said Osgood with a sob. She felt the tears pooling on the seat beneath her cheek.

"*You* didn't kill anybody," said Audrey. "Something beyond all of our control is happening here, and we're all doing our best to deal with it.

"I know," she replied.

"If Goddard killed—"

"The monster," countered Osgood. "The monster killed the nurse."

"Then it's not his fault, either," said Audrey.

"It's somebody's." Osgood struggled to shove herself into a half-sitting position.

"Let me help you," said Audrey, helping Osgood reposition until she sat in the center seat in the back of the Jeep.

"Thank you."

"Let's also get the seatbelt on," she added, assisting with that as well. "Because this one's driving is a nightmare."

Zack snorted. "I am compelled to remind you that I'm driving the getaway car from a hospital escape from a *monster*."

"Noted," said Audrey.

Osgood's phone buzzed, but she couldn't find it in her sling. She looked around. "Have you seen my—"

"You're sitting on it," said Audrey.

Osgood tried to grab at the phone but couldn't get a good purchase on it, reaching across her chest. She finally sighed.

"I've got it," said Audrey. She reached over and slid the phone out from under Osgood, then handed it to her.

The notification announcement was an email from **etbosgood@cyberlnk.org**. Osgood tapped it.

I've tried to reach you multiple times at the number your father gave me to no avail.

"Does this phone have a different number on it than my usual?" asked Osgood.

"Yeah," said Zack. "It's just a burner, until I can find where I put your regular phone and yank the SIM card. Sorry." His apologetic eyes met her good eye in the rearview mirror.

"No, uh, worries," said Osgood.

At the bottom of the email was a phone number and a signature, **Eliza Osgood**.

Osgood selected the phone number in the email and pressed on the small phone icon when it popped up. She tapped the speaker icon and then set the phone on her lap. Not a moment too soon, either, as she was certain her shaking would have made her drop it if she'd tried to hold on any longer.

"Hello?"

The voice was rich in timbre, and Osgood felt an immediate attachment to the woman who spoke the word. She wasn't sure she could explain what it was or how it felt, so she instead returned the greeting. "This is Osgood."

"Hello, Osgood; you've reached Osgood."

Osgood laughed. "You're my aunt?"

"It would appear that I am."

"Did you know?"

"Did I know about you?" asked Eliza. "I did. But not a lot. I knew that your mother didn't want us to have contact."

"One more reason to be pissed at Cynthia," said Osgood.

"I wouldn't be terribly angry," said Eliza. "She's right, I am a bad influence. I've also lived in Prague for most of your life. Returned to the States just over a year ago. Compelled to return to the homeland."

Osgood cocked her head at this timeline.

"Your father said you've mastered the doppelgänger."

"Mastered?" laughed Osgood. "I wouldn't say that."

"But you can create the thought-form?"

"I," Osgood looked at Audrey, then back at the phone. "I guess I'd have to say yes."

"One more in the line!" Eliza clapped.

"What do you mean?" asked Osgood.

"Oh, darling," said Eliza. "I assume your parents didn't want us to connect because I was interested in your abilities."

"My abilities," repeated Osgood.

"Well, yes," said Eliza. "My aunt had them, my grandmother had them. Surely you've been told of The Psychic Osgoods."

"Grifters," said Osgood, nearly by default.

"Not even close, darling," said Eliza. "In the Osgood family, the men may have carried the name, but it was the women who were exceptional."

33

"D o you think she'll come?" asked Zack, slinging his messenger bag over his shoulder and reach out his arms to her.

Osgood shrugged as best she could. "Why else would she want the addresses?"

Audrey took Osgood's left arm and helped her to the edge of the seat. "Hold on," said Audrey. She bent and pulled off her own shoes, then slid them onto Osgood's feet, first one, then the other.

"What about you?" asked Osgood.

"I can walk to the house in socks," said Audrey.

Osgood smiled at her and looked down at the blue and white gym shoes. "Lucky I have small feet."

"Maybe I have big feet," said Audrey.

"Why don't we get her inside," said Zack, with little remaining patience.

"I have *another* pair of sweats and sweatshirt for her," Albrecht called. He stood silhouetted in the front doorway, with his hands in his pockets.

"Did he throw me shade?" asked Osgood. "Did you just sass me, Albrecht?"

"Absolutely not, my dear," said Albrecht.

"We ready?" asked Zack. He waved his outstretched hands at her.

"Yeah," said Osgood. She flexed the muscles of her left arm enough to be lifted from the car.

Zack put a hand on her back, accidentally sliding it into her gown. "Sorry," he said, pulling back his hand as though he'd touched a stove burner.

"For fuck's sake, Zack," said Osgood.

Hesitantly, he returned his hand to her back and helped guide Osgood up the short walk from the driveway to the front door.

"Welcome back," said Albrecht. He held up sweats, folded and warm from the dryer.

"Bathroom?" asked Audrey.

"Fuck it," said Osgood. She shakily stood on her own and reached behind herself, trying to grab at the knot in the gown's tie.

"Well, let's close the front door first, at the very least," said Albrecht, sliding between Osgood and the door, shutting and locking it. At last, he slid in the chain. "How about tea?"

"How about a hot toddy?" countered Osgood.

Albrecht smiled. "As you wish."

"Have you filled him in?" asked Osgood.

"Not totally," said Audrey.

"I'll do it," offered Zack. He set his bag down and shuffled out of his shoes and coat, then vanished down the hall toward Albrecht in the kitchen.

"We doing this?" Audrey asked Osgood.

Osgood nodded.

Audrey tugged on the knot a few times before finally

undoing it. She pulled the snaps on Osgood's right shoulder over the cast, then slid the entire gown off.

Osgood couldn't miss the change in Audrey's face, nor her attempt to stifle a gasp when the gown came off. "Am I that bad?"

Audrey put her hand to her mouth. "Os...it..." She forced a smile behind the fingers and then put her hand on Osgood's cheek. "You're going to be fine."

Osgood looked down her body, seeing cuts and bruises, road rash, other dark areas, and of course, the crowning chest bruise. One bruise to rule them all. "Well, at the moment I'm naked in Albrecht's hallway, so I'd like to take care of that problem, if we could."

"Yes, right," said Audrey. She knelt and held out the sweatpants for Osgood to step into.

"Been quite a while since these positions, 'eh?" Osgood smirked.

"Does *anything* dampen your sexual urges, Os?" Audrey shook the pants at her, and Osgood stepped into them.

"Would you prefer that?" asked Osgood.

"Well," began Audrey. "No, not really."

"Just another in a long line of inappropriate emotional defense responses from Prudence Osgood," said Osgood.

Audrey said nothing and held up the sweatshirt. After some maneuvering, they decided that Osgood would keep her arm and sling inside.

"Looks like an amputation, then," said Osgood, snickering again.

"Really?"

"Yunno, I just pulled off, 'Exit, pursued by a monster.'"

"I can't argue with that," said Audrey.

"What do we do when he finds us?" Osgood asked, startling herself with the seriousness of the question.

Audrey opened her mouth a few times, perhaps to offer a

solution, perhaps to reassure her. She was waylaid by Albrecht's return with a steaming mug, wafting cinnamon and lemon into the air.

They moved to the sunken living room.

"What is your plan?" asked Albrecht. "To be clear, I don't object to you being here without one, I'm just hoping we have something."

"It is more than likely that in the next few hours a monster will arrive," said Osgood. She looked at all of them as the room went silent. "I don't *know* this," she clarified. "But I know it. When it happens, we will need to have some idea of what to do with him. With it." For the first time since her escape from the SUV, Osgood considered the fact that the thing that had come from her chest had taken Goddard, but she didn't know more than that. Was Goddard still present within? Was it just using him as a vessel, a vehicle? That brief interaction, their sexual hunger, had that been the catalyst? "It's possible that only I can see the monster, and you will only see Goddard." she continued. She felt that hang in the air, yet another thing that would need to be taken on faith. "I want to assure you that something else is driving him. I don't know if they've combined or if it has just taken up residence. If we *can* separate them..." She trailed off, putting her hand to her cheek and feeling the wetness of tears.

"We will, absolutely..." Audrey looked between Zack and Albrecht, who both nodded. "Try?"

"I don't expect miracles. And I wish I had more answers."

"Osgood." Albrecht leaned forward from his chair. "You ask too much of yourself."

"Yeah," said Osgood with a choked laugh. "Yeah."

"In proposal of a solution," said Albrecht. "I have some literature about exorcism and possession expulsion, both liturgical and layman."

"It's a start," she said.

"In the meantime," he offered. "I'd suggest you get some rest. You are welcome to my bed." Albrecht gestured toward the staircase. "It's memory foam, surely better than the hospital bed you've been in."

Osgood prepared to insist that she was fine, that she wasn't tired, that she needed to work, but she yawned immediately after opening her mouth. Hard to argue with that. "Thank you, Albrecht," she said instead.

"Always, my dear."

Osgood turned to Audrey. "Would you—"

"Of course." Audrey helped her stand.

"I will look for..." Zack trailed off. "Exorcisms, I guess. Didn't honestly think I'd ever be doing that."

After Osgood limped up the stairs, and Audrey insisted on checking out and cleaning the small gash in her foot, the two sat on Albrecht's bed, a king-sized island in a sea of a room that took up nearly the entire third floor.

"Waiting, now, I guess?" said Osgood.

"Well, resting, really," said Audrey. "For you, rest."

"What about you?"

"I didn't just have surgery."

"I also ran from a monster."

"I didn't do that, either." Audrey reached out and cupped Osgood's cheek in her hand. The gesture felt so warm, so loving, that Osgood closed her eye and snuggled in. "So," Audrey asked. "After we stop this monster and whatever else is happening, what're you going to do?"

"Optimistic," said Osgood.

"Trying."

"Well, I suppose," Osgood began, but then thought more about it. "It certainly wouldn't suck to be a part of a *successful* Spectral Inspector team."

"You *are* a part—"

"Please." Osgood held up her good hand and shook her head. "First I was absent, then I became the problem."

"Not the problem, the..."

"Yeah," said Osgood, when Audrey trailed off. "Not *intentionally* the problem, but you weren't running and hiding before I returned. And you weren't spending hours in hospitals before—"

"We didn't have you," said Audrey, who turned toward the enormous picture window wall of the upper floor. "It's not worth it without—"

"You did fine without me, before," said Osgood.

"No, I didn't!" Audrey's wide, glassy eyes said it all.

Osgood nodded and looked toward the window. She squinted at a reflection and held up her hand. "Man, that's bright."

"What is?"

"The reflection of the light," said Osgood. "Must be where I'm sitting."

"Let me..." Audrey didn't finish but jumped up and turned the dimmer by the door, and the lights of the room dropped to a fraction of their brightness.

"That didn't do it." Osgood covered her eye and looked to Audrey from behind her hand. "You don't see it?"

Audrey shook her head. Now her eyes said plenty about something else – the old chestnut, the "what if there's something wrong with Osgood?" look.

Osgood stood and limped over to the window. When she got close enough, she saw that it wasn't a reflection at all, but a brilliant blue beam of light shooting into the sky. She sighed. "The other beacons needed to be lit."

"What do you mean?"

"The shimmers I...Tulpa me, I guess...saw at the apartment. I think that's one of them."

Audrey squinted into the darkness, over the trees that

surround Albrecht's house. "I still don't—"

"I know. I think they're for me." Osgood pressed her fingertip to the window. "What direction is that?"

Audrey opened a compass app on her phone. "North...ish?"

Osgood nodded and moved to the west-facing wall. On that wall were two smaller windows shaped like pie quarters, something that had always tickled Osgood because of their resemblance to the two scariest windows of all time.

"You don't see those when pulling up," said Audrey with a laugh.

"Nope."

"They're like—"

"Yep." Osgood leaned into one and looked around, finding a tree selfishly blocking her view. She grumbled and walked to the second. "You know the real Amityville house."

"I know *of* it."

"Well, they swapped out their eye windows for squares. Too many people pulling up and taking pictures."

"Must suck to live in that house," said Audrey. "Even if none of it was true."

"Well, a family *was* murdered," said Osgood "It's the ghost story that was just a demented lie, cooked up by the Lutzes with Jay Anson over a bottle of wine." She turned back to the right eye of the wall and peeked out. Another tree blocked most of her view, but as she moved around, she could see eerie shafts of azure light poking through the trees. "It's there," she said, poking her finger against the window. She drew a sad face in the fog of her breath.

"The...shimmer?"

"Yeah. The crossroads beacon," she laughed. "Not to be confused with the blinking light above the

(it saw me and knew what I was and how it could use me to get out) "road." Osgood turned back to Audrey. "And if there were windows on that wall," she pointed south, "We...well, *I* would see the Bachelor's Grove beacon."

"Do you think they're landmarks?" suggested Audrey. "For navigation maybe?"

"I think they're ceremonial, like fires at a seance or whatever. Conjuring."

"A conjuring," repeated Audrey. "And you might be the harbinger?"

Osgood whipped her head back to Audrey as the memory of the eye downstairs returned, the horrid eye that had called her... "Harbinger," she said. "I thought the thing that took Goddard might be it. But maybe I am the harbinger."

Audrey waved her hands. "Why don't we sit back down."

Osgood nodded.

"We really don't know much of anything, yet. So, let's not worry about you being the harbinger, whatever that might mean."

Osgood felt her head grow swimmy as she nodded again. "I think... Whew, I'm tired."

"Yeah," said Audrey. "You've had a really rough—"

"Life?"

"Well, and day. And week."

"I have," said Osgood.

"Let's lie you down," Audrey offered, putting her hand low on Osgood's back to guide her toward the bed. "I'm sure the adrenaline of the chase has worn off, and now you're..."

"Just a patient after brain surgery." Osgood lay back on the enormous bed and smiled as Audrey pulled a crocheted afghan over her. "Don't go far," she said.

Audrey sat next to Osgood and held her hand. "I'm not going anywhere."

Osgood's eyes stayed open only a few seconds longer, then she drifted, and darkness fell.

34

"**M**otherfucker," Osgood says, turning in a quick circle. The bubble of artificial night surrounds her, and the roads disappear into the void beyond. Above her, the industrial yellow beacon, with its familiar *cha-click, cha-click, cha-click,* blasts its amber light north-south, then east-west. She puts her hand to her forehead to stifle the awfulness, to put pressure to the growing migraine. Why is she here? "No fucking way!" she screams into the sky—full dark, no stars.

Looking down, she sees that another unpleasant recurring element has reasserted itself. Here stands Prudence Osgood, naked to the world, at least the world in her

(kingdom)

mind. She feels pleased, at least, that her body isn't covered in bruises and cuts, her arm isn't in a sling, and blinking her eyes together, then separately, reveals that she can see from both. She reaches her hands up to her head and sighs with relief to find her hair, glorious and curly and so thick her fingers get tangled within the locks.

"Not so bad," she concedes. "But I'm sure I won't be alone here for long. After all, what would the point of that be?" She takes a deep breath and throws back her head to scream, "What would the point of that be?" again into the dark sky. She pauses when she realizes that the beacon is above her is gone, and the roads are silent. "Alright," she concedes. "What do you have for my...mind? I guess?"

Since they'd killed, well, since *Audrey* had killed The Lord of the Hinterlands, she'd not dreamed of this place, which had been a staple of nearly every night prior, at least, those when she hadn't managed to squelch it with whiskey or oxy. She realizes with the thought that she doesn't have many sober nights to choose from. Most of them were, well...

"Reel missing." Osgood laughs. She listens but can't hear even a returning echo of her voice. True emptiness surrounds her. There's no road or glow in the distance, no highway full of trucks air-braking, no defunct Amoco station with a beat-up Buick Skylark in the lot, just waiting to reenact her near-swansong when she'd met a semi at the crossroads.

"I getcha'," she shouts to the heavens. "Don't think I don't!" What does she want? She asks herself and is uncertain. "Besides waking up?" Yeah, that feels right. "Let me wake up! I've got shit to do! This is terribly inconvenient right now!" She begins to pace the crossroad, from one corner to another. "Fine, if no one is going to talk to me, I'll pace." She hears the soles of her feet slapping down on the pavement as she goes, a satisfying sound that quickly gets swallowed by the void. No resonance at all, here and now.

Has it shrunk? she wonders.

(As I built my kingdom,)

Collapsed into just this single remaining point? Like a video game glitch where she'd somehow wandered off the map and found a vast, barely programmed emptiness, devoid of characters, interactions. Just her and the dark.

(so have you built yours.)

Osgood grimaces and stops, folding her arms. She takes a moment to appreciate the very fact that she has two working arms and two working eyes. "Binocular vision," she tells the crossroads. "Helluva thing." She tucks her chin to her chest and looks down her body. She runs her fingers down her sternum, between her tits, where the horrid black bruise had once been, and stops just before it gets saucy. Curly hairs brush against her fingertips.

"I've decided I'll stand," she tells the darkness, feeling defiant and more than a little bit grumpy that she has only herself to defy. Couldn't this place at least give her that funhouse version of her younger self to go toe to toe with? Give her something to do here? What good is a dream with no plot?

She stomps. She clenches her fists. She screams into the sky. But it's not a sky, is it? Just blackness. No expanse, no distance. May as well be a ceiling, just out of her reach. And perhaps it is.

"If I had garments, I'd rend them in my displeasure!" Osgood smirks. *I'm funny in my dreams.*

Watch.

She whips her head around. Where had the voice come from? It had been low, a whisper, without discernible attributes.

"Watch what?" she asks over her shoulder. When nothing more comes, she asks it again, louder.

She sees something emerge from the darkness at one corner of the crossroads. But it's not moving, simply becoming visible. She feels the hair stand up on the back of her neck. Gooseflesh runs up and down her arms. Before her stands the screaming thing, the monstrous sculpture she'd seen once upon a time in Minnesota. Pitch black, with holes for eyes and a mouth that extends all the way to the ground in a perma-scream.

"I thought you were a representation of the Lord of the Hinterlands," she tells it, steeling herself and approaching.

The screaming thing doesn't move.

"Ahh, just a sculpture again, are we?"

Osgood yelps in pain and goes to a knee. She grabs at her foot and shudders from the pain radiating upward. A look at the bottom of her foot shows a jagged piece of black glass embedded in it. With a shaking hand, she grips and pulls it out, feeling woozy at the size of the hole in her foot. Wait, hadn't she hurt her foot? Where had that been? Outside the hospital, she'd stepped on—

"Did you move?" she asks the screaming thing, which seems closer than before. Now an arm is outstretched, long and thin, and at the end of that arm is a hand with a finger that could be nearly two feet long. The finger, white and bone-like, makes Osgood recall her vision of the teratoma's extension emerging from her head. She follows the point up and up into the darkness. She gasps when she sees it.

The quasar hangs in the void, an enormous disk of rotating gasses, orange and yellow and red, taking up nearly a third of the western sky, almost down to the horizon. The black hole in the center pulses and belches a particle jet toward her. It is larger now than it had been the last time she saw it, here in her dreams. She feels overwhelming dread surround her, crushing her with feelings of hopelessness, of unimportance. How could anyone's lives matter in a universe that could create that? Something that needed to be measured in lightyears not miles. She forgets the pain in her foot and sits bare-assed on the concrete. Chunks of asphalt and rocks dig into her flesh. From her seat, she stares, mesmerized, into the maelstrom. "I thought you were..." she begins, wanting to tell the quasar that she'd thought it also was the Lord of the Hinterlands, as though begging its forgiveness.

Begging? What? she asks herself. Osgood blinks a few times and realizes her eyes have dried out. How long has she been staring into the spiral? She lifts her hand to her chin and feels a blanket of saliva. She closes her eyes, seeing the negative impression of the quasar behind her eyelids. Somehow it still turns. How is that possible? Her breath quickens, and she feels the gooseflesh return. Panic sweat begins to form on her brow. "It's in my head," she says, and the realization sends another shudder through her.

Of course, it is, Lil's voice tells her.

"Lil?" Osgood opens her eyes and twists her head over her shoulder, hoping to catch a glimpse of the kind

(it was the women who were exceptional)

woman in white. Her great-grandmother. The truly Psychic Osgood. She isn't here, though.

It's all in your head, darling. This is a dream, after all, Lil's voice says in her mind. *But that doesn't mean it hasn't value. Watch.*

Again, the "watch" command. Osgood turns to the screaming thing, still screaming endlessly silent into the night. She takes a breath and turns in the direction it is pointing, back toward the quasar. It has solidified, the gaseous disk no longer spinning, the black hole no longer emitting its jet. Why has it stopped, she wonders? What is it doing?

"Watch," Osgood reminds herself. "Right, Lil?" She turns to the darkness. "Sure wish you'd offer a more concrete—"

Watch! Lil shouts in her head.

Like a shade being drawn, the disk begins to eclipse, hiding behind the pitch darkness of the sky. She notices it is happening at the both the top and bottom. Over a few seconds, the black lines creep toward each other, blanketing the sky in darkness. Closer and closer, until just a string of light remains, broken by the black hole in the center. Then that, too, is gone.

"What happened?" she asks the sky. "Lil? Please! What am I supposed to be learning here? Why did it—"

She feels a tug in her chest, as though someone has just blown an airlock and she is being sucked toward it. The tingles of static she'd felt in the presence of the Goddard-monster in the hospital. The smell of fire from the motel room. The aperture in the sky begins to open again, no longer flat lines, now jagged and inconsistent edges. The quasar has changed. The disk of gasses now has texture, form, variances and color changes radiating out from its black center, from deep orange to yellow like a flame. As the aperture opens wider and wider, Osgood's mouth goes dry, and she sees it for what it truly is.

The eye in the sky, an orb half-blind and half-mad, stares at her, its iris burning, its pupil a jagged black hole. She has been naked in almost every dream here at the crossroads, as though her mind wants to strip her of any protection. She's never really minded until now. That glare, that leer, it looks at her nude body and

(it sees me)

she cannot even begin to process the shame she feels. She tries in vain to cover herself, first her tits, then her pussy. Too hard to cover both. She is exposed, on display before the eye in the sky, the eye

(and knows what I am)

that sees and knows and judges her. Unblinking and unrelenting. She crouches, hoping that she can hide by being smaller. It seems to make sense, as she forces her body into a compact position with her arms around her knees, her ass hovering over the pavement. She ducks and drops her eyes after throwing it

(and how it will use me)

one last look. The iris has begun to radiate in streams away from the black hole, an endless flow, braiding and unraveling into eddies and

(to get out)

vortexes. The eye looks within her and pulls everything to the surface. The shame and guilt long she's long since rejected, forgotten, repressed. She sees her parents in the eye, reflected into her mind, the moments where she scrambled to find the right words to describe who she was, what she wanted, *who* she wanted, what she felt. The time she'd told them she was getting into ghost hunting with Audrey and they flipped out, reminding her of the shame brought to the family by grifting Psychic Osgoods.

The eye sees all of it, and reflects it, magnified, back to her.

Osgood.

She waves Lil's voice away, despite it being in her head.

Osgood, we

"No!" she shouts, realizing that the iris, bleeding yellows and oranges, is whirring like a fan. Like a jet engine! How on earth could it be so loud?

Osgood, we need

"I can't!" she screams, pleads with Lil, with the eye. "Just let it stop." She puts her forehead against her knees and sobs into her lap. Tears shower down onto her thighs and stomach, catching and glistening in the curls of her bush like morning dew.

Osgood! He's here!

The voice isn't Lil's, Osgood realizes. It's Audrey. She needs to go back to them, to help them. She slowly stands and turns her head toward where she knows the eye is, with her own eyes still closed. She takes a breath, feeling the wind kicked up by the engine of that iris, the black hole of the pupil. "Kiss—" she yells, getting drowned out by the din. She fills her lungs and compresses her diaphragm, then blasts her command toward the monstrous eye. "Kiss my lily-white ass, Sauron!" Then, for effect, she turns and bends over, giving her ass a slap. "Pucker up!"

35

"**N**ow is not the time, Os," said Audrey, pulling gently on her arm.

Osgood shook her head and allowed Audrey to pull her to a sitting position on the bed in Albrecht's bedroom. "Time for..."

"We survive this, I'll kiss your ass all you'd like."

Osgood snorts a laugh.

"Right now, we need to be in battle positions."

"I'm in no condition to—"

"I don't need you to fight," said Audrey. "I need you to hide."

"Why would I hide?"

"Why would you..." Audrey squinted at her. "I mean, do you not think he's coming for you?"

Osgood shrugged. She looked up from the bed at Audrey. "Here I am with one working eye, a giant stitched head wound, a broken arm, a gashed foot. Bruises and cuts everywhere." She shook her head. "What good am I doing any of you?"

"Os, are you giving up?" Audrey asked, crouching before her. "'Cuz it sounds like you're giving up."

"I..." began Osgood. She looked down at her hand in her lap. She could feel the guilt and shame hangover from the dream. What help could she possibly be? Being here would only hurt her friends. If Goddard got in, wouldn't he (*it*, she reminded herself, Goddardmonster) just start killing to get to her, to do...whatever it was hoping to do with her? "I don't know if I can do this."

"You may be beaten down, and I completely get that," said Audrey. "But there are three other people in this house who aren't. Who love you. And who are ready to beat the shit out of Sampson Goddard."

Osgood sniffed out a laugh. "You never did like him, did you?"

No, mouthed Audrey, shaking her head.

"I do wanna remind you that Goddard isn't at the wheel."

"I know. My comment was for effect."

"And if we're fighting, I'm fighting," said Osgood.

"That's a long way from giving up."

"Yeah, well," Osgood sighed. "I'm fickle."

"Alright," said Audrey, holding out her hand. "Come with me."

"What's the plan?"

Audrey waved her hand at Osgood, who took it and pulled herself to a wobbly stand. Audrey led her to the bedroom door, then to the hall overlooking the staircase that wound down two floors. She pointed at the landing below. "We've barricaded the staircases." A bookshelf and an upended couch blocked access below.

"Poor Albrecht," said Osgood.

"He said he's enjoying the adventure."

Osgood looked at Audrey with hesitation. "Shouldn't he be up here...with—"

"We thought it better to divide our strength."

"Alright," said Osgood.

"Here." Audrey lifted a black plastic and metal gun, which Osgood realized was a TASER, from a table near the stairs. She handed it to Osgood, then slung an aluminum bat over her shoulder. "We aim to debilitate him with electricity."

Osgood nodded.

"Recognizing that he is not, in fact, Goddard at the moment."

"So, if he gets up here, we zap and then clobber?" asked Osgood.

Audrey nodded. "And as a last resort..." she pointed at the table, and Osgood saw the real gun. "You good?" she asked as Osgood stared.

Osgood felt tension in her chest and throat, more than ever. "The gun makes it more real, somehow."

Audrey agreed.

"And safety, er..."

"Safety is off. It should be just a 'pull the trigger' thing."

"Fuck," said Osgood. "Great. Well." She wiped at her tired open eye. "Don't usually have to fight monsters, as a ghosthunter."

"We *did* kill an interdimensional being," said Audrey.

"You did," she told Audrey.

"We did." Audrey fixed her eyes on Osgood's and repeated it.

Osgood nodded, taking a long breath and slowly letting it out.

"We got this," said Audrey.

"Yeah?" asked Osgood with a laugh.

"We've got this," Audrey repeated quietly, seemingly to herself, as she choked up on the bat.

"Approaching!" crackled from somewhere, startling Osgood. Then she heard a hiss of static.

"Shit."

"It's the walkie," said Audrey. She lifted the walkie talkie off her belt to her mouth. "Os is up and has the TASER. We're, well, ready as we're gonna be."

"Us too," said Zack on the other end. "Found the last stun gun, so Albrecht has both distance and short-range..."

In the background, Albrecht chuckled. "Yeah," said the old man, his words dripping with sarcasm. "Albrecht is *all* set."

"I'm sorry," called Osgood.

"They can't hear you unless I press," began Audrey, but then she pressed the button and held it to Osgood's mouth.

"I'm sorry. To both of you. I love you."

"Yeah," Zack returned. "Love you, too."

"He's so awkward about that," said Audrey.

"When he said 'approaching...'"

"Goddard was standing at the end of the driveway for a long while, just staring at the house. That's when I came to get you."

"And now he's..."

"Not, I guess." Audrey shrugged, and for the first time tonight, Osgood saw the fear hiding beneath the combat-weary banality they both pretended.

A *bang*! So loud the entire house seemed to shake.

"Fuck," said Osgood.

Another *bang*! Then another. Then another.

"Aud," Zack crackled over the walkie. "Door's cracking."

"That's metal-lined! What on Earth?" Albrecht asked in dismay in the background.

"We've pushed both couches from the living room against the door, but I don't think it's going to last if he comes through."

The next *bang* came with a crash.

"Door's down!" called Zack.

"Tell them to fall back. We do have a fallback plan, right?" Osgood asked desperately.

Audrey shook her head. "Phase II is electricity," she offered.

More commotion from downstairs echoed up the stairwell. "Goddard stop!" yelled Zack in the distance.

Osgood watched Audrey adjust her grip on the bat, circling her hands. She looked down at the TASER in her own hand and moved her finger from the side of the barrel to the trigger.

"Hah!" exclaimed someone below.

A roar came, of anger or pain Osgood couldn't tell, but it sounded like a great beast was engaged in a brawl.

"Zack?" asked Audrey into the walkie.

Silence for a moment, then two, then three.

"Zack?" she repeated.

"Goddard's down," Zack said, following it with a giddy laugh. "It took both of our TASERS *and* the stun gun." His heavy breathing began to subside. "Man, he just looks like Goddard to me. I mean, more disheveled than he usually is, and he can take a shitload of volts."

"Zack," Albrecht said. "Step back."

"He's—"

"Zack!" This time Albrecht yelled it.

Another roar from below.

In the gap between the staircases, they saw commotion on the ground floor.

"Oh my god," said Audrey.

Osgood looked wildly from the commotion below to the walkie talkie. "Call him."

Audrey nodded. "Zack, are you—"

"Coming," said Goddardmonster over the walkie. His voice had grown deeper, full of gravelly vocal fry. Then all they heard was static.

"Zack," Audrey pleaded into the walkie.

Osgood stepped back from the stairs until her back slammed against the wall. She felt her panic rising. How long had it taken for this plan to go wrong? Three minutes? She thought of what the commotion below might have been, the thuds, the yells. She could see Albrecht, in her mind's eye, lying on his hall floor as she had, just days before. And Zack... Her thoughts were interrupted by the sound of something climbing the stairs. Albrecht's house had been constructed at the dawn of the 20th century, and with every creaky, plodding step the Goddardmonster took, it sounded its age. There was no question that the thing climbing toward them wasn't Zack or Albrecht, as the old house screeched in pain with each step.

"Okay, Os." Audrey shook her by the shoulder. "Os!"

"Do you think they're—"

"We need to focus," Audrey snapped. Her voice sounded desperate. "You need to go into the bedroom and shove—"

"No!" said Osgood. "Fuck no! You're not going to throw your body between it and me."

"Os, really, you're not strong en—"

"Audrey," Osgood said, her voice quiet but firm. "I will be by your side until he kills us." She laughed, strained. "Which may well be soon. But don't you wanna find out?"

"You're crazy," said Audrey.

"Fuck yeah, I am," said Osgood.

Audrey cautiously took a few steps away from Osgood and peeked over the rail. "He's on the landing below." She watched for a moment, then quickly ducked away. "Yeah, he saw me. Fuck! I'm sorry. Fuck!"

"Aud, he knows where I am." Osgood told her. "He followed us fifty miles from the hospital. He would find me up here, even if you hadn't looked down. He's coming directly to me. For me."

Audrey nodded, flicking her eyes between the railing and Osgood. Below them came more crashes, the screech of furniture sliding across hardwood, shelves breaking into kindling.

"Help me up," said Osgood.

The plodding began again, closer. One step, a beat, another, a beat, another. Audrey reached and grabbed Osgood's outstretched hand.

After a shaky deep breath that made Osgood wonder how many of those she might have left, she approached the railing and leaned over. The Goddardmonster stopped. For the moment, though, Osgood only saw Goddard, breathing heavily as he looked down at his feet. But then his head moved, tilting up toward Osgood's face. The flickering between forms began infrequently but grew and grew, strobing at her.

"Osgood, look!" Audrey pointed.

"Yeah, I see him," agreed Osgood.

"No!" said Audrey, with unexpected irritation. "His shadow!"

The shadow cast down the stairway wall indeed seemed to show the beast, unchanged, while the flickering blur of the Goddardmonster ripped Osgood's migraine back to the forefront of her mind. "You see the monster?"

"In the shadow, yes," said Audrey. She quickly reached into her pocket and pulled out her phone, snapping a photo.

The Goddardmonster smirked and resumed its climb, not turning its face from them. The creature itself still didn't have any discernible features, but Goddard's true face, appearing in the flicker, made her sick. His eyes had widened to the point where a full ring of white could be seen around his irises. His smile was so tight on his face, his lower lip had split. There was a splash of dark blood across his cheek and onto his shoulder and chest. Osgood wondered whose it was and if they'd survived the attack. She looked at the TASER in her hand. "Do you know the range?"

"I, uh…" Audrey stammered. "I don't."

"Sam!" Osgood called.

The Goddardmonster responded with a hideous chuckle from between clenched teeth. He climbed closer and closer. Six steps, five. Trying to measure her distance, Osgood waited and waited. Four steps. Three steps. She couldn't wait any longer, aiming the TASER at its orchid face and pulling the trigger. The metal leads shot out on their thin wires, hitting it. When the current blasted through him, his form stopped shifting. Only a man now, with wires on his forehead and upper cheek. A man who faltered, one foot sliding off the step. He fell to his stomach and slid down several steps, bouncing his chin as he went. For a moment, there was silence, but then he looked up. Blood streamed from his mouth, but he still grinned. He rose first to his knees, then his feet.

Osgood dropped the TASER and lunged for the gun on the table. Shaking, she pointed it at Goddard's leg.

"Last resort," said Audrey, her eyes darting to the gun and back, wild with fear. "I'm going."

"Aud, don't—"

But Audrey went, charging down several steps, swinging the aluminum bat from a long wind up. The sound when it hit the side of the Goddardmonster's orchid head was the same sound she'd heard on summer days playing softball. A rich, deep *thunk*. The creature swung around and crashed face-first into the wall, the flickering halting again. Audrey expelled a mighty cry as she swung again.

Osgood winced, seeing the bat near the back of Goddard's human head, and thought for sure that would do it. Two bat hits to the head would put anyone down, wouldn't it? But he caught it so fast Osgood hadn't even seen his hand go up. The flickering resumed, and she could see the monstrous orchid form clutching the bat in one calcified and broken hand. It yanked the bat away from Audrey and, with a single swipe of its other stumpy mitt, sent her tumbling down the stairs to crash into the wall at the turn near the bottom.

"Audrey!" Osgood yelled. She turned the gun toward the thing in Goddard's body, the hitchhiking thing, the parasite. She pulled the trigger, and a gout of blood hit the wall as the bullet passed through his left shoulder. For a moment, she saw Goddard's grinning face, his eye bloody on the side of his head where Audrey had hit him. He lunged for her, moving almost inhumanly fast and showing his slow ascent to have been a ruse. She heard the gun go off again as she squeezed the trigger, but she didn't know if it hit him, then Goddard was on top of her. With a quick slap, he knocked the gun from her hand. He shoved her down against the floor and wrapped his hands, and its stumpy hands, around her neck. It began to squeeze.

She immediately felt the blood flow to her head slow. Her migraine throbbed. The ringing that'd begun with the gunshot grew louder and louder. Tears poured from her eye as she stared into the horrid grinning face of Goddard, once a lover, once a boyfriend, once a partner, once a friend, now this. Then the orchid face usurped Goddard's and cocked its head to the side. She saw features for the first time, including multiple rows of iridescent black eyes.

"Why do you fight?" it asked in a voice garbled, so sticky and wet that she could barely understand it. Slimy brown-green blood splattered across her face and onto her glasses, turning everything before her to a darkened haze. "You will be the mother of legion. Like Mary of Nazareth, you will birth our deliverance."

As its grip tightened, she began to lose feeling in her body and face. Panic rose within her as she tried desperately to squeeze just a single breath through the constriction.

"You are the harbinger of a great arrival, an evolution of this world," said the Goddardmonster, its voice gleeful. "And it will tear you open."

Osgood heard a slam, like someone had played the world's most enormous bass drum, and suddenly she could breathe again. She gasped in breaths that felt like fire down her throat and into her lungs. She saw the Goddardmonster rise off her, a strangely comical look of confusion in those rows of irides-cent eyes. It moved up and backward, over her head, its hands pulled loose and flailing, before it crashed into the wall just behind her on the landing.

She brought her hand to her throat to make sure no tether remained, no rope, no spectral garrote cutting off her air. But nothing was.

"Slowly," said someone far away. "Breathe slowly."

Osgood slid her head up and down in a nod, but panicked as she still couldn't catch her breath. Then came another thunderous boom, and the air above her face shimmered like heat off blistering asphalt in the summer. She heard another crash over her head and a weak guttural attempt to speak. Then silence.

She reached her hand to her glasses to center them and wipe off the goopy brown. She lifted her head off the floor slightly as the form coming up the stairs came into focus.

The woman was tall and almost skeletally thin, clad in black turtleneck and slacks. She had a pale face with short white hair rising from her head like a mushroom cloud. In the middle of that nearly colorless face were dark eyes and lips, wearing a small smirk.

"Hello, Osgood," said the wraith. "I'm Eliza."

Osgood felt her eyes roll, and she dropped her head back to the floor.

36

"Here you go," said Zack, handing Osgood what seemed to her like an excessively large glass of water. She took it with both hands and began to gulp it down her burning throat. As she did, she looked at the bloody gash below his dark hairline and the bruise rising on his right cheek.

"Thank you," Osgood croaked. "I'm sorry."

"It's not your fault," said Zack. "It was my plan, after all."

Osgood pushed herself up to more of a sitting position against the wall in the upstairs hall, just feet from where she'd nearly been choked to death. Or had she? Had it just wanted her unconscious? Incapacitated. "Albrecht?"

"He got walloped and knocked out, but we think he's alright."

"We should." She coughed. "Paramedics."

"Well," said Zack. He looked over her shoulder into the room beside her. "I think it's more complicated than that."

Osgood knew who he was looking at, but not what the situation was. Her aunt had said few words after introducing herself, instead dragging the creature into Albrecht's bedroom for something. Osgood nearly tried to get up but remained where she was. Getting up could wait. Moving could wait.

"If Albrecht's..." she cleared her throat. "Badly hurt. We need..."

"I know, Os," said Zack.

Osgood gasped as she saw Audrey's head crest the landing of the third floor. Her face was so bloody that for a moment Osgood thought it had been skinned. She held a zipper bag of ice to her mouth and nose.

"It's not as bad as it looks," said Audrey. "Promise. Though I'm confident my nose is broken. Smashed directly against the bottom stair."

"Shit," said Osgood. She turned to Zack again. He interrupted her continued insistence on paramedics by tipping the glass toward her mouth. She obliged and drank more and more, finishing it.

"Good," he said.

"Are you..."

"I'm okay," said Zack. "This is not as bad as being shot, I promise." He creakily lowered himself to a seat next to her. "We really didn't have a chance. He played dead, then when he hit Albrecht, he got the stun gun. Put me down immediately." Zack looked down at the floor. "I should be the one apologizing for not having a better plan."

"Nobody knew how he'd attack," said Audrey.

Osgood knew that wasn't exactly true. She had seen Nurse Pollack's neck snapped. She'd known the Goddardmonster would be brutal. "I could see the monster," she said. "You could only see Goddard." She began to repeat her apology, to Zack next to her and Audrey sitting on the landing, when Eliza emerged from the bedroom.

"Where is your other friend?" she asked. When they didn't immediately answer, she snapped her fingers at them.

"Um, he's downstairs," said Zack, adding a tentative, "ma'am."

"What room?" she asked.

"Living room, left of the front door."

"Thank you." She moved past Audrey and seemed to float down the stairs. They heard no creaking wood as she went, only the light footsteps of a ballerina.

Osgood shook her head. "She saved my life."

"Probably all of ours," said Audrey.

"How'd she...stop...him?" Zack asked, haltingly.

"I have no idea," said Osgood. "But whatever she did, it sounded like an enormous drum."

"Huh," said Audrey. She pointed at the room behind Osgood. "What'd she do in there?"

"Don't know," said Osgood.

Zack stood and approached the door. They heard him exhale, long and slow.

"What is it?" asked Osgood, craning her neck to look in the room. She saw the bed, but not much else; there were still black splotches in her vision from the attack.

"Goddard is on the bed," Zack told them. "It's like...he's frozen."

Audrey stood and looked over Zack's shoulder. "That's unsettling."

"Alright, dorks," said Osgood. "Help me up so I can see."

Zack shook his head at her. "You should probably stay—"

"In the hospital," said Osgood. "Yeah. They told me. Please help me the fuck up."

"I take it that we didn't win?"

They all turned to Albrecht, shakily climbing the stairs with Eliza's assistance.

"Depends on how you define 'win.'" Osgood pointed at Eliza. "*She* won."

"The fight isn't over yet," said Eliza. "And we've miles to go."

Albrecht coughed and nodded.

Osgood felt fresh tears, seeing her friend, her mentor, so frail. His eyes looked sunken, his face wan. A jagged cut had dried closed, stretching from his scalp down in front of his ear to his lower jaw. Flecks of dried blood listed against the white of his beard.

"We're still all alive," said Audrey. "That's a win so far."

"Indeed," said Eliza.

Zack turned and looked her up and down. "So, you're..."

"Eliza Osgood. Need anything further?"

He opened then closed his mouth again. "Maybe..."

"It is excellent that you called me," said Eliza. She helped Albrecht sit on the top step, then clapped her hands. "We've much to do."

"What's your plan?" asked Osgood.

"And why do you think you're in charge?" Zack snapped but went silent and looked away when Eliza flicked her eyes toward him.

"The man in there—" She extended a long pale finger toward the open bedroom door.

"Sam Goddard," said Osgood.

"He has an entity inside him, and it has a strong hold."

Osgood nodded.

"We can likely extract it, but I will need multiple hands on deck."

"I've got one for you," offered Osgood, lifting her left hand.

"Yeah," said Audrey.

"Good," said Eliza. She looked to Zack, who gave her a reluctant nod. She nodded back to him and stepped past Albrecht and Osgood to the bedroom door, closing it. She crouched, and Zack returned to sitting on the floor. "I will need you all to do exactly as I say, if we expect to make it through this. He and the entity are tethered together, but it is not actually here."

"What do you mean?" asked Osgood.

"The entity is a shade. Its physicality is brief and serves only to protect its host or travel short distances."

"A ghost?" asked Audrey.

"Not unlike a ghost," said Eliza. "But never was it alive on this Earth. Inhuman entities, what many call demons or monsters, are from otherspace.

"The margins," said Osgood.

Eliza looked at her silently.

After a moment, Osgood continued. "The space between this world and the next."

"Ah," said Eliza. "Yes, then. Though it isn't the 'next' world. It's infinite worlds. And the space between is a seething void, filled with the lost and angry. Restless spirits and entities."

Osgood wondered when to tell them about the eye in the sky.

One thing at a time, assured Lil.

"Think of that space like the ocean, so impossibly vast it seems empty. That is, until there's blood in the water, and then the frenzy begins." Eliza grew more animated as she explained. "There are places in this world where the border to..." She held out a conciliatory hand to Osgood. "...the margins has been rubbed thin. Supernatural energy on this side calls to those on that, who come to scratch and knock and bang, desperate to either return or come here anew."

"Ghost hotspots," said Audrey.

"And they look for any way out," said Osgood.

"Yes." Eliza nodded. "They crave it."

"It came out from within me," Osgood told her. She pointed to her bandaged head and chest.

Eliza nodded

Osgood was surprised Eliza didn't have follow-up questions about that. "Then it took him."

Her aunt gave them another robust single nod and stood. She pressed her palm against the closed door, her eyes staring unwavering at it. "I cannot promise that we can save the man. It's possible that the thing holding him has protected him from his injuries, which looked substantial. Once we separate the two, he may die."

Osgood took that in, recalling the moment he'd sidled up to the bar beside her, just days before. Why hadn't she been nicer to him? Why was she always such a cunt?

"The entity," Eliza continued, as though death was a foregone conclusion, "so long as it cannot take another host, will dissipate and fall back into..." she looked down at Osgood and smiled for the first time since her arrival. "The margins. I like that."

"Thank you," whispered Osgood, distracted.

"It's good," said Eliza. "Alright. We cannot afford to wait much longer. I would advise all of you to tend to your wounds as best you can, and we will begin in..." She closed her eyes, cocked her head at the door, "ten minutes' time. Osgood, may I have a moment with you?" She gestured toward the stairs. "Downstairs, please?"

Osgood nodded and reached with her good hand. Eliza took it and lifted her surprisingly easily. On shaky feet, Osgood stood before her aunt and found they lined up almost precisely, nose to nose, eyes to eye. Eliza smiled, and Osgood returned it. "So lovely to meet you, Osgood. We've much to learn about each other. But that will need to happen at another time."

Holding her hand, Eliza guided Osgood down the stairs, past a large crack in the drywall where Audrey had landed. Albrecht's second floor landing opened into his spacious office, and Eliza deposited Osgood into an oversized easy chair in the back corner. Her aunt sat on the ottoman before her, then leaned forward and put her fingers on Osgood's knee. "Lil told you to contact me?"

"Oh," said Osgood, shaking out some cobwebs. "Yes. She told me to tell my father to—"

"You know who Lil is, then?"

"My great-grandmother," said Osgood. "But she's young."

"Yes," said Eliza. "She speaks across time. Not often. I find it fascinating. She wasn't the first talent in our line, but she was the first Osgood." Eliza lifted her fingers on Osgood's knee until only the tips touched. "But we've no time for this now. That entity upstairs wants something from you. I'm not certain what that is, but he is quite determined."

"It said I was to be the mother of legion," said Osgood.

"Interesting." Eliza waved her hand. "It's of no consequence, however. It will not get what it desires."

Osgood smiled. "You're very confident of that."

"This is not the first extraction I've done."

"We thought it might be like an exorcism."

"Without religious context, I suppose." Eliza pointed to the ceiling above her. "That entity is not a Christian 'demon.' It would likely laugh off, or not even respond, were we to apply the Rites of Exorcism to it." She put her hand to her cheek. "No, it needs to be shoved from this world. It will lie, it will fight, but the only reason it can do those things is because of your...how do you know him?"

"Ex-boyfriend," said Osgood.

"Well, that must be awkward."

"The monst— entity came out in the middle of sex."

Eliza's face showed no surprise or judgment. "Quite awkward, indeed."

Osgood nodded, then looked down at her lap. "He's going to die?"

"I don't know," said Eliza, her voice clipped and matter of fact. "I am sorry."

"I feel responsible," said Osgood.

"Don't," said her aunt.

"I—"

"Lean forward, please," Eliza said, interrupting her.

After a moment's hesitation, Osgood leaned toward her.

"Thank you." Eliza slid Osgood's glasses off her face, going blurry in the process, then cupped her hand over Osgood's bandaged eye. "Close your eyes, please."

"I can't see out of that—"

"Both, please."

Osgood did as she was told. In the darkness, she felt the pressure of the hand on her face and saw blooming purples amidst the black. She could hear Eliza mumbling, very quietly, in a language Osgood didn't know. A cold hand took her left, and Eliza's thumb traced shapes on Osgood's wrist. She heard a distant jingling sound, then felt Eliza slide her thumb across her cheek under the edge of the bandage.

"Open."

Osgood opened her mouth.

"Your eyes."

Osgood opened her eyes.

"Hold still." Eliza reached behind Osgood's head and felt around with her short nails. Finally, she managed to pull up part of the bandage and unwound the gauze covering Osgood's eye. After a moment, all that remained was a cupped pad, which fell to Osgood's lap.

Immediately, Osgood squeezed that eye shut.

"No, no," said Eliza, as she slid Osgood's glasses back onto her face.

"It's fucking bright!" said Osgood.

"It isn't, you just have not used that eye in a while."

"No," said Osgood.

"Please, open."

Slowly, Osgood opened her left eye. All was blurry, but as she opened it wider, things began to come into focus. "They told me it might take a few weeks to recover my vision fully."

"Occasionally science is...less than a science," said her aunt. "However, I boosted the energy flowing to your eye. You will still likely take multiple weeks to be back to normal, after tonight."

"Oh," said Osgood.

"Magic is also less than a science."

"Magic," repeated Osgood, hearing the skepticism in her own voice.

"What exactly do you think I am?" asked Eliza.

"My father said you think you're a witch."

"Oh, Basil," she said. "He's right, I do think that. Because it's true."

"You're a witch."

"I think, therefore I am."

Osgood laughed, then closed her right eye, using only her left. Such a relief to have both again, binocular vision.

A pained roar from above crashed through their silence.

Eliza tilted her head back so far that her face appeared parallel with the ceiling. "It's time." She fixed Osgood with an intense stare. "Are you ready?"

"I," began Osgood. "As ready as I'll ever be for an exorcism."

"An extraction. A push."

"Yes," said Osgood.

"Good." Her aunt held out a hand. "Then let's begin."

37

"What a lovely day for an exorcism," said the Goddardmonster, holding steadier than before it his insectoid-flower form. It seemed restrained to the bed by nothing, but it held its arms and legs out like some horrifying alien simulacrum of Vitruvian Man. It threw its head back and laughed uproariously.

"It would be," said Eliza, setting a large black bag on the floor next to the nightstand. "The Christmas season is excellent for exorcism, as it imbues its own psychic energy." She clapped her hand down on the Goddardmonster's head, shoving him down into the squishy memory foam of the mattress. "But that is not what we are doing tonight."

"You're fun," said Goddardmonster.

"I just need to know," said Osgood. "Does anybody else see the monster?"

Zack and Audrey both stared at Goddardmonster, then turned back to Osgood. "No," said Audrey. Zack concurred.

"Me neither," said Albrecht, in a chair near the windows, gauze wrapped over his head and ear and under his jaw. He held a leather-bound book open in his lap. The text was written by hand on dark pages.

"Only you," said Goddardmonster to Osgood.

"No," said Eliza. "I see you."

The alien rows of eyes rolled up toward Eliza, and Goddardmonster didn't seem to have anything to say about that.

She leaned down over it, whispering.

It began to squirm and laugh, but there was desperation in the laugh. "Who the fuck are you?"

Eliza didn't answer, just continued to whisper. Without altering her position, her hand shot out behind her in the direction of Albrecht.

"*Daemonium, vade*," said Albrecht.

"Again," said Eliza.

This time the old man threw his words with more force. "*Daemonium, vade!*"

"No," said Goddardmonster, with obvious relish.

"Next," said Eliza.

"*Veniat Helias liberans eum!*" yelled Albrecht, his voice growing less shaky with every phrase.

"Zack, Audrey."

"Yes?" asked Audrey.

"Stand near his arms, either side."

"That sounds dangerous," said Zack.

"Don't you still have a stun gun?" asked Eliza.

Zack held it up and nodded.

"If he does anything I don't like," Eliza began, then looked down at Goddardmonster. "Do you understand me?"

Goddardmonster just laughed.

"I want you to hit him, hold, hit him, hold, then one last time."

Zack nodded slowly.

"Audrey," said Eliza.

"Yes?"

"Gun."

"What?"

"Please bring the gun."

Audrey left the bedroom and returned, gun in hand.

"Point it at his head."

"You won't kill the piggy," said Goddardmonster.

"You don't know me," said Eliza.

"Wait," said Osgood. "No."

"Hold on!" exclaimed Zack. "I've got something!" He rushed out of the room. Osgood watched the door.

"I don't have time for this," said Eliza. "Osgood. Show him from whence he came."

"What now?"

"Here!" Zack rushed back in, a large wooden crucifix in hand, as though he were rushing to a vampire hunt.

"Where did you get that?" asked Albrecht. "Did you bring it with you?"

"I...found it," said Zack.

"Zack," said Eliza.

"Back, demon!" Zack put the crucifix directly in front of Goddardmonster's face. It didn't flinch, merely snickered in reply. Zack's own face fell. He pulled back the crucifix, shook it, and pressed it forward once again.

"I've no use for your god," said Goddardmonster.

"Zack," Eliza repeated, quiet but firm.

He looked at her, forlorn. She waved him back. Zack took a step back and dropped the crucifix to the floor.

"Osgood," Eliza commanded. "Show him."

"Yes," said Goddardmonster, with deep hunger in its voice. "Please do."

"It wants me to," said Osgood, feeling the situation rapidly spiraling in the wrong direction.

"It's pretending to—"

COOPER S. BECKETT

"No," said Goddardmonster. "I do want her to. Show me your tits, Spooky." It turned back to Eliza. "Doesn't she have amazing tits?"

Eliza returned her hand to its forehead, bent down, and whispered again. The creature squirmed as she pointed to Albrecht. "One, two, three."

Albrecht nodded and held the book closer to his face. "*Daemonium, vade! Veniat Helias liberans eum! Tenebrae tuae vadat!*"

"It's. Not. Working," said Goddardmonster, its voice guttural and deep, seeming furious now.

"Audrey," said Eliza. "Put the gun against his head."

"What?" asked Audrey.

"Please."

Shakily, Audrey brought the gun up, aiming in toward Goddardmonster's head. The creature leaned forward to press its head against the barrel.

At that moment, Osgood saw Goddard, that horrible grin plastered on his face, his eyes wild. "No!" she said. "You can't!"

"Osgood," said Eliza, still calm.

"Pull the trigger, cunt," said Goddard to Audrey. His voice had lost its monstrous roar, but it dripped with immense hate. "Or better yet, put it under your chin and blow your own fucking head off, so I don't have to compete with you for this one's snatch." He flicked his head toward Osgood without taking his eyes off Audrey.

Audrey's face shifted, from fearful, pained, as she held the gun on him, to a scowl Osgood knew too well.

I am Audrey's fury, thought Osgood.

Goddard seemed dumbfounded as Audrey hit him once, then again, then again with the gun stock. After the third, with everyone in the room looking at her, she dropped the gun to her side.

His face lost the surprise, then he laughed, choking on his blood, his nose flattened against his face. "So. Fucking. Easy!"

"Eliza—" said Osgood, stopped by Eliza holding up her index finger.

The finger then went to Albrecht, who repeated his three Latin phrases.

In a flash, her ex-boyfriend vanished and the Goddard-monster returned. It shot its calcified hand up and grabbed Eliza by the throat. "You have no idea what I am, what I serve."

Eliza grabbed at its hand, punching down on its face with her other.

Zack seemed to snap back into focus and pressed the button on the stun gun, shoving it between the creature's legs. He hit it, then released, then hit it again, and again. It writhed and twisted.

Eliza stepped back with a cough. "Page...page two, Albrecht."

Osgood went to her. "What should I—"

"*Vade,*" said Albrecht. He hesitated. "*Vos hinc interea.*" He looked up. "I don't know this, below. Is it still Latin?"

"No, it isn't," said Eliza. "But that's alright." She turned back to Goddardmonster, squirming on the bed, yowling in pain with its legs pressed together. She slapped her hand onto its forehead again. "Please, Osgood. Show it."

"But," Osgood shook her head. "It wants me—"

Goddardmonster roared. "*Aperiam in porta,*" it called. "*Aperiam in porta.*" Then it turned to Osgood, showing Goddard's face again. "I will eat him from the inside as you bear fruit."

Again, Eliza whispered to it, and Goddard's face contorted in what appeared to be extreme pain. Then she screamed directly into his face. "*Absisto, daemonium absisto. Daemonium, vade! Veniat Helias liberans eum! Tenebrae tuae vadat!*" Eliza's hair seemed to lengthen and flow, tossed by unseen and unfelt wind. She continued to scream but had moved from Latin to something Osgood had not heard before. Some of it sounded like modern language, other bits seemed like the clicks and glottal stops of forgotten tribes. Whatever she was saying, it bothered Goddard, and the monster returned, turning its face to Osgood.

"*Aperiam in porta*," it growled. "*Propterea domini idolonorum dant advenit!*"

"Guys," Osgood said. She put her hand to her chest. Something was different. Something was happening.

Eliza continued to scream at Goddardmonster, her voice growing deeper and deeper, her eyes wild and black.

The Goddardmonster repeated its own refrain over and over, sounding more and more desperate until, abruptly, it stopped speaking. The thing on the bed tensed all limbs, shooting them out and shuddering them as though trying to make a snow angel. Then it bent, chest up toward the ceiling, and Osgood saw a separation begin, the monster leaning out of Goddard, who was screaming below.

"*Recedere!*" screamed Eliza. She pointed back to Albrecht, who repeated his shaky refrain.

The creature howled and mewled and shook as it slid forward, separating from Goddard. It flailed its limbs as it emerged, slicing and scratching at his body, the bed growing red with his blood. Then they were two, the monster above and Goddard below.

"*Sororibus continebit, sororibus continebit, sororibus continebit!*" called Eliza, then returned to the unknown languages.

Osgood saw her rise and was sure that, if she looked around the side of the bed, she'd see her aunt was levitating off the ground. She felt awe as the monster above Goddard, surrounded by light, began to grow more and more compact. Suddenly, Osgood's diaphragm spasmed and she dry-heaved, falling to her knees.

"Os," said Zack, rushing to her side. "Os, what—"

The creature opened its maw and the voice of the damned came forth, echoing through the room. "*Tempus est!*" Then it yowled one last time and vanished in a pop, air rushing in to fill the vacuum.

"Holy shit," said Audrey. "Did you see that thing?" She looked to Osgood, who nodded that she had. Then, seeing Osgood on her knees, Audrey rushed to her side.

"What's happening?" asked Albrecht.

"I don't know!" Osgood felt another rough spasm of her diaphragm. She spat out thick yellow liquid. "Something's wrong!"

Eliza lowered back to the carpet, entranced still.

"Eliz—" The pain was indescribable, and Osgood felt herself reeling back, her body trying to get free of the pain within it.

Her aunt snapped from the trance and moved to her. "Osgood."

"Something's wrong!" she said again and heard a tear, as she felt the most searing pain she'd ever felt. The scent of fire burned into her nostrils. She screamed and fell to the floor, her eyes rolling up into her head.

Remain calm, Osgood, said Lil in her mind.

Osgood nearly laughed at the suggestion that she might be able to do that, but the ripping pain continued.

I am with you.

Eliza reached her hand out, putting it on Osgood's forehead. "Please stand back, and give her some—"

Osgood spasmed, again and again, flopping on the carpet like a fish on a boat deck.

"Fuck," cried Audrey.

Something poked up, pushing against the fabric of the sweatshirt she wore, pressing out harder and harder until it lifted the neck away from the body and Osgood could see straight down her front. Between her breasts, a bony midnight blue form pushed up from between ragged bits of skin, yawning open to reveal the dark. "Something—" she gasped, closing her eyes at the pain and the horror. "Something's coming!" Osgood pulled up her sweatshirt, exposing her tits and the thing between them to the room. The creature's emergence caused her arm to slip out of the sling and flop to her side, tugging painfully.

"Oh, good Lord!" exclaimed Audrey, who promptly vomited behind the bed.

"What the fuck?" asked Zack, stumbling backward.

Osgood looked into Eliza's eyes, the same shade of brown as hers. There were tears in them. "Help me," whispered Osgood.

"I don't think I can," said Eliza, covering her mouth with her hand.

Osgood spasmed again, and her glasses flew off, so the world was blurry when she saw the midnight-blue thing tear through her chest as it emerged. It seemed so impossibly tall, impossibly huge. She felt a sticky tentacle slide over her nipple and up to her face. *What do I do?* she asked Lil in her mind, but Lil had gone silent. She saw the thing step out of her and move directly to Eliza, but she couldn't move to see what happened. She heard Albrecht shouting, but it was muffled. Her vision began to fade, but before it did, something as red as a cooked lobster rose from her chest. As her eyes went dark, she found she could see them in the darkness, in the void. Lines of...things...stretching back forever, waiting to emerge, to come forth into the world, waiting for their turn at the gate, all under the watchful eye in the sky.

As the commotion around her grew, Osgood felt surprisingly calm. Her breath slowed. *I think I'm dying,* she thought to herself. *For really reals this time.* She knew, however, what she had to do, though she really didn't want to. But she heard the screams and crashing of her friends, and the things in the room with them, and she knew that she had to be quick or it wouldn't matter.

After all, she'd done this before, hadn't she?

Osgood bent and flexed, in ways she wondered whether she'd always been able to do, or only for this, only when it counted.

Could eat my own pussy, she thought in a wild moment of insanity, as her face somehow pressed into her chest, blocking the

(gate)

wound. She slid forward, her ribs separating and her organs moving away as her body turned itself inside out. She saw it in the distance, not just a vision, but real. The black void, the darkness, the margins. She scraped past her bones, feeling them dig into her head, against her scars. So very painful, but not as painful as before, as the emergence of that—

The darkness swallowed her, and her thought was lost to the void.

38

A woman floats in liminal space. Nothingness, a void.

In the vastness of that void, the space and the black, it would be easy to think herself small and pointless. An ant in the afterbirth. But she doesn't. Not now, not today. Today—whatever "today" might mean in this timeless space—Prudence Osgood has surprised them all, hasn't she? "I closed the fucking gate," she screams into the darkness, at the hulking forms barely visible in their queue, their waiting line. Those entities, those things, those monsters looking for the easiest path out of the margins. Sharks in the water. They slouch toward her, tumbling through the vast soupy expanse, gnashing their teeth and roaring with fury.

Osgood realizes that, as much as she's flirted with death in this wild life of hers, here may truly be her final destination. How unceremonious an end for Prudence Osgood, to be torn apart, devoured in the margins. She asks herself what she should do and hears nothing in response. She calls out in her mind, to Eliza, to Lil. *Help required, SOS.*

Still come the beasts.

"Wait," she tells herself. Her voice echoes, but off what,

she has no idea. It should just go on forever. Her life, here in the margins, is less important, isn't it? Back there, back in the world, her already-wounded friends are fighting honest-to-god monsters. And here she is, in the space between. She must help. But first, she must deal with the charging creatures. As they near her, she can see the flailing arms and tentacles, claws and teeth, wild eyes of all colors. They can't use her as their gate any longer, but they'll think nothing of tearing her apart.

She closes her eyes, breathing slowly to stave off rising panic. She should be able to do something. After all, she'd accidentally built herself a full representation of the intersection that had nearly killed her. She'd built it as endless punishment for her various sins. If she could do that *unconsciously*, she should be able to... She lifts her hands, the way she'd seen her aunt hold hers, the way characters in cartoons, in books, in D&D, have always done. *Cast magic,* she thinks.

"A wall," she says. Uncertain what she'd thought would happen, she's still disappointed when absolutely nothing does. The beasts come. Again, and again, Osgood tries to create a wall, a barrier, anything that will keep the creatures from devouring her, or worse, using her for their nefarious plans. "I'm useless! Jesus fucking Christ, what's the point?"

She closes her eyes and thinks of her love, the one person more important than anyone, anything in the world. In Osgood's mind, she sees Audrey flying down the stairs after trying to protect her from the Goddardmonster. She sees Audrey ready to fight the things emerging from her chest. She sees Audrey at the door of her hospital room, looking over her shoulder and agreeing, "Me too."

That moment, when love had begun. At twelve and thirteen, respectively. With Britt Ekland and *The Wicker Man* playing on a nineteen-inch black and white television. In the barely-finished basement of the Osgoods' new suburban home. Her father behind them as they lay on the floor, couch cushions under their heads. Blanket pulled up to their necks. Hands held, in case Sergeant Howie should come up against any real monsters in this film that her father had called, without shame, "the greatest horror film of all time." The sergeant hadn't, though. His biggest antagonists were his own holier-than-thou attitude and a woman trying to show him her wiles. And then her father had snapped off the TV, pulled the tape out of the VCR, and taken it upstairs with him, emphasizing how late it was and how they ought to sleep, reminding Prudence of church in the morning. There in the semi-dark they had lain, looking at each other. Prudence had felt the tingling between her legs, and wondered if she needed to pee again, or if she might be able to rub against a pillow to get that weird floaty feeling. All she'd wanted, then, was to be Audrey's knight. The one who'd fight the monsters and slay the dragon. Who'd rescue Princess Audrey. Wake her with a kiss.

Now, if only she can actually do it. Fight the monsters, slay the dragons.

Osgood opens her eyes. She exhales rapidly, at first not understanding what she sees. She's in a room. Unpainted Sheetrock walls, with some studs still exposed. An unfinished ceiling showing the support beams of the floor above. A nook containing a 19-inch Zenith with rabbit ears and a UHF dial. Below it, one of the first VCRs ever available, a top feeder. Her father had bought it the day Sears had begun carrying it. Spent several hundred on it. She looks around and sees the rest of her basement in Rolling Meadows, Illinois. Behind her is the ratty brown couch she's fallen asleep on so many times. Over the back is the steadily unraveling afghan, knitted by a great-great-aunt she'd never known.

The sense of home wells up within her. Home, the way it hasn't been in ages. Not since she'd come of age, learned about herself. Since they'd stopped understanding. But this place, this room, this was refuge from the darkness, from the pain, from her parents' fights, from her own fights with her mother. This was the place she and Audrey could be alone together. The place she'd sucked her first dick and eaten out her first girlfriend. The scene of her first orgasm. The place where she'd cried after Alan Haring asked why she thought he liked her, when she wouldn't let him touch her barely budding breasts. The place she'd watched the first Gulf War begin. The place where she'd seen *Twin Peaks*, and *Halloween II* as the late-night WGN movie. The place she'd taped movies off HBO and Cinemax during those random free weekends, making special note of anything that was rated R for "strong sexual content." This place had encapsulated the dawn of her sexuality and all that had followed. This place held love, passion, pain, yearning, regret, and contentment.

This place is home. This place is safety.

"No wonder I built this as my new kingdom," Osgood says, her voice reflecting off the Sheetrock walls.

She reaches forward and pulls the power button on the television, hearing the snap and hum as it slowly brightens. Onscreen is an old monster movie, all waving limbs and squishy—

No! It isn't an old monster movie at all, though, it's Albrecht's bedroom, and things are attacking her friends. They're fighting hard, but they're outgunned. She squints at the blurry image, through the rolling picture and static. Eliza is doing her best to keep the monsters at bay, but she needs help.

"Lil!" Osgood calls. "We could really use you!"

Lil doesn't answer.

"I need to be there," says Osgood, repeating it again for good measure, or to tell the cosmos, or to simply manifest it like *The Secret*. "Tulpa," she tells herself, closing her eyes again. "Tulpa, Tulpa, Tulpa." She can see herself in her mind, not her current self but her past, the version she loved being: the purple-haired firebrand, clad in a t-shirt and jeans, red Chucks and maroon leather coat. That version of Osgood can do anything. That version of Osgood can leap from world to world.

She feels the dial of the TV in her fingers, and she twists it. Nothing but blaring snow on the next channel, and the next, and the next. Then water, people, a gull overhead.

Osgood opens her eyes and squints at the daylight. Before her is an elaborate fountain, full of cherubs and enormous fish diving and spitting water. She feels the strangest sense of déjà vu and reaches out, feeling the water, cold against her fingers on this hot sunny day.

"Osgood!" calls a voice behind her. "Prudence Osgood! *The Spectral Inspector*, right?"

Her heart beats fast. The sense of déjà vu overwhelms her, accompanied by rising dread. She needs to move, move through this, whatever it is, move through the miasma, and return to Albrecht's. Descend from this place. Descend to the world.

Tempus descensus.

What? she asks the voice in her head.

Tempus decensus, it says again. This voice isn't Lil's, or Audrey's, or her mother's. This voice is hers.

"*Tempus decensus,*" she says, then again, then again. She hears commotion behind her. She turns to the young Indian man, holding up his phone to videotape her. She knows what this is, where she is, when she is.

She smiles and turns back around. It truly is time to descend. She continues to repeat the Latin phrase. The sounds of static snow around her, growing louder and louder to a cacophonic screaming fever-pitch, then she's gone from there, and the channel changes. The same but different, new places and old, across the country and around the world, Osgood travels the Tulpa highway in her mind, looking for the place, the time, she needs to be. Through diners and theatres and crosswalks and studios. On mountain tops, in penthouses, in churches, in slums. It feels at once as though it takes an eternity and no time at all.

When she opens her eyes, she has descended. She stands in the doorway to Albrecht's bedroom, with oodles of unearned swagger. Well, maybe a little bit earned—she has found her way here, after all.

"Don't leave me out," says Osgood. The things in the bedroom turn and charge toward her.

39

A woman is in two places at once. Here and there. Both in her recreated basement in the margins and attempting to fend off creatures in the bedroom at her mentor's house. The double vision is nauseating, and she stumbles to a seat. Something swings at her with a sharp claw and tears down her arm. Osgood feels the pain, but her arm is fine in the margins.

"What the fuck do I do here?" she screams at the television.

"Fight!" says Eliza, pulling her to a standing position in both worlds. They stand shoulder-to-shoulder in Albrecht's room, marking a line between the creatures and her friends. She looks over her shoulder and sees them, battered and bloodied. She yearns to touch them, hug them, tell them that somehow this will all be all—

The roar of the red one, crusted with scabs and barnacles, draws her back. It swings at her, its eyes wild and alien, enraged. She can feel its fury directed at her for closing the gate, for fighting the emergence, the evolution, the birthing. Osgood had a role to play, and she'd refused it.

"Osgood, are you here?"

Osgood turns to her aunt in Albrecht's bedroom. "I'm right here."

"What?" asks Eliza.

"I..." Osgood turns back and sees the creatures on the television in the basement of her formative years, bearing down on two women, all shlocky movements and goopy flesh.

"You're here," says Lil.

Osgood turns from the monsters, from her aunt, from that world, and sees her great-grandmother, younger than Osgood is now, descending the stairs into her basement hide-away. The tether is severed. She no longer sees both places, feels both places. She's out of the world and back into the margins.

"I need to go back," she pleads with Lil.

"Yes," says Lil.

"Now!" Osgood exclaims. She points at the TV behind her, wildly swinging her arm. "They need my help!"

"You've severed the tie," says Lil. She raises her hand to point at the TV. "Congratulations."

"What?" Osgood looks back. On the television, she still sees her aunt and herself taking on the creatures. Her aunt blasts them with energy, and the Osgood on the screen leaps onto one, kicking and punching at it.

Osgood blinks at herself, then at Lil. "I don't understand."

"The thought-form lives, independent of you."

"My...Tulpa?" asks Osgood.

"Whatever you'd like to call it," says Lil. "I am so proud."

"I don't understand," says Osgood again. "Help me."

"I am," says Lil. She points again at the TV, and Osgood watches in amazement as one of the creatures slams into a wall.

"You can—"

"The energy in that world is a beacon," says Lil. "It calls to them, but also to us."

Osgood opens her mouth to say something, but she isn't sure what. "I need to go back."

"Yes," says Lil.

"Can you tell me what I need to do?"

"No," says Lil. "I cannot."

"What good—" Osgood stops herself before finishing that sentence.

She watches as Lil, her great-grandmother, the original Psychic Osgood, fights the creatures through the television with her grandniece, as effortlessly as if she were playing a video game. That's "what good," isn't it? Lil isn't here to help Osgood return, she's here to send aid to Eliza in the other world.

"I need to find it, on my own, don't I?" Osgood asks. "The way back."

"There are places that are thin, and in those places, it may be possible to break through." Lil moves forward toward the TV with a level of concentration on her face that amazes Osgood. "To open the gate, they had to create a thin place, utilize every available tool. That's why it was in you, because he'd opened you up and created a hole."

"The Lord—"

"I wouldn't elevate him like that." Lil looks over her shoulder for only a moment. "I watched you overcome, you know. The moment I saw you here, I knew who you were, what you were. I chased the dragon every moment I could, to see you, to be with you. To nurture your gift."

"I. I don't know what to say."

"Nothing is needed, my dear," says Lil. "You are an Osgood, through and through."

Osgood can feel the yearning tug at her; she wants to stay,

to ask more questions, but her friends are hurt and need help. "I need to find a hole."

"Yes," says Lil.

She gives her great-grandmother one last look and climbs the stairs, out of her basement hideaway. She reaches the door and cracks it open, slowly. On the other side is her apartment in Andersonville. Her living room, the way it had been before she fell into the margins. She doesn't even know where to begin to find this hole. Her anxiety grows. She knows one thing above all others: if her friends are going to die there, she will stand with them. She will not leave them alone and afraid, even with her Tulpa and Eliza fighting along-side them. She needs to be there. Herself. For real.

Osgood stammers as she rounds the doorway to her office and comes upon herself fifteen months ago, sitting behind her grandfather's desk in sweats and a tee, speaking silently into her microphone. Osgood cannot hear herself but knows in an instant *when* she is. If she left this room and went down the hall, she'd find Nora lying naked in bed, where she'd left her over a year before to do some podcasting, to speak about her experience.

Perhaps she can stop this entire train, here and now. Stop this Osgood from being pulled into the margins in the first place. From being used as a vessel. Maybe she can take it back. Take it all back. Instinctively, though, she knows she cannot. It happened. She can't make it un-happen. She still might be able to fix the present, if she hurries. Maybe she can use what's about to happen to make her own hole.

She sees her past self growing distracted. It happens soon, doesn't it? She's reading the press release about the new In the Shallows album. Osgood remembers that, and little beyond.

"It happens here," she says. She moves around the desk, crouching next to herself. She is amused by the wafting scent of sex, of lube. She leans in and sniffs deeply. At her closeness, the other her flinches. Osgood cocks her head. She wonders if she could feel the hole herself, maybe ride through it, before this older version of herself does. Would she end up in the past? Would time exchange one Osgood for another? Or would it just open—

The past version of herself leaps back, and Osgood realizes she'd touched her chest, right where the hole is...or will be. This is the way. She's suddenly certain of it. To pull herself out, she must pull herself in. She moves toward the other Osgood, poor naive Osgood who is celebrating a win and a fuck, Osgood who has yet to spend empty time in the margins, who has yet to see—

Osgood shoves her hand into her younger self's chest, and her vision doubles and trebles and quadruples. She's there, in the past, feeling her chest pains, feeling that sharp lash of

("*Aperiam in porta*")

pain as she sees herself beating down a creature in Albrecht's bedroom; as she stands beside the monstrous Prudence at the crossroads; as Audrey stabs the Lord of the Hinterlands in the face; as she and Audrey duck away from falling crystals from a rigged chandelier at the Waverly Hotel; as she sits in the waiting room with her father, wondering if she'll survive brain surgery; as she opens her chest and births the orchid creature with Goddard's tumescence rapidly receding inside her; as she lies on the floor of Albrecht's front hallway, eyes closed; as she goes up to a boy, Danny something, in junior high to tell him that she likes him, only for him and his friends to laugh in response and walk away; as that same boy, the next year, begs to go to the eighth grade dance with her, because now she has tits and all the little piggy boys want to be able to tell their friends they got some over-the-bra action; as she tells her mother she likes girls and begs, pleads, with Cynthia to support her, just this once; as her father shakes his head and goes upstairs, leaving her with her mother, who proceeds to tell her absolutely everything she's ever done wrong; as she accepts her high school diploma, convinced this means the world will get better because she can move on and move in with Audrey in the city, maybe; as she stands, naked in the darkness, before the great and terrible eye, the eye that knows she may be its gateway to the dimension it left eons ago, before humans had even crawled to land in their earliest forms, gasping their first gasps of air, left to slumber until the world was ready for its new master.

(It saw me and knew what I was and how it could use me to get out!)

Osgood knows, too, and she pulls the ripcord in her younger self's chest, apologizing for the pain that's to come, the agony, the terror, the fight, but she hopes it'll be worth it at the end, when they defeat these things, and all will come out in the wash. One must believe in possibilities, after all.

They tumble and fall together and apart, her and her past-selves, Tulpas and doppelgängers, another joins, then another, falling and tumbling through the dark world of endless night. Empty eternity. It's terrible and terrifying, yet also, perplexedly, comforting. She resists the comfort and pulls at the space around her, finding it solid, not empty. The void is liquid and alone again Osgood swims, propelling herself through, knowing movement only by feel, as visually nothing has changed.

Until it does.

She feels a tremendous pain as she falls flat on her back on a slate floor. Above her is a dark smoking hole, ragged edges smoldering. On the other side of the hole, she sees herself. That poor version of herself, panicky in the darkness, clothing shredded, pain in the chest. Maybe she can retrieve her, too, so she doesn't have to find her own way.

Osgood reaches into the hole above her, grabbing hold of the t-shirt worn by her other self and pulling. The other screams and falls toward her, through the smoldering gap, then is gone. As hard as she finds it to comprehend, Osgood knows where she's gone. She's here, on the floor of Albrecht's foyer, days ago. She knows because she remembers it now, all of it. The time in the darkness, the connection with herself, meeting Lil, and of course, the eye. She remembers the things tearing open her chest and head to get inside, under the eye's watchful gaze. She remembers screaming and crying, being told that it would be alright. Lil had been there with her, holding her hand, attempting to comfort her.

But most of all, she remembers looking down into the darkness, when all hope was lost, and seeing herself. She didn't recognize herself at first because of what had appeared to be a white cap. But she'd been grabbed by that white-capped version and pulled, falling down and out and crashing into Albrecht's floor, where he'd found her, unconscious, hours later.

Lying in the same place, days later, now, she just hopes she can end this.

40

"I know what to do," Osgood said, feeling a strange and confident calm wash over her.

The creatures turned from her aunt to look at her. She thought she saw surprise on their faces, but how could she possibly tell? Regardless, the things that had emerged from her chest focused their attention on her. She threw her aunt, and Audrey and Zack protecting Albrecht in the corner, a firm look. "Chase them," she said. Their eyes all wide, they each gave her a nod. "Come get me, fuckers."

The blue thing roared and the red one screeched, a deafening sound that made Osgood hold her hands to her ears, only to find the noise was inside her head. She rushed through the bedroom door and slammed it behind her. On the floor near the stairs, she saw the gun and dropped to her knees to grab it. She threw a look over her shoulder and watched as the door thumped, then began to bend and split, finally shattering and blasting open.

First was the midnight blue thing. It saw her, and she saw it, and then Osgood charged down the first flight of stairs. She waited on the landing as the creatures seemed to debate which was to go first before following her down, the red one tumbling as it came—she thought at first it was falling, but then it became clear this was how it moved. She pointed the gun at the blue one, took a breath and held it, and shot twice. The first bullet went wild and ricocheted off something, the second struck the blue thing right in what she thought was an eye. It hesitated, blocking the red thing behind it, as black goop leaked out of the hole, then it resumed its chase. Osgood rounded the landing and headed toward the next flight.

"What're we doing?" shouted Zack above her.

"Chasing," said Eliza.

Osgood heard a deafening thud and watched as the two creatures slammed into the wall before the landing, then fell down the last few stairs. It caused them to hesitate for only a moment, though and then they were back up and moving.

"Lil!" shouted Eliza.

A horrifying crash sounded, and the red thing flew backward, its crusty upper portion cracked like a lobster shell, exposing wet pink innards. It hesitated, grasping at itself with claws and tentacles, but then continued. Osgood fired again, hitting the blue thing in another eye, spilling more black sludge.

"Foyer," Osgood yelled up to her friends.

"Whatever you say, Os," Audrey shouted back.

The final flight of stairs was the longest, and Osgood tried to take it without looking back. She was close to where she needed to be, she knew, and to get there she had to stay ahead of—

When the tentacle wrapped around her ankle, she knew she wouldn't make it. The grip felt tentative, uncertain, like that boy, Danny something, who'd felt her up when they were freshmen, and who had told all his friends about Pru's "supple jugs." But then it grasped in earnest, and Osgood felt suckers pulling at her skin, a needle prick in each. Venom began to flow; she felt its heat and pain shooting up her leg as she crashed forward. She hit the wall first, then tumbled back to the stairs. As the red thing held her ankle, she didn't move when she fell, just swung around, directly forward, smashing her face into the staircase. She saw stars and glorious fireworks and felt blood spurt from her nose. She needed to get up, to take them all the way down, to get them to—

Well, she didn't quite know to what. Or where this plan had come from. But she needed to make it down the stairs.

"Osgood!"

That was Audrey, above her. She wanted to call out, to tell her what to do, but found her mouth full of blood and broken teeth.

The red thing came forward and grabbed hold of her other limbs. The tentacles weren't slimy as she'd thought they'd be, instead the warm, dry texture of a hairless cat. Then the suckers took hold, and the pinpricks began. She felt the venom doing its work, paralyzing her from the waist down, stillness creeping up her body.

Two booming blasts from above sent the blue thing tumbling over her. She couldn't see it, but she heard as it hit the turn in the stairs beyond her. She'd been so close to the first-floor landing. So close to the foyer. She lifted her head and looked at the blue thing. It moved shakily but began to lift itself off the stairs almost immediately. It roared at her, and she felt spittle fly from its gaping mouth, splatting into her blood-wet face. She felt electricity shoot up her legs from the tentacles and marveled for a moment that this thing might be electric.

"No, Zack!" shouted Audrey.

The red thing smashed a claw into Zack's face, sending him back up the stairs. The TASER bounced from his hand. Osgood reached an arm out and caught it, surprising herself, and jabbed it toward the blue thing as it began to climb toward her. It moved shakily and slowly, but relentlessly. She zapped it once, then again. It reacted less and less, then finally took the TASER from her as easily as one would take a toy from a toddler.

"We can't reach you," yelled Eliza. "I am so very sorry, Osgood!"

She wanted to tell them that it was alright, it would be alright, but she couldn't speak and didn't know why she felt such confidence. The blue thing blocked the light above her and, with a quick swipe of its claws, tore her shirt away. With startling precision, it carved a line down her chest. She felt the skin catching on its claw and ripping. Once the line was drawn, filling her with relentless agony, she lifted her head toward the beast and spit a tooth at it. "Fuck you."

The thing roared at her, then grasped either side of the line in her chest and yanked. She felt her ribs shatter as it pulled, the blood in her mouth nothing compared to the blood in her lungs. She knew this was it, the actual end. She'd failed. So close, but so far. If only she could— She coughed, and the light began to fade. The things digging into her were angry and she didn't know why. So much didn't make sense. What had her plan been here? Why did she do this in the first—

Her eyes rolled, like the martyrs before her, and then it all made sense.

At the foot of the stairs stood Prudence Osgood, her head bandaged, her arm in a cast.

I am not Osgood, she realized. She'd been the bait.

And that was alright. It would all be alright.

The Tulpa took one last agonizing breath and died.

 ⊘ 41 ⊘

"**O**sgood!" screamed Audrey above.

There was commotion on the stairs, but Osgood, down below, waited for the right moment. Watching her

(self)

Tulpa be torn apart on the staircase did strange things in Osgood's stomach, but she supposed that she'd seen so much weirder lately; this might just be her new normal.

Lord, I hope not, she thought. She wanted to reach out to her friends above, to make sure they knew she was still here. She wondered that they hadn't noticed the hair on her duplicate, the clothing. The full use of both limbs. Trauma can make you miss the fine details, though. She threw a glance over her shoulder to make sure the hole still churned. It cycled and roiled around, spitting sparks off the burnt edges. She assumed the earlier version of her had fallen through, just days before. *Otherwise, I wouldn't be here, would I?*

"Lil," she whispered, are you with me?

I am, said Lil in her mind.

Above, she heard Eliza call to Zack and Audrey, pulling them back. Lil must be with her as well.

"This is going to work, right?" she whispered. She waited and waited for a response, but none came.

On the stairs, the two creatures slowed their dissection of the Tulpa. Osgood wasn't sure how she knew, but she sensed they were confused. They poked around in the Tulpa's open chest, looking for their gate. Not finding it was apparently not something they'd considered.

Footsteps on the landing above her, moving away from the staircase. Osgood watched the ceiling as they went, two sets. Thank god, Zack and Audrey would be out of harm's way.

She took a few deep breaths and then stepped into the stairwell. "Wondering where your gate is?"

The two creatures whipped their heads toward her. The blue one looked incredibly battered, with multiple eyes missing. The red one slouched down toward her, beginning to tumble. They didn't hesitate. The moment they recognized her and what she was, they charged.

She felt the air pressure change as the enormous creatures slid down toward the landing, toward her. *Toward the end*, thought Osgood. "Eliza!"

Her aunt silently descended the stairs behind the creatures, her hands both held in front of her like shields, fingers splayed wide. Their eyes met, and Osgood saw visible relief in hers.

They haven't killed me yet, Osgood thought.

Thank the goddess, said Eliza, in Osgood's mind.

Shall we, ladies? asked Lil.

Osgood laughed and reared back, stepping into the foyer as the creatures approached. Back further and further until she felt her stomach lurch and drop, the way she'd always felt on those parachute rides at the carnival. She realized she'd stepped into the expanse of the hole and quickly jumped backward, until it was between her and the creatures. The blue one roared at her, but she could hear the shakiness in it. Much of the sense of menace was gone, though she knew it could still reach forward and tear open her chest just as easily as it had the Tulpa's. The red thing just gurgled and gnashed teeth that she couldn't see. Their charge continued onto the landing and into the foyer. They seemed to gain speed as they hit the flat ground. For the first time, Osgood's confidence wavered. She saw Eliza still a quarter of the way up the stairs. She honestly had no idea what Lil was planning to do. And these things were charging faster than she'd expected, as battered as they were. What if they made it? What if they moved right past the hole and attacked her, then ripped her chest open? Would that reopen the gate? Her breath quickened, and her heart pounded. *Fuck, they're coming fast*, she thought as the creatures neared. She saw the blue one's claws catch the light and glint, razor sharp and ready to tear her open. *Fuck, fuck fuck fuck fuck.*

My darling, said Lil. *May I?*

May you what? thought Osgood, who shook her head and decided, "Do whatever you need to!"

She felt something slide into her. It slid into her legs and arms, then her chest and head, as though putting her on like a costume. After a moment of terror, of a desire to shake off this intruder, this interloper, she experienced a sense of deep, profound calm.

Her left hand went up, and through her, Lil told the creatures, "Stop."

Osgood's eyes widened; her voice had been completely different. Lil was here, speaking through her, puppeteering her. How fucking wild!

Eliza reached the landing and pointed her hands at the creatures.

They were infuriated by the command, but the things yowling before Osgood did stop, right beneath the hole. She wondered if they knew, if they could see it, if they could sense it. She wondered if Eliza could.

I can, Eliza told her.

"You don't belong here!" her aunt shouted from behind the creatures.

"This reality is not yours," added Lil.

"Get—" Osgood began, but was silenced by both her aunt and her great-grandmother's assurances that they had this.

"*Daemonium, vade!*" shouted Eliza.

Osgood felt her head pounding as the creatures spoke—a hissing, gnashing sound that made her sick to her stomach. *Weee... are not... daemons...*

"That is unimportant," said Lil. "You are banished."

The creatures began to gargle and snort, and Osgood realized they were laughing. She felt nauseous.

"You think that's funny?" asked Eliza, a sassy tone in her voice.

"It would appear that they do," said Lil.

"Shall we?" asked Eliza.

"We shall."

The two women, one speaking through Osgood, together called "*Eicio, expulso, expello. Eicio, expulso, expello!*"

Osgood joined the chorus, realizing that two different voices were coming from her body at once. *How incredibly surreal*, she thought. "*Eicio, expulso, expello!*"

From the stairs, Zack and Audrey took up the call. "*Eicio, expulso, expello!*"

The creatures reared back, ready to throw their full weight and attention at Osgood. Their gate, their grail, their Mary.

Osgood closed her eyes. She felt her hand thrust forward, feeling it push against something incredibly powerful. She opened her eyes again and saw pure light emitting from the center of her palm. It had frozen the creatures, bathed in the light of power. From behind them, Eliza also projected light.

The shaking began, first barely noticeable, like a snowplow passing out front, then growing and growing. Zack and Audrey held onto the banister to keep from falling down the stairs, Audrey—forever impressing—with her phone out, recording it all. Eliza wavered and steadied herself. Osgood, somehow, remained stick-straight, unmoving.

The ember-lined rim of the hole in the world began to undulate and cycle, then turn, first slowly, then faster and faster, spinning into a vortex of light. Osgood would have thought it a hallucination if not for the papers and clothing around the vortex being sucked into the maelstrom.

"*Eicio, expulso, expello! Eicio, expulso, expello!*"

The creatures began to change, elongate, tugged toward the center of the hole, tugged from beyond, tugged toward where they belonged.

For a moment, the sound became overwhelming, the crashing of things around the hole, the screaming of the creatures within, the voices in unison expelling them out, the whirring of the vortex itself. Then, without warning, the sound ceased. The room was dim in an instant. The vortex was gone. The creatures were gone. Silence.

Eliza stepped forward. "Grandmother," she said, her face hopeful and open.

Osgood hugged her but she knew that it was more than just *her* there, that Lil and Eliza were having their own physical reunion. She felt Eliza shaking with tears, then she pulled back and sniffed, resuming her stoic demeanor. "Thank you."

"You were exceptional, Eliza," said Lil. "It has been such a delight to see you come into your own."

"You'll..." her stoicism failed, and Eliza smiled through the tears. "Talk to me... soon?"

"Whenever you need me, I'll be there," said Lil.

Osgood lurched and fell to her knees as the spirit left her body. She reached out, hoping to...what? Catch it? She slumped, feeling loss.

For you, as well, Prudence, said Lil in her mind. *If you need me, I'll be here.*

"I want to know more, though!" called Osgood, as she felt her great-grandmother's spirit receding.

"Then it's a good thing I'm here," said Eliza.

Osgood nodded. Eliza helped her stand.

"So," said Zack from the stairs. "Could someone explain to me what the fuck just happened?"

As Eliza tried to explain, Osgood stepped away, moving past them on the stairs, then past Albrecht, sitting quietly on the upper landing, his worry giving way to joy at seeing her. She promised she'd be back and continued to the third floor, stepping over the chunks of broken door, to the bed where Goddard lay.

His breathing was shallow and stuttery, and she took his hand. He looked up at her, his eyes rolling in their sockets.

"I'm sorry," she told him, kissing his forehead between gashes. "I never meant— I'm so, so sorry."

Wind whistled from his throat, but no discernible response came. Before the rest of her motley crew had climbed the staircase to join her at his side, she'd watched the last vestiges of life drain from his eyes. With his hand in hers, Osgood allowed herself to sob. Sam Goddard, who'd really loved her once, who'd wanted so desperately to help find her, who'd gone bewildered to the Heartland Motel with her, who'd suffered so needlessly and vastly for error in judgment, had died.

Audrey put her hands on Osgood's shoulders, squeezing lightly. Osgood put her hand over Audrey's and pulled her down into a kiss. She tasted both of their tears. Then Osgood looked back to her dead friend, as Eliza gestured over him, sealing his wounds and banishing his bruises. After a few moments, he looked like he might be just sleeping.

Osgood put her palm to his cheek and found it cold.

She broke down again.

42

*C*arol of the Bells had always been Osgood's favorite Christmas carol. While a surprising number of songs for the season dropped into minor chords, *Carol of the Bells* stood alone in its vaguely ominous tones. Osgood was listening to the song on repeat, streaming from her phone as she sat in her plush papasan chair in the window nook of their apartment, wrapped in a microfiber bathrobe she'd received from Audrey. Through the windows, she watched Christmas Day dawning on Clark Street. Several fresh inches of snow had fallen in the past several hours, and few vehicles braved the street. The liquor distributor had stopped by around four, though. Nothing said "family holiday" quite like a desperate need for liquor. Osgood wondered how full their own stashes were. She hadn't had a drink since the incident. But today was a holiday. And today her... She clenched her jaw. Today her family was coming. Here, to her apartment, a space that had only begun to feel like hers again in the past few days. She'd invited Eliza as well, to help buffer against her mother, as they both apparently drew similar levels of Cynthia's ire.

"I've got your back," her aunt had assured her.

She lifted the mug of hot chocolate to her lips, considering what would go best with it. Rumchata? Baileys? Maybe some 43, if she wanted to go a little wild. But it was only just after 5:00 in the morning, so perhaps she ought not begin her drinking now.

"What're you doing up?" asked Audrey, yawning and wiping the sleep from her eyes. She leaned against the hallway doorframe as she blinked.

"Still not sleeping much," said Osgood.

Audrey nodded. "Want company?"

"Yours? Always," said Osgood. "There's water on the stove, but you might need to reheat a little."

"Coffee?" asked Audrey.

"Hot chocolate." Osgood held up a mug rimmed with a black and white chevron pattern. "I know it's heresy in this mug."

"I think Dale Cooper would approve, after what you've been through," said Audrey, then disappeared down the hall to retrieve her own. When she returned, she climbed into the papasan chair with Osgood, who laid her head against Audrey's chest.

She heard her friend's heart beating and felt tremendous comfort. "Do we need to have my family for Christmas?"

"For a family Christmas?" asked Audrey. "Yes. If mine are coming, yours are, too."

"You get along better with—"

"You didn't tell your parents that an interdimensional being killed your sister."

"No," agreed Osgood. "I am a constant disappointment, though. And Albrecht is *definitely* coming?"

"He said he would," said Audrey. "I don't know why he'd lie."

Her old friend, her mentor, had spent two weeks in the

hospital nursing the wounds of the fight. He'd told the perplexed staff he'd fallen down his stairs. "They don't dare challenge me," he'd told her on her first visit. "But they won't allow me Scotch."

"I'll see what I can do," she'd told him and returned the following day with a bottle of Lagavulin.

"You're too good to me," he'd said.

"I mean, you do remember why you're here, right?" she'd asked. "I nearly got you killed."

He'd put his hand on hers and repeated himself. "You're too good to me."

Thinking of Goddard still made her choke up. Eliza's glamour had fooled the medical examiner, who still was mildly suspicious but determined the man had died from an embolism. Thankfully, Zack had been able to surreptitiously snip out the security footage from the hospital's servers, cutting out the nurse's murder. It was an unfortunate price, but he didn't need to be charged with anything post-mortem.

Though she'd last seen him peaceful, first in Albrecht's room, and then in his casket, when she closed her eyes, she saw his rolling eyes, the eyes of the martyr. They haunted her in the dark.

Maybe that was why she wasn't sleeping.

"You shouldn't blame yourself," Zack had told her, home for the first time since the incident.

"Maybe not," Osgood had said, "But I will."

"I know you will." He'd put his hand on her shoulder. "I think these events would've happened this way regardless. If not Goddard, someone else. If not Albrecht's, somewhere else."

"That doesn't help," Osgood had said.

"I know. But it will in time."

"If I'd let the cordyceps run me," Osgood had told him,

"then Goddard wouldn't have been involved. I would've lit the beacons, opened the gate."

"No," said Zack. "You would've collapsed from the pulsing brain tumor and had to break yourself out of the hospital with a monster at the wheel."

"We don't know that."

"No," he'd said. "That's kind of my point. We don't know what could've or would've happened. All we can do is accept this timeline and move forward."

On Christmas morning, Osgood ran her fingers through Audrey's hair.

"What are you thinking about?" asked Audrey.

"That I could've gotten you all killed," said Osgood.

"That's..."

"True?"

"No," Audrey said. "You didn't do it. Those things from the margins did."

"To get to—"

"Os..." Audrey sat up in the chair and looked down at Osgood. "I am just as responsible for this as you are."

"How do you figure?"

"We went chasing my sister down the rabbit hole."

"But—"

"No!" Audrey pressed her hand to Osgood's chest to stop her. "The only reason *any* of this happened is that my sister disappeared. And if you want to blame someone, let's just go ahead and blame the band who made a deal with the devil to be famous. Goddard is one more victim. Maybe, *hopefully,* the last victim of Rhapsody in the Shallows' greed."

"Alright." Osgood frowned. "But I don't think I'll let go of the blame so easily."

"I know," said Audrey. She leaned down and kissed Osgood's forehead, then cheek. She hesitated for a moment, then kissed her lips.

Surprised, Osgood also hesitated, holding her lips still for a chaste kiss, but when she felt Audrey's tongue, she fell into it. Their kissing was as it always had been, intense, awkward, silly, with breaks for laughter, noses bumping against each other, Osgood's glasses falling off her face. It also was as natural as it had been before, from the earliest moments in her parent's basement.

"I know you don't want a relationship with me, but—"

"Shut up, Pru," said Audrey.

Osgood couldn't though. "I don't think I'd be able to manage a relationship so—"

"Let it be what it'll be. It's Christmas! Now will you shut up and make out with me? Do I need to put on *The Wicker Man?*"

Osgood shrugged. "Couldn't hurt."

"Fuck you." Audrey sniffed out her disapproval and stood to walk away.

"Wait," said Osgood, grabbing her hand and pulling her back, into a kiss that deepened.

Later, much later, the two of them lay in each other's arms in Osgood's bed. "Merry Christmas, Osgood."

"Merry Christmas, Audrey."

Audrey sat up, pulling her shirt back on. "We should... you know, before Zack."

Osgood nodded.

Audrey pulled on her pajama pants and walked to the door.

"Aud."

She turned back.

"I know that you don't love me like I love you."

"What makes you think that?" asked Audrey.

Osgood hesitated. "I just know."

"You shouldn't tell others how they love, Pru."

Osgood nodded.

"I've never loved anyone the way I love you," said Audrey. She walked back over and kissed Osgood one more time. "Never."

They looked into each other's eyes, and Osgood knew that her hopes for the future, for love, for a relationship, for possibilities, weren't in the cards for them. She smiled at Audrey. "This was the best Christmas present I've ever gotten."

"Very sappy this morning, Os," said Audrey.

"I've been places," said Osgood. She nodded to emphasize the point and surprised herself with her own earnestness. "I just want to stay where I am."

"How about bacon," asked Audrey.

"Bacon would be wonderful," said Osgood. She watched as the love of her life went to cook Christmas breakfast.

She turned back, toward the dark corners of her room, and saw Goddard's eyes, rolled up at her. His breath whistled. "I'm sorry," she told him, as she'd told him every night and every morning. As she'd told him in the darkness in every room. She jumped from one distraction after another to forget those eyes for a few moments. As soon as she was alone and could think about what had happened, what she had done, he came back. She didn't know if he was a ghost or just a nagging hallucination brought on by her guilt. Either way, she wished him gone but knew that this was her penance. This was the price for her part in his death. She had survived. Zack and Audrey had survived. Eliza and Albrecht had survived. Osgood squeezed her eyes shut, feeling tears roll down her face. She accepted the price today, as she had every day since his death.

Prudence Osgood took her penance.

Dying to know what happens next?

There are as many stories in The Spectral Inspector 'verse as there are things that go bump in the night.

*Sign up at the address below and **Be a Specterino!** Then you won't miss a single thing, including exclusive shorts, early access to novels in progress, artwork reveals, conversations with the author, and more!*

SpectralInspector.com/news

In the indie publishing world, reviews are more important than anything! If you enjoyed Osgood Riddance and are looking forward to future Osgood adventures, please post a review where you bought the book and on Goodreads! It's free and it helps a lot!

Prudence Osgood Will Return in

Osgood as She Gets

The Spectral Inspector
Book III

ABOUT THE AUTHOR

As a queer non-monogamous writer, Cooper S. Beckett endeavors to create characters that reflect the diverse lifestyles of his friends, his partners, and himself. If he can pit those characters against monsters and cosmic horrors he's all the happier. From a young age, his obsession with horror movies and books seriously concerned his mother. It probably still does. Given a choice, he would rather winter at the Overlook than the Waldorf. Like Lydia Deetz, he has always thought of himself strange and unusual, and is thrilled to be putting that foot forward in his Spectral Inspector novels.

He lives in Chicago with his wife, constant, and binary star, Elle, their dog Egon, and their black cats Xander and Willow.

Want short stories, updates, and discounts in your email? Sign up today at CooperSBeckett.com/news

CooperSBeckett.com

"Prudence Osgood is a true heroine for our times – gritty, complex and sharp-witted, vulnerable but never broken. A darkly captivating mystery infused with the warmth of well-loved characters and an undercurrent of creeping dread."
  - Claire C. Holland, I Am Not Your Final Girl

"Cooper S. Beckett has created a wonderfully disturbing world in this ominous mystery brimming with fractured friendships and nightmarish scenes."
  - Lisa Diaz Meyer, All Roads Shattered

"Touches on many of my favorite things: cults, weird conspiracy theories, sex, vinyl backmasking, 90s pop star breakdowns, ghosthunters, inter-dimensional beings... all wrapped up with crackling dialogue & relatable characters."
  - David Sodergren, The Forgotten Island

"A phenomenal book! It's CreepyPasta by way of Stephen King and sticks the landing on LGBT+ characters. Creepy, funny, clever, and captivating. You'll love this!"
  - Tyler Hayes, The Imaginary Corpse

"A bourbon soaked supernatural mystery leading to a heart pounding climax. Prudence Osgood is a force to be reckoned with in any dimension. The ethereal ending was filled with beautiful imagery. A truly great read!"
  - Joe Tassone, FearScale

"Beckett lends his unique voice to the horror genre, weaving a tangled mystery filled with dark turns into even darker places."

   - Summer Johnson, *The ABCs of Death*

"Sometimes delightful. More oftentimes, deliciously dark. But always anchored by a small group of compelling, misfit characters that you will never stop rooting for, especially our unlikely heroine, Osgood."

   - Julieann Stipidis, *Horrormonal*

"A masterfully vulnerable and relatable 21st Century horror story. Combines classic and contemporary horror elements with a moving exploration of the vulnerability of maintaining and rebuilding relationships after personal trauma."

   - Flynn Bailey, *Adult Salad*

"Queer heroine Prudence Osgood is intriguingly flawed, yet one can't help but root for her success. The story is captivating, twisted, and sure to keep you awake at night!"

   - Angela Elmore, *By the Bi*

Made in the USA
San Bernardino,
CA